From a Desert Playa

In This Series

That First Heady Burn
True Vermilion
The Dark Shill
A Stack of Sawbucks
The Hillside Roble
The Peroxide Pomp
The Incidental Twin
Brawl in Bardo
The Window-Shade Job
The Convenient Patsy
The Artisanal Grifter
Shrink in the Shadows
Project Chartreuse
From a Desert Playa
The Tired Canary
A Desperate Frame-up
Trail of the Blue Agave
The Saucer-Heads
The Satin Squeeze Play

DAGMARMIURA.COM

From a Desert Playa

From *a* Desert Playa

George Bixley

DAGMAR MIURA
LOS ANGELES

Published by Dagmar Miura
Los Angeles
www.dagmarmiura.com

From a Desert Playa

First published 2022

ISBN: 979-8-89195-012-2

ONE

G IG WORK FOR THIS insurance company was his bread and butter, so Slater wasn't going to pass up the opportunity to show his face at a reception, even though he'd never been invited to one before. Riding up in the elevator to the event room on the forty-sixth floor, he checked out the other passengers. A man in an evening suit and two women in long dresses. After business hours in an office tower they were obviously headed to the same party. His handler, Della, had told him what the excuse for the event was, and he hadn't bothered to retain that piece of information, but it had to be about someone important if everyone was dressed up like this. In jeans and a faux leather jacket Slater looked totally out of place. But he couldn't do much about that now.

At least he looked the part of what they paid him to do, euphemistically called field work: he dug into claims that were too lurid for the suits, or handled the rough stuff the bean-counters didn't want to dirty their hands with.

The elevator doors rolled open, and Slater followed the others as they stepped off. Standing in front of the big 46 plastered on the wall was a burly guy in a dark suit, with a red beard, his head shaved bald. He ignored the well-dressed trio as they walked past him but then stepped in front of Slater.

"Sir, this is a private function."

He knew better than to react, but he couldn't help

himself. Slater stepped close to the guy and slapped him hard, left and then right, a solid kovac.

The bouncer hadn't expected that, and took half a step back, but then grabbed for Slater's arms—not quickly enough, as Slater nimbly sidestepped out of his reach. But the guy managed to catch hold of his sleeve, and yanked at it.

"You think I don't belong here because I'm a brown guy?" Slater snapped, trying to wrench himself free. He had his father's dark coloring, and among the privileged it was often assumed he was the help. Sometimes that gave him an advantage, allowing him to pass undetected in high-tone places as a gardener or a busboy, but in a situation like this it was a barrier.

Before the bouncer could escalate, Della appeared, and put her hand on the guy's arm. Trim and with her hair styled back around her ears, Della was pushing sixty, and tonight wore a royal-blue dress that emphasized her cleavage.

"This is my guest," she said. "You need to back off."

The guy must have known who she was, as he let go of Slater's sleeve, and glanced at her sidelong, then glared at Slater, his lip curling into a sneer.

Della shot Slater a look. "Don't make it worse."

She knew him well, he realized, or maybe she'd read his body language, his instinct to go after the guy again. Instead Slater adjusted his jacket, and pointed two fingers at his own eyes, then jabbed a finger at the bouncer—a tacit *I'm watching you.*

Della looped an arm through Slater's, and pulled him away, guiding him into the event room and the crowd of guests.

"I can't take you anywhere," she said, leaning into him.

"Your orangutan started it."

"You know it's not a race thing, right?"

Slater frowned. "What are you talking about?"

"You think you're not welcome because you're a brown guy. There are plenty of Latin folks working at Cudahy Mutual."

He took a breath. It was true, he knew. This wasn't a segregated place. Even the tony women he'd ridden up with on the elevator were Latin.

Della stopped at the end of the line of people waiting for the bar. "You seem like you need a drink."

"Is it open bar, at least?"

"I need to circulate. Relax, and have fun. We'll catch up later."

As she stepped away, Slater surveyed the crowd, and the dramatic floor-to-ceiling glass flanking two sides of the room. Interrupted only by a couple of pillars, the big windows revealed the hilly neighborhoods north of downtown Los Angeles as dusk settled in. He'd never seen this view before, as it was higher up and on a different side than Della's office. The company must rent a dozen or more floors in the building.

When he got to the front of the line, the harried bartender, clad in a black vest, glanced at him and said, "What'll it be?"

"Booze. Whatever's easy."

"Red wine," she said, and poured from a bottle into the same kind of plastic glass she was using for all the drinks, then handed it to him. Slater dug out a single and tucked it into the tip jar before he stepped away. He probably shouldn't be drinking, but it fit with his booze rules: he was still working, but it was after five, and he was sort-of with other people; he could have the one.

The conversations were loud, likely fueled by the open bar but also because people all knew each other, standing in small groups that filled the wide room. As he surveyed the crowd, a woman subtly looked him over, her expression dubious. It wasn't unjustified—he was underdressed, and even though he'd just walked in, he'd already managed to make a scene.

Stepping over to the windows, he stood gazing out at the city. What the hell was he doing here? He'd wondered if he'd got the invitation by mistake, an email blast to a list that he shouldn't have been on. He wasn't good at schmoozing, and there was no way to tell who the important players were anyway. The only people he knew here were Della and her extremely aggressive guard dog, Crystal. He'd spotted her from the bar line, standing across the room, her streaky peroxided hair in an updo.

"That's a hell of a view," a guy said, stepping up beside him.

Slater looked him over. Lanky, with great dark hair, he was wearing a trendily cut suit and had a drink in hand.

"You called it," Slater said.

"So is the denim and leather a statement about not being an office drone?"

"It's more like I didn't bother to read the invitation." He gestured with his glass. "Who knew there was a dress code?"

"There's not," the guy said, leaning toward him. "It's just that most of these people are coming from their boring office jobs."

Slater glanced behind them, scanning the outfits. That was totally not true. Most people were in evening wear, dark suits and formal dresses, not office drag. This guy was obviously trying to put him at ease.

"Do you fit into that category?" Slater said. "A bored desk jockey?"

He laughed. "Not always bored, but yes, I have a desk downstairs. I'm Luís."

"Slater," he said, and Luís reached over to tap their glasses together.

"I'm thinking you're in the field."

"I investigate fraud."

"So you're a contractor?"

"Intermittently," Slater said. "When there's work."

"You must deal with Mark, maybe, or Della?"

"Della's my handler."

"I don't know her that well, but I know everybody to some degree. I work in payroll. We're known as the gossipy department." He waved his glass. "Are you working on the mining camp thing for her?"

"What's that about?"

"It's way out in the desert somewhere. A big hairy creature is stomping around at night and disrupting their operations. A bigfoot. Cudahy Mutual is paying out because of the production delays."

"I should definitely be on that investigation," Slater said. "I've worked with some squatchers."

"Seriously? Bigfoot hunters?"

"They're more like contactees. The preferred term is actually *hominid cryptid*. *Sasquatch* is specific to the Pacific Northwest, and *bigfoot* is a misnomer. Proportionally the creature's feet aren't oversized."

Luís laughed. "I can't believe you know all that."

"So you must know Della's receptionist, Crystal," he said, glancing over his shoulder, just in case she was within earshot. "What's her damage?"

"'Damage' is the right word." He lowered his voice. "Crystal is a whole thing. But I really shouldn't be gossiping."

Slater's eyes narrowed. "And yet you know you want to, and I know you want to. Cut the static and fill me in, brother."

Luís furtively glanced behind them, then leaned

closer. "Crystal was a sheriff's deputy."

"She doesn't seem like the type."

"It takes all kinds, right? Anyway, she got fired for negligence."

"It's really hard to can those people. It's like trying to kill a dandelion. Whatever she did must have been pretty egregious."

"I don't know the details, but Cudahy Mutual was involved, and Della must have felt responsible, because she gave her a job after. You know how you can still get a title for your car even after it was in a wreck and the insurance company wrote it off?"

Slater frowned. "That's called a salvage title."

"Like that. Della gave her a salvage job. Nothing to do with security work." He lowered his voice to a whisper. "She pays her way too much."

A woman stepped up to them, a smile on her face, her eyes booze-bleary, and put a hand on Luís's shoulder.

"You have to come and talk to Dave."

Luís held Slater's gaze for a moment, clearly more interested in him than whoever Dave was.

"Let's talk later," Luís said, and let himself be pulled away.

Slater knew what that meant, recognized that glint in his eye. Slamming the last of the acrid wine, he stepped into the crowd and set his empty glass on a table. Della was with a couple of suits, standing with one hand on her hip and her head cocked, listening to one of them talk. As he approached he winked at her and double-clicked his tongue.

"You'll excuse me," Della said, and stepped toward Slater. Resting a palm in the small of his back, she leaned in. "You saved me."

"They did look a little lifeless."

"Did you get a drink?"

"So what's happening at the mining camp? I heard about the hairy cryptid situation."

Della frowned. "You mean the bigfoot. Who told you about that?"

"Everybody here works for the same company, Della. Is it something you can pull me in on?"

"Maybe. It's getting to be a problem. I thought it might resolve itself, but that's not happening."

"So let me resolve it," Slater said. "What's going on?"

"Cudahy Mutual is paying out for late deliveries from the mine."

"The delays are because of the creature?"

"Bigfoot is part of the story. I can't seem to pin down the actual problem. Right now I've got a forensic accountant digging through the paperwork."

"But he hasn't given you any insight."

"She," Della said, "and no, she can't figure it out. The mining company and the transport company still work on paper. It slows everything down."

"It sounds like you need me."

She nodded. "Come in and see me tomorrow."

As Della looked beyond his shoulder, he saw something flicker in her expression. Disgust, maybe, or a similarly visceral negative reaction. She masked it almost instantly before she spoke.

"Hey, Cat," Della said, and squeezed Slater's arm as she stepped around him.

A woman in a print dress, Slater saw, turning to watch them exchange greetings. He moved a few steps from them and looked over the crowd. Crystal wasn't far away, wearing a strappy black cocktail dress. He never would have pegged her as a cop, with the expensive haircut, the elegant jewelry. As he watched, an odd kind of ballet played out. The woman that Crystal was talking to turned away, in the process elbowing a man next to them. His arm jerked upward, splashing the contents of his glass onto his suit jacket.

The woman who'd done it didn't even notice as she walked off, but Crystal's eyebrows shot up, and she briefly stepped sideways, reappearing a moment later with a wad of napkins in hand, pressing them onto the guy's lapel. In the noisy crowd Slater couldn't overhear what was said, but it looked like sympathy and concern. The guy took the napkins, and Crystal relieved him of the now empty glass and stepped over behind the bar. By the time he'd finished patting the booze off his jacket, she was back with a full glass, and handed it to him, and touched his arm.

Slater had never seen that side of her, the kindness and the competence. No way had Crystal learned that in the sheriff's department. There was more than salvage going on with her.

A woman stepped in front of him, drink in hand, blocking his view. In her forties, she had on a dark dress with lamé panels on the front, her hair carefully styled to tumble on her shoulders.

"I get what you were going for," she said, gesturing toward Slater with her free hand. "It's totally working."

"What, now?" he said, frowning at her. He couldn't quite tell how inebriated she was.

"The look you're working. It's tight."

Another woman called to her, and flapped her arm, and she whirled around and stepped away, leaving Slater on his own. Scanning the room, he spotted Luís, standing in a small circle of people, and maneuvered through the crowd until he was close, and facing him. He had to wait a while, until Luís wasn't the one talking, but eventually he looked over and met Slater's eye.

Slater held his gaze and raised his eyebrows. A smirk on his face, Luís extracted himself from the conversation and stepped toward him.

"You," he said. "Have you been networking?"

"I've actually been working a look and I didn't even know it." Slater waved at the crowd. "So have you put in enough face time?"

Luís frowned. "You want me to leave with you?"

"I want to fuck you."

His eyebrows shot up. "Your mother should have named you Frank."

"I told you already. The name is Slater."

"So no foreplay, I take it."

"Listen, Luís—if you want to sit in a window and drink coffee, or walk on the beach, or go wine-tasting in Paso Robles, or whatever it is that you people do, I'm not your guy."

"You people?"

"Civilians. Normies." Slater pointedly looked around at the crowd. "Squares."

Luís chuckled. "I guess I can respect the direct approach. Let's go."

They walked together to the elevator, where a couple of women stood waiting. Luís murmured a perfunctory greeting as they stepped up.

"I live in Westlake," Slater said, "unless you can do better."

His face visibly reddened. "My place is a few blocks from here. We can walk."

"Are they going to shut down the parking lot? I don't want to leave my ride if it'll get trapped."

"It's open all night," Luís said. "Your car will be fine."

As they stepped onto the elevator, one of the women glanced at him, and suppressed a smile. Luís went to the back wall, and Slater stood next to him, and subtly leaned into him, shoulder to shoulder. Luís didn't budge, and gradually Slater shifted more of his weight, until Luís was fully supporting him. Gazing up at the floor indicator as the numbers ticked downward, he could see Luís in his periphery, grinning, still red-faced.

They followed the women off the elevator in the lobby, and as they pushed through the door to the street, one of them looked back and spoke.

"Have a nice evening, Luís."

Luís nodded to her and turned in the opposite direction. Walking abreast, Slater inhaled the sharp night air.

"I'm thinking you're going to be the focus of the office gossip tomorrow."

"Undoubtedly," Luís said, and chuckled. "You'd better be worth it."

They stopped at a street corner to wait for a crossing signal.

"Why did you pick me?" Luís said. "There were lots of guys there."

"I don't remember it that way. You were the only man in the room."

He chuckled. "I know that's just mack. But I'll take it."

In the next block he pushed through a heavy glass door and led the way into a foyer. It was one of the ornate Renaissance Revival office buildings from the first gilded age that had recently been converted to tony lofts. This would suck, Slater thought, living so close to your office. You'd have to work hard to stay aware of the world outside this little neighborhood.

Upstairs Luís's place was laid out like a loft, one big room with a kitchen space near the door and a bed next to the windows. Through a doorway at the side he could see the corner of a bathtub.

"It's not fancy," Luís said, "but it's home."

"It's fancier than where I live. Light-years fancier."

"Do you want a drink?"

"I want you." Slater stepped close, and ran his hands

inside his jacket, along his belt. He nuzzled his neck, then met his mouth, and pulled him closer, grinding into Luís with his burgeoning woody.

Luís pulled back. "I should tell you I'm poz. I mean, HIV-positive."

"I know what 'poz' means," Slater said. "What's your viral load?"

"It's not undetectable. But I'm working on that."

"So we'll be careful."

Sliding his arms around his back, he pulled him close, exploring his mouth, taut and warm and perfect.

"Come on," Luís said, and led the way toward his bed. "Do you want to fuck me?"

"Once you're out of that suit."

Luís reached for his own belt buckle, but Slater pushed his hands away, unbuckling it for him, then fumbled with the zipper and shoved his pants down. Luís pulled off his jacket and unbuttoned his shirt. Once Slater had his own shirt off, Luís pushed him onto the bed and climbed up to straddle him. He undid Slater's belt, and pulled open the fly of his jeans, and moved down to take him into his mouth. Hard already, Slater lay back and got into it. After a minute he sat up and put a hand on the back of Luís's neck.

"If you want me to fuck you, you have to stop."

Grinning, Luís got up and pulled Slater's jeans off, then grabbed a condom. Once Slater had rolled it on, and found the lube, he shifted next to him, one arm under his neck, exploring with a finger, and then moved closer, and penetrated him. Luís winced with the intensity of it, and Slater went slowly at first, soon building up to pounding him. With his nose buried in Luís's sweaty hair, Slater came, pressing into him, then pulled back, panting.

As Luís turned toward him, Slater grabbed his cock, stroking him as he worked his mouth. Luís soon climaxed, groaning and straining into his fist.

Rolling onto his back, Slater folded one arm over his eyes and caught his breath. He started to doze, but Luís's voice soon brought him back to consciousness.

"Do you want some vitamin R?"

Slater lifted his arm to focus on him. "What the hell is that?"

"Ritalin."

"I don't do dope."

"It's a medication. Not a party drug."

"You know damn well it's both."

"Suit yourself," Luís said, and got up, and padded into the bathroom.

"Isn't that an upper?" Slater called to him. "How are you going to get any sleep?"

"It doesn't affect me that way." He stepped out of the bathroom again, his naked form silhouetted in the light from the doorway. "It just takes the edge off."

When he climbed on the bed he wrapped an arm around Slater's chest. The warmth of his body felt perfect. This was the best moment, right after the energetic part, the feeling of being sated, the brief interval before he had to engage with the world again. Eventually he got up and found his jeans.

"You can hang out," Luís said, watching him dress, his head propped on one arm.

"I have to go."

"Can I see you again?"

"You're too close to my source of income," Slater said, pulling on one of his boots. "If you get pissed at me, I'd never work again."

He chuckled. "I can't imagine that I'd get pissed at you."

"You say that now, Luís, but lo, they always do. It's just a matter of time."

Once he was down on the street, he walked back to the Financial District, and into the lobby of Cudahy Mutual's building. As promised the garage below was still open, and his sleek black Thunderbird was waiting for him, where he'd left it, unmolested. A classic car wasn't the best ride for his job, especially when he needed to be low-key or blend in, but he loved it, loved the long profile, the throaty engine, the cherry interior.

Slater drove up the ramp to the street and navigated across the chasm of the 110 freeway to gritty Westlake, and into his alley, and waited as his garage door rolled up. The private garage, basically unheard-of in this neighborhood, was the main reason he kept this crummy apartment.

Once he'd parked and waited for the door to roll down again, he trotted up the two flights to his pad, a small one bedroom with a kitchen counter at one end, a thrift-store sofa and recliner, and a bedroom off the side. From the kitchen cupboard he pulled out a fifth of bourbon, surprised that it was already half empty. Not that it mattered; on the shelf its twin sat unopened. Pouring out his paltry ration, he eyeballed it until there was a generous half an inch in the bottom of the tumbler, and then slammed it, relishing the burn in his throat, the vapor in his nose. He hated measuring it like this, but these were the new booze rules, and he had to admit the moderation had brought him some stability.

He poured out a little more, just enough to savor, then went to his recliner, and set the tumbler on the carpet while he pulled his boots off. As he stretched out, he lifted the glass and held it on his belly.

Going to that party had been worth it, he decided. He'd scratched up some work, and he'd found a hookup. And now he had the only other thing that mattered—a sweet heady snort of bourbon.

TWO

S LATER WOKE IN HIS bed, with daylight streaming in the filmy window overhead, not quite sure how he got here. It took a minute for full consciousness to sink in. He didn't have a headache, he realized. That was always a good sign.

He had a meeting today, he remembered, and got up, inhaling sharply at the sudden cold air. After he'd washed up, he put a mugful of tap water in the microwave, then dumped a spoonful of brown powder into it and swirled it around. After a couple of gulps of the tepid ersatz coffee he went to get dressed. Yesterday's jeans were still passable, he decided, and he pulled on a dark-green dress shirt.

A minute later he trotted down the stairs to his garage, and fired up the Thunderbird, and backed into the alley. Della's building was just a few minutes' drive, and when he nosed into the parking garage, he saw the valet was on duty, clad in a red vest. Pulling up to the curb, he climbed out and handed the guy his keys.

"Seventy-seven, seventy-eight, seventy-nine?" the valet said, stepping toward the driver's door. It took Slater a moment to figure out what he was talking about.

"It's a '78."

"Such a sweet ride."

"Not when it breaks down. It spends lots of time in the shop."

"The curse of the classic car."

"Be gentle with it," Slater said, and went into the elevator, and hit the button marked 34.

Trotting toward him from the parking lot was a guy wheeling a bicycle. Still in his twenties, at most, he had his natty hair slicked back, and a close-cropped beard, and a Roman nose.

"Hold the elevator," he called.

Slater leaned forward and pressed the DOOR CLOSED button, but the guy got there in time to thrust his front tire into the gap, and the doors bounced open again. Maneuvering his bicycle inside, he reached across and pressed the button for a lower floor. Great musculature, Slater saw, revealed by his trendy tight pants. Basically fuckable.

"Is that a fixie?" Slater said, looking over the bicycle.

"Yeah." He smiled. "It's a lot of fun, but you have to pay attention."

Slater scoffed and looked up at the floor-number readout. "Idiot," he muttered.

"Excuse me?" the guy demanded.

"I said you're an idiot. Riding around in LA traffic with no brakes means you're an idiot."

"You don't get to judge me."

"The paramedics will, after you crash that thing into a concrete wall."

"Fuck you," he snapped.

"No thanks, toots. I've got better sex options."

"That's not what I meant."

"You shouldn't take it personally," Slater said, raising his eyebrows. "Lots of people are stupid."

The elevator doors rumbled open, and the guy pushed the bike out, his mouth a tight line.

"Make sure you carry your ID with you," Slater called after him. "For when your skull explodes like a watermelon on the pavement. That way they can call your mother."

He turned back, one hand on the bike's yoke. "Asshole," he shouted.

"Spread out," Slater said through his teeth, as the doors rolled closed.

Stepping off on Della's floor, he found Crystal at the front desk, wearing a red blazer today, with her hair tied back.

Looking up, she frowned in recognition. "She's been waiting for you."

"You make it sound like she has nothing else to do."

Crystal huffed and rose, then walked into the hallway and toward Della's office.

"I've actually been here before," Slater said. "I can find her myself."

Crystal didn't respond to that, and he followed her into Della's office, briefly glancing at the expansive view of the basin out the window behind her desk. Concrete and asphalt and bits of greenery stretched to the hazy horizon.

Della was standing at a file cabinet along the wall. As they stepped in she rolled it closed and shifted her glasses up onto her head. She was wearing trousers and a gray tweed jacket.

"Are those the same pants you were wearing last night?"

"Of course not," Slater said.

"You fill them out so nicely."

"Seriously?" Crystal demanded. "You're flirting with him?"

"It's not like it's going anywhere." Della sat behind her desk. "Slater is forbidden fruit." Eyeing him, she added, "That's not a slur. It just means you're unattainable."

"More like strange fruit," Crystal said, and looked him up and down.

Slater put his hands on his hips. "Do you kiss your mother with that mouth?"

"Have a seat," Della said, raising her voice. "Crystal is going to join us."

"Does she have to talk?"

Crystal sat in one of the chairs in front of the desk. "I just hope that poor accountant had a long hot shower this morning."

"What are you talking about?"

"Gossip spreads quickly." Della raised her eyebrows. "You and Luís were seen leaving the reception together."

"That doesn't mean anything." Slater dropped into the other chair. "Luís wanted to show me some of his etchings."

Della chuckled. "So—recently Crystal has been taking on more responsibility. I want to read her in on this case."

His brow furrowed. "Keep an eye on the petty cash."

Crystal ignored that. She had a tablet in hand, he saw, and crossed her legs, propping the device on her knee and tapping at the screen.

"We're paying out on insured delivery dates," Della said, and scooted her chair closer to her desk. "The mining company in Nevada is having trouble delivering product on time. They claim the problem is with the transport company—they don't show up at the scheduled times. The transport company says it's the mining company."

"Where does the hairy creature fit in?"

"You mean bigfoot? The mining company says it's making trouble at the camp. An oversize creature that walks like a person and damages equipment late at night." She sighed. "It sounds far-fetched. I can't get a straight answer, and yet we're obligated to pay out on it."

"I thought bigfoot lived it the forest," Crystal said. "Not out in the desert."

"Hominid cryptids appear all over the place," Slater said. "In the Mojave, up at Big Bear, the Anza wilderness. Native Americans have stories about them everywhere. The early Spanish and the Anglos saw them too."

"How would a guy like you know something like that?" Crystal said, her brow furrowed.

"You don't know what kind of guy I am."

"Oh, I think I've got your number."

"Slater worked with bigfoot people," Della said. "He tracked one of them down."

She raised her eyebrows. "You tracked down one of the creatures?"

"I tracked down one of the people who was looking for the creatures." He waved a hand and looked to Della. "So who's your client? The mining company?"

"It's actually the company that's buying the product. They're insured with us for the delivery schedule. That's part of why it's been hard to get a straight answer. We don't have a direct relationship with the mining company or the transport company."

"What exactly is the mine producing?"

"Palladium," Della said, raising her eyebrows. "It's a valuable metal. Most of the world's supply is mined overseas, but this outfit found a way to obtain it in Nevada from a salt pan. They use some kind of revolutionary technology."

Slater scoffed. "I've heard that one before. Self-driving cars, flying to work in a drone, utopian equity wrought by staring at social media posts."

"So you believe in bigfoot," Crystal said, "but not in Silicon Valley."

"I never said I believed in bigfoot. It's certainly no more outlandish than the blue-sky bullshit the tech industry is selling us."

"It's not blue-sky," Della said. "In this situation Mott

Minerals is actually doing it. They built a functioning system to extract palladium in a novel way at this site. It's called the Elmer Mine."

"Are you sure it's legit?" he said. "Maybe the mine isn't producing as much metal as they've promised, because their paradigm-shifting technology doesn't actually work."

"We wondered about that. But several people at the site have told me they're on target."

"You went out to this place?"

"I talked to them on video calls, and I've seen documentation."

"They've made several full deliveries, haven't they?" Crystal said.

Della nodded. "So we have evidence that it's working."

Slater shifted in his chair. "What's the transport company's side of it?"

"It's an outfit called Seligman Trucking. They told me they need to use a special vehicle."

"An armored car, I'd think, if it's valuable cargo."

"Not a fully armored car," Della said, "but a vehicle with some security measures. On the highway it looks like a regular van."

"That alone is a security measure," Crystal said.

"It's also reinforced for the weight, I'm told, and has a big engine."

"Where are they based?" Slater said.

"Here in town. Vernon."

"I'll go talk to them."

"The person running the show there is named Rita," Della said. "I do not like her."

"You've met in person?"

"Just once. There's something off about her."

"Bad vibes," Slater said, and nodded. "Noted."

Della smiled. "The mining company has a presence

in town too. A transit warehouse. The contact there is a guy named Hernán. He handles delivery of the product once it arrives from the mine. He's also the only employee at that location."

"That's definitely suspicious. Can you send me the details?"

"I'll share whatever files I've got on both companies."

"What's your part in this?" Slater said, eyeing Crystal.

"Right now, looking at you, it's just trying to keep my breakfast down."

"Crystal is following the process," Della said. "For now it's a learning experience."

Slater rose. "I'll be in touch."

Downstairs the valet brought his car around, and Slater palmed a fin, slipping it to him in exchange for the keys. Driving up the ramp into the daylight, he navigated to the Fashion District, and pulled into the surface lot across from his building. A hundred years ago it had been an office tower, but today it was mostly small clothing factories. As he walked through the lobby a few day laborers were still hanging around, waiting for gigs upstairs cutting and sewing and carting fabric.

He rode the ancient elevator up to the ninth floor and walked around behind the shaft, glancing at the lettering on his office door:

SLATER IBÁÑEZ
MAXIMILLIAN CONROY
INVESTIGATIONS

The lights were off when he unlocked it and stepped inside. There was a small office each for Slater and his business partner, Max, and in the front office was a desk that their part-time operative Etta sometimes occupied. Next to the monitor on the desktop sat a little plaster statue of Rey Pascual, a skeleton wearing a crown and holding a scythe. It had been a gift from the woman he bought pupusas from, intended to bring him luck. Rey might look a little out of place now, Slater thought, since Etta had renovated the office for them.

She'd found classic art deco desks for all three rooms, and put up crown molding, and slapped some color on the walls—taupe in the front office, and mustard yellow in Max's, and a dark turquoise in Slater's. The overhead fluorescents had been replaced with 1930s hanging fixtures. For the first time in the years they'd rented it, the place felt finished, not just a utilitarian space to do paperwork and meet clients.

Slater eyed the bony figure and clicked his tongue as he walked by. "How you doing, Rey?"

At his own desk he settled into his chair, then pulled up the files Della had shared, and started to click through them. Someone had made notes on the documents. Della, maybe, or the accountant she'd mentioned. They mostly contained hard facts—names and job titles and contact details.

Scanning the info about Hernán, the guy who worked for Mott Minerals here in town, there was no home address for him, but his cell number was listed, along with the office address and phone number. Pulling out his phone, Slater dialed his office.

"The Los Angeles office is closed today," a man's voice explained on the recording. "Feel free to leave us a message or call back."

Reading from his computer screen, Slater thumb-typed Hernán's cell number.

"*Bueno*," he said when he picked up.

"My name is Ibáñez," Slater said. "I'm an insurance investigator. Regarding the Elmer Mine."

"How did you get this number?"

"Why is your office closed in the middle of the day?"

Slater demanded.

"We take a half day off on Fridays."

"I thought you were the only one who worked there."

"OK, sure. So I take a half day."

"You need to meet with me, Hernán. Preferably today."

"I'm not really around. Can we say tomorrow? I'll be in the office."

"You'd better not be dodging me."

"Dude," he said. "Chill. I said I'm available tomorrow."

"If you're concealing anything, there will be consequences." Not waiting for a reply, he ended the call.

Seligman Trucking looked like a bigger enterprise, he saw, digging through the file on his screen. LA was their home base. It was definitely big enough to drop in without calling ahead.

The sound of keys rattled at the front door, followed by Etta's voice calling out a greeting. When she stepped into his office, Slater sat back. Curvy, and with her black hair cut short, she was wearing a rugby shirt and jeans. Not waiting for an invitation she dropped into the chair in front of his desk.

"What up, pup?" she said, grinning at him.

"I've got a question for you. Say I have some money in the bank that I have to give to someone. How would you do that?"

Etta's eyes narrowed. "Write a check? Is it a checking account?"

"I think so."

"Do you have checks?"

Slater pursed his lips and thought about it. "Not that I'm aware of."

"How can you be so canny about some things and so obtuse about money?"

"This isn't about money," he said, waving a hand. "It's about banking. I understand money just fine."

"Banks let you instant-transfer funds, but it has limits, unlike checks. How much is it?"

"Fifty grand."

"They're never going to let you transfer that much through an app." She shifted in her chair. "Go into your bank and ask them what to do."

Slater huffed. "It's so damn complicated. I'll just pull out the cash."

"Has Max been in?"

"I just got here. Are you working with him today?"

"He said he might have an assignment for me."

"You've been working with him a lot," he said. "How that going?"

"It's great. I love the work. I'm learning things all the time."

"Has he got you hankering for a concealed-carry permit? I know you've been to the gun range."

"Max says I should know about firearms, and be comfortable around them, but I don't need to carry one. Unless I get my PI license."

Slater nodded. That was very good news. Etta was skilled at this work, but it felt like they were dragging her into the cesspool. Exposing her to all the lowlifes might turn her into one. Like Slater was, and like Max was. This city definitely didn't need a middle-school teacher walking around packing a rod.

The muffled rattle of keys in the door made Etta sit up.

"Speak of the devil," she said.

Max stepped in and greeted them. A burly guy with mousy brown hair, he was wearing a gray suit with a necktie loose at the collar. His sidearm bulged under his suit jacket.

"Are you ready to do some work?" Etta said.

"First I wanted to talk about the safe."

Max gestured to the squat black box bolted to the floor in the corner of Slater's office. It was an old-school antique with a dial and faded gold-leaf lettering on the door, and its presence here when they'd rented the place had sealed the deal, as it was one of the basic requirements in their business. All they'd had to do was get a locksmith to come in and retool the tumblers.

"What about the safe?" Slater said.

Max stepped over and squatted in front of it, shielding it with his body as he dialed in the combination. They'd built up trust working with Etta, but not enough to let her know how to get into the safe.

Twisting the handle, Max pulled open the heavy door.

"Have a look at this," he said, and stood erect. "There's almost a hundred grand in here. I counted it yesterday."

"Sweet," Slater said. "Money's got no odor."

Max nodded. "No odor at all."

"What does that mean?" Etta said, her brow furrowing.

"We work in the gutter," Slater said. "Lots of the stuff we do, the people we deal with—it stinks. But the money we get for it doesn't."

"Clean as it is," Max said, "there's no room in here for anything but cash."

It actually did look pretty tight, Slater realized. Neat racks with intact currency straps and messy elastic-bound bundles of greenbacks filled the shelves.

"Does that include your bounty for taking down Galliform?" Etta said.

"They put that directly into my bank account," Slater said. "That's why I'm having trouble with it. Cash, I know how to deal with."

"I contest that remark," Max said, and waved at the safe.

Slater chuckled. "I guess we're both pretty good at this business."

"Earning it, yes, thank Darwin. But we're still keeping track of it on the back of an envelope, even though we have a damn lawyer-slash-accountant."

"O'Dowd said that was fine as long as we write everything down."

Etta raised a hand. "Who's O'Dowd?"

"Our lawyer-slash-accountant," Slater said. "She's not a crook, but she's just sleazy enough for this business."

"My point," Max said, "is that there's too much cash. We need a plan to deal with all this."

"I'll talk to the Russians." Slater leaned back in his chair and laced his fingers behind his head. "We can either put up pepper-spray traps or knockout-gas traps." He pointed to the ceiling above the safe and then above the doorway. "If anyone tampers with it, boom."

"You're going to pepper-spray anyone who wanders into your office and happens to touch the safe?" Etta said.

Slater frowned. "You're right. With pepper spray, a crook could still escape with the cash. Knockout gas it is. Svetlana has this Soviet-era stuff. It works great—when you're out, you're out. We'll need to get gas masks for ourselves, though."

Max held up a palm and took a breath before he spoke. "Before we go there, how about we do something with the cash?"

"Like what?" Slater said. "Buy drapes? Etta already redecorated."

"I talked to O'Dowd," Max said. "She wants us to smurf it into our bank accounts. If the tax people notice, we can say it was a bunch of small jobs and we didn't bother to get receipts."

"That's actually mostly true." Slater waved at the

open safe. "Fine by me. Have at it."

"We both have to." Max stooped and pulled out a rack, and fanned through a chunk of it, and handed Slater a stack of C-notes. "Take two grand and put it in your personal account. I'll put two in mine and two in the business account. We'll do it again in a few weeks."

Slater stuffed the cash in his pants pocket. "So complicated."

"And yet slightly less complicated than knockout-gas booby traps." He took a pen from Slater's desk and scribbled on the envelope they used to keep track of the cash. "It is kind of amazing that when we started out, this little number 10 contained all the money we had in the world."

"It's the same envelope?" Etta said.

"We've added sheets to it," Max said, flipping through the taped-on pages, "but yeah, this is it." Tossing it back in the safe, he stooped to close the door and spin the dial.

"You two are working a window-shade job?" Slater said.

"As usual."

Etta followed Max into his office, and Slater locked his computer, and got up, and went down to the street, hustling across to the parking lot and climbing into the Thunderbird. His bank was a few blocks away, near the wholesale fashion mart.

He never came in here, he realized, looking around the place. There were fewer tellers now, with big hulking self-service machines instead. Once he'd waited in the line for a human, he slid the sheaf of hundreds across to her.

"I need to deposit this."

She stared at him for a moment. "Do you have a bank card, or an account number?"

Slater dug out his cards, and found the right one, and handed it to her. "I also need to give fifty grand of what's in that account to someone else. How can we make that happen?"

She swiped his card and stared at her computer screen. "The funds are there," she said finally. "It's a checking account. Do you have your checks?"

"I don't think so."

She talked it over with him, explaining the options, and a few minutes later he walked out with a piece of paper in his pocket that was worth fifty grand.

THREE

CLIMBING INTO THE THUNDERBIRD, Slater checked the address for Seligman Trucking on his phone. The navigation app told him to drive a few minutes south on surface streets. The neighborhood was the sprawling warehouse district south of the 10 and toward the river, with wide boulevards for semitrucks and long single-story structures amid the acres of paved yards. Slater pulled up at the address, a white and windowless building like all the others, with SELIGMAN in big blue letters on the side facing the street. A black steel-picket fence surrounded the whole place.

Some city agency or industry group had tried to spiff up the gritty district by planting trees along the verge. They were still saplings, from the look of them maybe a *Chitalpa*. It was a good choice for street trees, as they grew fast and didn't hog up the water.

The wide vehicle gate was open, and as Slater walked toward it a box truck lumbered out, its engine roaring. Plastered on the side was the Seligman logo, in the same blue and the same bland typeface as on the building. Once he was through the gate and in the yard he could see that the big garage bays along the side of the building were all open. He walked along them, then stepped inside and looked around. At the far end were office windows, he saw, just past the last big door. In one bay a couple of guys in dark coveralls were standing in front of a cube van, the hood up, a rolling tool rack parked nearby.

Box trucks were lined up along the wall.

Before he could walk back to talk to the mechanics, a woman came out of the office, headed directly toward him. Tall and bony, she had a pinched expression, and her black hair was in a tight bun, the way beat cops wore it when they were on duty. Slater stopped and watched her approach.

"*No contratar*," the woman called to him.

"*No comprendo*, sister," Slater said, exaggerating the final *o* to sound as Anglo as possible.

She stepped up to him. "We're not hiring right now. You can be on your way."

"I'm not one of your damn flunkies to shove around," Slater said. "I work for Cudahy Mutual Insurance, and if your name is Rita, you're going to have to talk to me."

She gave him the once-over. "Do you have a business card?"

Slater dug one out of his hip pocket and handed it over, and Rita glanced at it briefly before she spoke.

"What do you need to know?"

He waved his arm at the garage. "Seligman Trucking seems to be a sizeable setup."

"There are forty-odd employees. And it's 'suh-*leeg*-mun.'"

"Are you the only manager?"

"Not the only one, but I'm the one who deals with the Elmer Mine. Go on, say it: 'suh-*leeg*-mun.'"

Watching her, Slater's eyes narrowed. Her expression was deadpan. Why did he need to practice pronouncing it? She was acting like a grade-school teacher, or a control freak.

"Is the company based in the town in Arizona with that name?"

Rita folded her arms. "It's named after a person. The founder. He lived in Los Angeles a century ago. This is the company's only property."

"Do you specialize in secure transport?" Slater glanced around the garage space. "I don't see any armored cars."

"The secure vans we use for Mott are a niche service. We only have a couple of them. Most of our business is about local transport with these box trucks and intercity transport with traditional semitrucks and trailers."

"Who drives the van to the Elmer Mine and back?"

"We send a team of two," Rita said. "A driver and an armed guard. The guard does some of the driving."

"How many people work in those roles?"

"We always send the same two men. Mott doesn't hire us very often. A few times a year. It's a long drive." Her brow furrowed. "Do you actually know where the mine is? In remote northern Nevada. Miles and miles on dirt roads to get to it."

"I need to talk to those two, and you'll need to show me their personnel files."

She shook her head. "I can't do that. You can interview them here in the office, but neither one of them is in today."

"You're going to show me those files," Slater said intently, "or I'll have your insurance voided."

Rita frowned. "Cudahy Mutual isn't our insurer."

"You don't think we all share information? Mess with me and I'll hang you out to dry so fast it'll make your head spin."

In truth he couldn't really do that, and he wouldn't even try. But the seed of doubt was there, visible now in her expression.

"I can't let you take any files, but I guess I could let you look at them here."

Slater gestured widely. "Lead on."

She walked toward the office, with Slater close behind. Inside the broad window onto the garage floor was a big cluttered desk and grimy worn office furniture. Rolling open a file cabinet, Rita riffled through the contents, and pulled out a manila folder, then another, and set them on the desktop.

"You can use the guest chair," she said, gesturing to it, and then walked out.

It was surprising that she'd left him alone, but the office door was open, and his back was to the window into the garage—she could still keep an eye on him. He sat and shifted the chair closer to the desk.

The files on the two men were comprehensive, he found, with lots of stuff about wages, and copies of their tax forms, and for one of them a copy of a concealed-carry permit. From the photos on the driver's licenses they both looked like idiots. The one without the gun permit, Bender, might be fuckable in the right circumstances, but the armed guard, Vitale, looked like the kind of guy he just wanted to punch in the face.

Glancing over his shoulder, no one was in sight, so he pulled out his phone and photographed the licenses with their photos, and some of the other pages in the files that had details like addresses and phone numbers.

Once he'd seen enough he rose and walked around behind the desk. Rita had an old-school blotter calendar on her desktop, and she was using it, with appointments written in blue ink dotting the grid. Mostly they were people's names written next to times, he saw as he looked it over. The weekends were blank except for one entry, for tomorrow: "taiko." Wasn't that about drumming? Maybe it meant something else. Briefly pulling out his phone, he snapped a photo of the blotter.

There were drawers on either side of the kneehole, and he tried one, but it was locked, as were the ones on the other side. He stood erect when Rita spoke from the doorway.

"What are you doing?"

"I've been through the files," Slater said. "I need to see the vans you use to transport the palladium."

"Well, they're not in my desk," she said, scowling, and waved for him to follow.

Rita walked out onto the lot, and farther in from the street, where she stopped next to a semitruck. Beside it, almost hidden from view by the hulking vehicle, was a white cargo van. Unlike the larger vehicles, it had no markings. On the driver's side, near the back, was a dark tinted window.

Stepping behind the vehicle, Rita grabbed the handle and pulled open the double doors. From the way they swung he could tell they were heavy.

"The cargo box has steel all around," she said, "to harden it to cutting and blasting."

The floor was scuffed wooden boards, and the interior walls were unfinished steel plates, with the compartment completely sealed off from the seats up front. The tinted window on the side was just a feint, he realized, as it was completely blocked by the steel armor.

"Why is it built so secure?" Slater said. "Why not just use a regular armored car?"

"That would attract a lot of attention on desert back roads. This design allows the cargo to move around unnoticed."

"Palladium must be valuable."

Rita waved a hand. "Extremely."

"How much of it do you transport in one trip?"

Glancing around, she lowered her voice. "They ship it in ingots. About this big." She held her hands a few inches apart. "A run is usually about a hundred twenty of them. The insured value is seven million."

"All this looks pretty straightforward," he said, and rapped his knuckles on one of the doors. "Why are there unexpected delivery delays?"

"That's about Mott. They don't know what they're doing. They give us the wrong information and then blame it on us."

"What kind of wrong information?"

"The date a shipment will be ready. I always double-check now because the story tends to change." She threw up her hands. "Sometimes I send the team up there in one of these vans, and they have to wait for three days, in the middle of nowhere. Sometimes Mott is on the phone screaming at me because there's no vehicle there to pick up a shipment, even though they never asked for one."

"Who do you deal with at the mine?"

"It changes all the time." Rita sighed. "There's one named Mo. She's in the office. Hilda is another. I talk to her on the phone sometimes. She's got a quick temper."

Slater glanced into the back of the van again before he spoke. "I might be back."

Reaching for the doors, Rita folded them shut. "Whatever problems your client is having are about Mott. What I'm doing here is simple. I send a vehicle when they request one. That's all there is to it."

Watching her, he could see the sincerity she was trying to muster with her firm tone, her intent gaze.

"OK," he said, and walked toward the gate to the street.

Slater climbed into the Thunderbird and started the engine to get the air blowing, then pulled a yellow pad out of his satchel and made some notes—the names of the staff at the mine that Rita had mentioned, Mo and Hilda. Pulling out his phone, he looked at the photos he'd taken of the personnel files, zooming in on the details.

Interesting that she always sent the same two people. It left room for temptation. Businesses that entrusted workers with valuable stuff usually mixed things up, changing the personnel and the shifts and the responsibilities. That way no one got familiar enough with the system to exploit the weak spots.

The address in the personnel file for the driver, Bender, was a post office box. That was next to useless. No home address at all was listed for the guard, Vitale. Why wouldn't his employer know where he lived? Maybe Rita hadn't shown him everything. In any case these chuckleheads were making it difficult to visit them in their natural habitat.

Slater dialed Bender's personal number and listened to it ring. A voice-mail recording answered. Using his authoritative tone, he identified himself and said, "You need to call me back and set up an interview."

Vitale didn't pick up either, and Slater left the same message. Next he pulled up the paperwork that Della had sent him, but after a minute of trying to dig through it, he huffed in frustration. It was too much work on the small screen. Before he could set it down and drive away, it rang in his hand. It was one of the guys he'd just left messages for.

"Vitale," Slater said when he picked up.

"I got your message," he said. "I'm not sure what I can tell you."

"You make the runs to the Elmer Mine in Nevada. I need to talk to you about that. Are you around today?"

"Are you working tomorrow?" Vitale said. "I'm free in the afternoon."

"Where do you live?"

"I'm going to be out running errands. Can I meet you downtown?"

Once he'd set up the meeting, and ended the call, Slater pulled into the street and drove back downtown, heading up Broadway. The afternoon traffic was always sluggish, and it was always worse on Friday. He parked in the surface lot behind Andy's building and paid the attendant the flat evening rate.

Walking around to the street entrance, he went up to Andy's floor and knocked on his door. It took him a minute to get there. As he pulled it open, Andy flashed that easy smile. He hadn't shaved in a few days, and his hair was a perfect tousled mess. His metabolism ran hot, so even though it was winter, he was wearing his usual boxer shorts and a tank top.

Andy's loft was mostly one big room, with the original wooden floors from when it had been a textile warehouse, and big multipane windows, a bed, and a desk with an impressive array of computer monitors. A little kitchen table sat under the windows.

"I wasn't expecting you," Andy said, and dropped into his desk chair.

"I brought you something." Slater dug in his pocket and handed him the banker's check.

"Fuck me," Andy said, once he'd scanned it. "Fifty grand. That's half the ... reward for catching Galliform."

"You did half the work."

"I can't believe they actually ... paid you. I thought those bounties were just ... bait to get tips from people."

"I had to push for it," Slater said. "As soon as I told them I was thinking of taking it to the media to claim that they'd scammed me, they caved."

"That would do it. Nobody who needs the ... public's help wants bad press."

"It was pretty hard for them to weasel out of it. Four federal cops watched me clobber the guy."

"Why a cashier's check? Don't you have ... your own checks?"

"You're the third person who's asked me that today." He threw up his hands. "They're probably in a drawer somewhere. Most of my jobs are in cash. The banker convinced me to do the check. She said giving you five racks would be a hassle for you."

"I guess you never have to … pay me to work for you again," Andy said, setting the check on his computer desk.

"Of course I have to pay you. That's a separate thing. This is the gravy. Your Uncle Sam showing his appreciation for your hard work."

Andy laughed. "Who am I to argue with … the will of the American people?"

"Speaking of work, can you look into a couple of knuckleheads for me? I have names and photos and Social Security numbers, but for some reason no home addresses."

"Sure. Are they lowlifes?"

"You tell me. They work for a transport company. I want to know if they're dirty or connected to anybody shady. I'll send you the details." Slater pulled out his phone and took a minute to share the photos he'd taken of the files on Bender and Vitale.

"Do you have time … to mess around?" Andy said.

"It's Friday night," Slater said, tucking his phone away. "Don't you have a date with that gunsel Kyle?"

"He's coming over on Sunday. You should too."

"Kyle is such a sweet little twink." He put his hands on his hips. "He makes my teeth ache. I'm afraid I'll catch diabetes."

"You have such a delicate and sensitive … constitution. I'll be here to protect you, petal."

Slater chuckled. "You're really into the three-way thing."

"It's like I can … have my cake and eat it too."

"Kyle doesn't seem all that into it."

"He shows up," Andy said. "And so do you."

Watching him talk, seeing the spark in his eyes, Slater

could feel his heart pound. He knelt in front of him, and put his hands on Andy's thighs, hot to the touch and run through by his random muscle movements.

"I show up for you. Not for him."

"That's what ... he said."

Slater leaned in and met his mouth, taut and warm and perfect. Andy's woody was tenting his boxers, so he shifted closer, pulling him against his belly. As Andy pulled off his shirt, Slater mouthed his chest and his neck.

"Let's get ... horizontal," Andy said, and Slater pulled back.

Stretched out on his bed, arms behind his head, Andy watched him undress.

"Let's go, son. This dick isn't ... going to ride itself."

Slater had to chuckle. He took his time undressing, moving deliberately, making a show of it for Andy. By the time he was naked, Andy was rock hard.

Climbing on top of him, Slater lowered his weight onto his body. He knew it turned him on. Mouthing his neck, his nose in his hair, he ground his cock into his thigh.

"Want to smoke me?" Andy said.

Slater shifted down the bed, and took him into his mouth, and worked him, keeping a forearm firmly across his knees to fend off the involuntary muscle spasms. As Andy climaxed, he thrashed around, his CP making it seem more chaotic than it really was.

When Slater sat up, Andy grabbed his cock and stroked him. Slater mouthed his neck, and breathed in the heady scent of his hair. Their mouths locked together, Slater came, breathing hard, then pulled away, and rolled onto his back.

"That didn't take long," Andy said.

"You know why."

He ran his hand across Slater's belly. "Do I?"

"It's because you're sexy, and you're an extremely good kisser. Just thinking about you puts lead in the pencil."

Andy chuckled. "Good to know."

His arm folded over his eyes, Slater drifted off for a while, stirring briefly when he felt Andy pull away. He was vaguely aware of the sound of him at his computer, and when he finally sat up, it was dark outside. He grabbed his shirt and pulled it on.

"That was fun," Andy said, swiveling his chair toward him.

"I have to go." He pulled on his jeans, then squatted to tie his boots.

"See you Sunday?"

"If I remember to take some antinausea medication," Slater said as he rose. "I'll need it, right, because I'll have to deal with Kyle."

"I understood the implication."

He leaned in to kiss him. "Bye, beautiful."

It wasn't much of a drive to Westlake. Once he'd waited for his garage door to roll down, he trotted up to his apartment, and ditched his boots. In the cupboard the fifth waited patiently for him, golden and gleaming. When he poured out his ration it looked like barely more than a taste. But he had to make it work. Grabbing his laptop, he got comfortable in the recliner. He closed his eyes and took a sip, savoring that delicious burn. He could already feel his body starting to relax.

Setting the tumbler and its paltry contents on the carpet under his hand, he pulled open his computer and looked up *taiko*, the word that Rita had written on her calendar. There didn't seem to be any other meaning besides the drums. They came in different sizes, but mostly it was about the big ones, played on their own as a type of performance.

When he searched for local taiko events, he found a class happening tomorrow afternoon. It aligned with the time Rita had written down. That had to be it—Rita was taking a taiko class. The venue was a public park along the Arroyo.

Slater thought about it for a minute, then fished out his phone and texted Etta:

I need you on a case tomorrow. Do you have time to strategize in the morning?

Etta's response came soon after:

Yes! I'll be in the office first thing.

Slater thumb-typed a reply:

I won't. I have a thing to do. I'll be in around 11.

FOUR

W AKING TO THE BUZZ of a text message, Slater
rubbed his eyes and scrabbled for his phone
on the bedside table. It was from the driver,
Bender:

I got your message. I'm working today. I'll contact
you when I get a day off.

"Idiot," Slater muttered, and forced himself to throw
off the covers and confront the cold air. Once he'd
washed up, and nuked a mug of water to make pseudo
coffee, and pulled on his clothes, he hustled down to
his garage. Backing the Thunderbird into the alley, he
waited for the door to roll down, then headed toward
Seligman Trucking.

Obviously the company didn't take Saturday off,
as the vehicle gate was open, and the bay doors were
rolled up. There were people in the truck yard, and as
he walked into the building, he could see Rita sitting in
her office. Maybe he'd been wrong about her going to
that taiko class. But that was still hours away. Toward the
back a guy was working under a cube van that was up on
a lift, but otherwise it was quiet.

Rita stepped out of the office. Her face clouded when
she recognized him. Wearing a dark nylon jacket, her
hair was bundled tightly again. If you were going to keep
your hair so tightly bound every day, why not just butch
it, the way Etta did?

"What are you doing here on the weekend?" Slater said.

"I'm here when there's work on."

"Your man Bender said he'd be in. I need to talk to him."

Rita frowned. "He told you he'd be here? He's on his way to Natron, or on the way back."

"Where's Natron?"

"Up the 395 in Inyo County. They mine borax or boron or some such." She waved a hand. "Bender's on a job, and his job is driving. Why would he be hanging around here?"

Thinking about it, the guy had said he was working, not that he was at the office. Slater had made a stupid assumption.

"When will he be back?"

"He'll drop off the truck sometime this evening. I won't be around."

"So I guess you're not always here when there's work on."

Rita dropped her chin, a smirk playing on her lips. It was the first time he'd seen a crack in her facade.

"Work's not all I do," she said. "We should go out sometime. Get to know each other better."

Slater frowned. "I'm on dick, sister, so you can cut the crap."

He knew she wasn't really interested. It was just a tactic to influence him, gain an advantage, take charge. That alone was noteworthy.

Her eyes hardened. "You can be on your way, then." She turned to walk back to the office.

He stood for a moment, and looked around the garage, then walked out to his car. It wasn't a completely wasted trip—he'd learned that Rita was up to something.

Driving north, Slater turned onto Washington and

paralleled the metro train for a few blocks, the riders in the windows with their eyes closed or gazing out absently at the traffic, then turned into the Fashion District and parked across the street from his office. The attendant wasn't around, but they never bothered him anyway, as long as he bought a pass at the start of the month.

Instead of crossing the street he strode to the end of the block and headed into Skid Row. Along the cross street he walked in the gutter, avoiding all the tents cluttering the sidewalk. The encampment was quiet at this hour, at least. If you lived in a tent it was probably the best time of day to get some sleep.

His destination was a new construction, out of place and towering over the neighborhood's sagging old commercial buildings. There was shelter housing on the upper floors, he'd been told, and downstairs was meeting rooms and offices. Walking through the lobby, he found the right room and stepped through the open door.

A dozen folding chairs were arranged in a circle on the carpet, most of them occupied by the losers who'd shown up already. Slater took a chair, strategically not directly across from the instructor, or whatever he called himself—coordinator or facilitator or something equally milquetoast. A yoga-skinny guy in a billowy white cotton blouse, he was sitting bolt upright, his blond hair held back by a clip. He'd told them his name was Integrity, but no way had his mother put that on his birth certificate. He looked more like a Chad or a Brandon or a Tyler. "Integrity" was the New Age equivalent of a street name.

Integrity caught his eye and smiled. Slater looked away, and folded his arms, and set his teeth, trying not to scowl. Normally he'd never be in a place like this, but he had no choice. He'd slapped around a lowlife and got caught. Usually those guys never went whining to the cops because they were up to something worse, but how was Slater supposed to know he was a police informant? Of course they'd press charges after hearing his "poor me" tale of woe. The prosecutor's office had a diversion program, and they'd offered to let Slater take this mindfulness class instead of going to court. It was painful, but he knew it was a lot better than sitting in stir.

Scanning the attendees, most of them were lowlifes, and mostly men, and likely here for the same reason he was, on diversion from the crowded jail system. He'd picked this class for the location, near his office, but since it was on Skid Row, lots of these people were clearly homeless.

"Welcome, everyone," Integrity said, his calm dulcet voice just above the level of the conversations. He waited a moment for everyone to quiet down and focus on him. "I invite you to sit up straight. If our chakras are aligned, light can penetrate deep within."

Slater dutifully sat up, along with the others, some of them grunting and looking physically pained at the process.

"Today we're going to continue to invite awareness," Integrity went on. "That will allow us to invite other supportive practices into our lives, so that we can make better choices. Let's all close our eyes and invite mindful breathing."

He talked them through the exercise, step by step, breathing slowly and deeply. Slater followed along. It was weird to be aware of the process. Breathing was something his body already knew how to do. It didn't really seem like something he needed help with.

"Mindful breathing allows us to invite nourishment into our lives, and then transform negativity," Integrity said, as if reading his thoughts. "I invite you now to welcome contemplation and deep reflection. This will allow us to get to the root of why inner negative attachments are present for us."

Slater opened one eye. Integrity had his eyes firmly closed, his hands in the air with his thumbs and index fingers in little circles. The guy was dead serious about this.

After leading them through some more breathing techniques, Integrity said, "I invite you to open your eyes." He smiled at them, looking around the circle. "We all have things to be grateful for, no matter what challenges we face. Let's talk about that. Harmony, what are you grateful for?"

Harmony had her shopping bags piled next to her, and wore a vinyl rain jacket over a print dress. It was hard to imagine how that little chair was holding up her oversize bulk.

"I'm still here," Harmony said, her raspy voice jarring and loud after listening to Integrity. "This neighborhood wants to grind me into dust. But I'm still here."

"Indeed you are," Integrity said. "I'm so glad you are." He turned to look at Slater. "Slater—what are you grateful for?"

It was surprising that the guy actually remembered his name. He'd only been here once before. But then he probably had to—despite all the soft edges, the justice system needed to know who actually showed up.

Slater raised his eyebrows. "Nothing."

Integrity smiled. "Are you sure about that? Like Harmony said, you're alive on this earth. Isn't that something to be grateful for?"

"Gratitude is weakness, man."

Anger flashed in his eyes. There it was. This guy could suppress it, or deny it, or lie to himself that it wasn't in him, but there it was. Everyone had it.

"That's not where we're at in this group," Integrity

said, holding his gaze, his tone unperturbed. "I'll give you a moment to connect with your feelings, and invite calm, to nourish yourself." He looked away. "Who else can talk about what they're grateful for?"

FIVE

N HOUR LATER SLATER walked back to his office building and into the lobby. The factories ran on Saturday, and a few day laborers were hanging around, chatting and waiting for gigs. When he walked into the office Etta was on the front desk. She'd turned the statue of Rey Pascual around, facing her now, positioned next to the computer monitor. She must like the little guy.

"Your car was in the lot," Etta said. "Where were you?"

"That new building on Skid Row. I had a mindfulness class."

"Right—I remember. You're lucky that's all you have to do. Is it working?"

"Totally. Can't you tell?" Slater waved an arm. "I feel completely blissed out. I've actually been able to invite imperturbable calm into my life, so I won't have to go back."

Etta frowned. "Like I tell my kids, I'm dubious of that assertion."

"It's true. I've cleared a week in my calendar too. I'm going to spend some time inviting clarity by staring at my navel. If you can do it for seven days straight, all the wisdom of the universe comes shooting out in a blinding beam."

Etta laughed, then sat up when a knock came at the door.

"Are you expecting someone?" Slater said.

"Nope."

He pulled open the door to find a man wearing a black T-shirt, and jeans, and pointy-toed boots. Still in his twenties, maybe, his dark hair was slicked back. He was kind of buff, and his face was contorted with anger, his fists balled. It was a pose meant to intimidate, but from his stance it was clear he didn't really know how to throw a punch.

"Are you Max Conroy?" the guy demanded.

Slater jutted his chin. "Who's asking?"

"My wife kicked me out because of you," he said, raising his voice.

"I bet she kicked you out because you were screwing someone else."

"That's nobody's business but mine. That woman was my meal ticket."

"Simmer down," Slater said. "Maybe your side piece can pay your bills."

His hand still on the door, he started to pull it closed, but the guy threw a punch. Slater saw it coming, and blocked him with his forearm, and quickly struck his chin with his other fist. The guy's head spun, and he stumbled back.

"You don't get to hit me, *cholo*."

Slater lunged at him, and grabbed the front of his shirt, and slapped him hard, left and then right. "I am not a *cholo*."

"Stop it," he shouted, trying to fend him off.

"You'll take it, and you'll like it," Slater growled, and pushed him away.

He stumbled back, one hand on his cheek, panting. "Why did you show her those pictures?"

"I didn't show her anything, dipshit. I'm not Max. But I bet the pictures were of something real. Your wife already knew some part of it, or she never would have called Max."

"Fuck you," he spat, "and fuck Max."

"You should be pissed at yourself, Tex, not at Max."

The guy scoffed and pushed his way into the stairwell.

Behind Slater, Etta was watching from the office doorway. "I'm so glad you've invited calm into your life this morning. I can see it's really taken root."

He followed her back inside and flipped the deadbolt. "That actually was pretty calm. If I'd been perturbed I would have used a haymaker on him and thrown him down the stairs. Do you know who he is?"

"I've never seen him before. I don't think I worked on that case."

Etta followed him into his office and sat across from him.

"So what's the job?"

Slater explained what he was working on. "The honcho at the transport company is a woman named Rita. I thought you might be able to get close to her. She's taking a taiko class this afternoon at a park along the Arroyo. That one in Hermon."

"What does she look like?" Etta said.

"Let me see if I can find a photo of her." On his computer he looked up Seligman Trucking's website, and sure enough, there was a head shot of Rita among the other managers. "Check your phone."

Etta tapped at her screen and then studied the image. "She's a lot older than me."

"Does that matter to lesbians?"

"How do you know she's a lesbian?"

"She seems that way," he said, and gestured vaguely.

Etta frowned. "What were the indicators?"

"She was wearing a tool belt with a circular saw and a belt sander hanging off it."

"Bullshit. Even if I believed that, it doesn't make her gay."

"Rita actually hit on me," Slater said. "But I could tell it was just to see if she could get leverage."

"That makes her sound straight."

"She did it the way a lesbian would think straight women act. Like in an old movie. Even better evidence is that she didn't look at my crotch even once."

Etta chuckled. "So you're completely irresistible to straight women."

"It's not about attraction. But they usually check out the merch. Unless they're not shopping in that aisle."

"You're completely delusional. Did you know that?"

Slater waved a hand. "I need to get into her phone. If you can install some Russian software, I might be able to get into her company files."

"How does that work?"

"With a QR code. You scan it with her phone and it brings up a website. Click the link to install the software. You might have to do a couple of permission overrides. I'll text you the code. Whatever you do, don't install it on your own phone."

"That sounds like a ham-handed thing to do," she said. "I should be able to manage it."

Slater dug out his phone and tapped at it.

"It means I'll need to get my hands on her phone," Etta said.

"That's the part that takes finesse."

"I'll need to get the code to unlock it, and then I'll need a minute alone with the device. Do you have a technique to get a phone pass code?"

"That's the thing about getting friendly with someone. If you're sitting very close, it's hard to hide your screen without looking paranoid. For most people the instinct to play nice overrides their concerns about security. It's why con artists are able to thrive."

"So what do I do?"

"Just ask to see some photos or something."

She pursed her lips. "I guess that might work."

"Even if you're sitting opposite, you can detect the pattern. Watch my thumb."

Slater held his phone with the screen tilted up and out of her view, then tapped at the numbers on his screen.

"I get it," she said. "Top left, then bottom right. That means 7, then 3, then 5 and 6."

"Even if you're not completely sure of every digit, you can try a few variations before it locks you out."

"I'm not sure how I'll even get possession of it. But I'll see what I can do."

"What's it going to cost me?" Slater said.

Her brow furrowed for a moment. Finally she said, "Three dollars?"

"That works."

"Plus the cost of the taiko class."

"Fine," he said flatly.

Etta sat forward. "I guess I should sign up for that class. Then I'll have to think up an excuse for abandoning Safiya today."

"You don't tell her about working with Max and me?"

"She knows that much." Etta rose. "But I'm not going to tell her the operation is to romance another woman."

Checking the clock on his phone, Slater saw that he had time to go to Doris's before his meeting with the transport company goon. He rode down to his car and headed toward the freeway, accelerating on the ramp and driving north a few exits to hilly Mount Washington.

Doris's Buick was missing when he pulled into her driveway, but her stupid boyfriend's stupid Boxster was here, parked at a douchey angle. Slater pulled up tight to its rear end, even though he could have parked beside it, and climbed out, then walked around to the gate into the backyard.

The roses were looking sharp, and the bougainvillea hedge at the side wasn't throwing out canes the way it did in warmer weather. In the little shed he pulled on a pair of work gloves, then heaved up a bag of wood mulch and carried it out to the yard.

Kneeling in front of the bed of ornamentals, he spread the mulch on the surface, massaging it in with his fingers. The soil smelled vibrant and alive. This was way more calm-inducing than sitting around with Integrity and his bland version of mindfulness. Proximity to the dirt was what recharged him, through his hands and his knees and his boots.

The back door to the house swung open and Albert stepped out. Gray-headed and balding, he was trying to compensate with styled muttonchop sideburns. His whole look, and that affable smile, made Slater want to punch him in the face.

"Why do you leave so much space around the plants?" Albert said, leaning on the railing. "Is the mulch not supposed to touch the stalks?"

"It's technical, Albert." He sat back on his heels. "I don't think you'd understand."

"I have a medical degree. I might be able to wrap my mind around the logic of gardening."

Slater sighed impatiently. "There are native bees and other insects that need access to the soil. You have to leave room for them."

"That doesn't sound so difficult to grasp."

"This is about the nuances and complexity of nature, not bloodletting and amputations."

His face clouded. "You know damn well that's not what I do."

"Where's Doris, anyway?"

"Out with some of her girlfriends."

"If you iced her and tried to hide her car," Slater said, "it'll all come out. You know that, right? Even if you torched the Buick and rolled it into a canyon, the cops can still ID the vehicle, and it'll come back on you. Whatever you steal from her they'll find when they search your place."

"You don't think very much of me, do you."

"That's quite insightful, Albert. I hope you're that smart about your patients."

"I love your mother. More significantly, she loves me. You need to get comfortable with that. You only get one mother in this world."

Slater chuckled. "It's funny that you think your presence could in any way impact my relationship with Doris. You're like a silverfish crawling around behind the furniture of our lives."

"I'm not saying I'm a threat to you," Albert said. "But pushing me away means pushing her away."

"When I get word of the first teardrop that falls because of you," Slater said, jabbing a gloved finger at him, "I'm coming for you."

"Always a pleasure to see you, Slater." Albert stood erect and went back inside.

"Idiot," Slater muttered, and went back to the mulch.

When he was done with that he grabbed a bucket and poured fertilizer into it, the low-phosphorous kind for citrus trees, then massaged it into the soil in a wide circle around the trunk of the lemon tree. He sprayed water over the dirt and the mulch for a few minutes, then coiled up the hose and packed everything back into the shed.

Usually he washed up in the house, but no way was he going to give Albert the satisfaction of playing the gatekeeper. Instead he slapped the dirt off his knees and went out the side gate. Freaking Albert. Such a creep.

Climbing into his car, he backed into the street and headed toward the freeway. It would be better to have something from Andy about Vitale, the armed guard, before he interviewed him, but he wasn't going to nudge Andy. The guy did good work, and Slater could take another run at Vitale if he turned up any dirt.

Vitale wanted to meet at a coffee place near the library, which seemed a little suspicious, but then lots of people lived far from where they worked. If Vitale lived in freaking Fullerton or some distant exurb, this was definitely a better choice.

He had to cruise the streets a while for a parking spot, and eventually found one a few blocks away. As he walked into the coffee place he scanned the clientele. Lots of the tables were occupied, with loud conversations filling the air, and he soon spotted Vitale, sitting with his back to the side wall, staring at his phone.

At the counter Slater ordered an espresso and subtly watched Vitale while he waited for it. In his forties, he looked Anglo, and had dark hair. You had to wear it shorter than that when you were balding. Straight guys were so clueless. Even though it was warm enough inside, Vitale wore a light jacket over a collared shirt, the way Max did sometimes. Slater couldn't see the telltale bulge from here, but he was likely dressed that way to conceal his sidearm.

Vitale never glanced up, obviously unconcerned about their impending meeting. Once he had his coffee in hand, Slater stepped over to his table and pulled out the chair.

Watching him as he sat, Vitale set his phone down. "You're Ibáñez? What exactly does your company need from me?"

"It's all about the delivery delays, Vitale. And you're

the one who's in that van every time."

"I also drive that van half the time."

His gaze was level, not intimidated even a little by Slater's tone. This guy was no civilian.

"So why are there delays?"

"The mining company keeps changing the story," Vitale said. "I'm sure Rita told you that. They change the pickup date when we're already on the road, or we get there and they tell us we'll have to wait another day, or longer. We're not paid to wait around."

Interesting that he knows he'd talked to Rita, Slater thought, watching him talk. That meant they were comparing notes.

"So it's all about Mott's incompetence," Slater said.

"What else would it be? We don't do the scheduling."

"What does the hairy creature have to do with it?"

Vitale scowled. "Did Mott's people tell you that? As if that's the cause of their problems. It's a great excuse, isn't it? A paranormal entity that you can't detain and you can't talk to. They might as well say ghosts did it, or the holy spirit."

"So you've never seen evidence of the creature."

"All I've seen up there is evidence of bullshit."

"Run through the procedure for me," Slater said. "The trip up there, the pickup, the delivery."

Vitale sat back and took a breath. "It's not that complicated."

Slater raised his eyebrows. "Indulge me."

"Rita usually gets the pickup request a couple days ahead. We get on the road after traffic, like 9 p.m., and get to the mine around 8 a.m."

"So the drive takes eleven hours."

"With stops for gas. I usually drive the first half. The mine people load the cargo into the van."

"Do you get a look at it?"

"The ingots are on a pallet. One of us has to make sure the count is what's on the bill of lading. That only takes a few seconds, then they cover it with a tarp and tie it down in the back of the van."

"You come back the same day?" Slater said.

"As soon as the load is secured and we've eaten a burrito."

"Do you always take the same route?"

Vitale waved a hand. "It depends on the weather. In summer we go up the 395 through the Sierra. In winter through the Cajon Pass and around Death Valley."

"What time do you get back to the city?"

"We usually leave the mine around 9 or 10 and get to Mott's depot at 8 or 9 p.m."

"Who do you deal with at the depot?"

"A guy named Hernán." Vitale chuckled. "He's not very bright."

"He's the only one who receives the stuff?"

"The only employee Mott has in LA, I'm told. He unloads the pallet and locks it in the safe."

"A pallet loaded with palladium fits in a safe?"

"I guess it's more like a vault. By volume it's actually not that much stuff. Enough to fill a barrel, maybe, if you stacked it right. But it's extremely heavy."

"Like rocks?"

"Heavier. Think solid metal."

Slater nodded to his sidearm, its bulge visible under his jacket. "Have you ever had to use that rod on the road, or at the mine?"

"Not yet." A smirk played on his lips.

He drained his little cup and stood up.

"That's it?" Vitale said.

"For now."

SIX

SLATER WALKED OUT TO the street and headed toward where he'd parked. He needed to compare Vitale's story with what Bender had to say. Why hadn't that guy called him back? Once he was behind the wheel of the Thunderbird, he dialed Bender's number, and got voice mail.

"You need to talk to me," he told the machine. "If you're avoiding me, I will hunt you down."

Swiping through the case files on his phone, he found the office address for Mott Minerals. It was just outside downtown, past the 10, in an old industrial neighborhood. Shifting into gear, he pulled into the traffic and headed south.

Any business that dealt with semitrucks would have long ago relocated farther out, where there was room for them, but this central district was still bustling with light industry and warehouses. Slater parked at the curb in front of the address, a single-level structure in grimy white-painted stucco. There was no sign, only the numbers painted above the pedestrian door, next to a vehicle entrance with the shutter rolled down. The building wasn't neglected, just old, he decided, and the steel shutter actually looked new.

Slater walked to the door and tried it, but it was locked. With the heel of his fist he pounded on the glass, then cupped his hands to shield his eyes, and looked inside. The interior looked dark, but then a figure appeared, hustling toward him. He flipped the deadbolt and pulled it open.

Still in his thirties, his Latin hair was in a trendy style, high on top. Basically fuckable, Slater decided. His brow furrowed as he stepped back for Slater to enter.

"I'm Hernán. You're from the insurance company?"

"That's right."

Not bothering to lock the deadbolt again, Hernán led the way down the hall to an office with a pair of desks. The room was wood-paneled and had ancient shoe-blackened carpeting, unrenovated in decades. It didn't look like the kind of place a cutting-edge tech company would be caught dead in. One of the desks was empty and disused, but the other looked lived in, piled with paper and a computer monitor and several fist-size rocks.

"Sit down," Hernán said, and waved to the chair in front of his desk. He dropped into his chair, and scooted it closer, then folded his hands on the desktop. "Can I see your badge?"

Slater's eyes narrowed. "I'm not law enforcement. I work for an insurance company."

"They don't give you a badge to investigate insurance?"

"I investigate insurance fraud, not the insurance itself. There's no badge. But I can show you my business card." He half rose and pulled one out of his hip pocket, and handed it across the desk.

Hernán studied it for a moment. "You got one of each."

"What are you talking about?"

"An Anglo name and a Latin name. Like my family—kind of Latin but pretty much assimilated. For birthdays it's empanadas and hot dogs both."

"I can't really call myself Latin," Slater said.

"I hear you. Some of my uncles don't even speak English." He waved a hand. "It probably makes sense, right, because they live in Mexico, but it makes communication quite challenging."

Slater watched him talk, irritated but not quite ready to react. Normally his instinct would be to slap some sense into the guy—the kovac was a precision tool to sharpen someone's focus—but he wanted to hear how this would play out.

"My sister speaks the language," Hernán went on, "but that's probably because her first husband spoke it. He made her get her tubes tied after their kid was born, then she divorced him, and now there's a new man, and he wanted kids, so she had the procedure reversed. Can you believe that? It seems so extreme."

Slater leaned forward, but before he could say anything, Hernán spoke.

"I don't know why everyone thinks it's all my fault." His eyes grew wide. "I just do what I'm told."

Slater gestured impatiently. "What's your fault? Are you still talking about your sister's tubes?"

"Nothing is my fault," he said intently. "The problems at the Elmer. Those truckers and other people want to put it on me."

"So you do what you're told," Slater said. "Who tells you what to do?"

"Technically my boss is in the head office. Gary. We've actually never met. I just talk to them for the HR stuff. Day to day I deal with the people at the mines."

"There's more than one mine?"

"Half a dozen across the West," Hernán said.

"Is that what the rocks are about?" Slater said, gesturing to them on his desktop.

He beamed. "That's right. Ore samples. Not from the Elmer, though. They're not mining ore."

"So the head office isn't at the Elmer Mine."

"The Elmer is in Nevada," he said slowly, as if maybe Slater wasn't quite paying attention, "and Mott Minerals head office is in Denver, or Colorado, or one of those."

"Who do you deal with at the Elmer?"

"Mostly Mo. Sometimes Hilda. Those two usually arrange the shipments."

"And once it gets here, you sell it?"

"Head office sells it. I just deliver it."

"You drive it somewhere?"

Hernán shook his head. "The buyer comes to pick it up. That usually happens the next day. The day after those truckers bring it in."

"So all you do is watch the trucking crew unload it," Slater said, "and then watch the buyer load it up again?"

He frowned. "You make it sound so basic. It's not. I have to do the unloading, and lock up the vault, and unlock it again, and take care of the office."

"How many shipments come through here?"

"Three or four a week, but from the Elmer only once in a while. I'd say every couple months or so."

"So why are there problems at the Elmer?" Slater said.

"It's not about them—it's about the transport company. Seligman. Those dopes call and say they're coming, and then they don't show up, and no one answers the phone. Once Mo said they left the mine at 9 a.m., and they didn't show up here until 2 a.m. I had to come back in the middle of the night."

"Is it always the same crew on the truck?"

Hernán nodded. "One of them is a damn bully." He deepened his voice to mimic him: "'You need to put down the meth pipe, you little fairy, and learn to use a calendar.'"

"Is that Vitale, or Bender?"

"I don't even remember their names. There's a black one and a white one. The black guy doesn't say much, but the white guy is mouthy. He always carries a gun."

"Vitale," Slater said.

"I don't smoke meth." He waved a hand. "That's such a stereotype. Just because I like to shake my booty sometimes in places where there's guys."

"There's no crime in that. Does Seligman handle the shipping from the other mines?"

"Each one is different. Gary said they try to get a local transport company, but the Elmer is so remote that there aren't any. So they use a company from LA."

"Have you been to the Elmer Mine?"

Hernán chuckled. "The farthest into the desert I've been is Palm Springs. There's some fun hotels there, and great menswear stores. The last time I went I bought a swimsuit. It has these little stripes on it." He gestured in the air. "High cut. I think that's coming into style again."

"High cut is always in style," Slater said, and raised his eyebrows. "Did Mo or Hilda mention a hairy creature at the camp?"

His expression sobered. "They said bigfoot comes around and smashes stuff. Nobody managed to take a picture of it, but Hilda said it smells really bad, so they know it's bigfoot. She saw it one night walking around at the edge of the camp."

"Is she the only one who's seen it?"

"I don't think so." He shrugged. "Like I said, I haven't been up there."

"Can you show me the vault?"

Hernán pursed his lips. "I guess that would be all right," he said finally, and stood up. "There's some stuff in there. As long as you don't steal it."

Slater followed him down the hall, and watched as he produced his keys and unlocked the door into a roomy garage bay. It had a concrete floor, and a high ceiling, and the tall steel shutter he'd seen from outside. There was at least enough room to park a box truck. At the far end of the space was a gray-painted vault door with a big five-spoke handle and an electronic keypad, and parked at one side was a little yellow forklift.

"You drive this baby?" Slater said.

"A-yup. I had to get a license for it."

"Do you administer the security recordings?" He pointed to the camera mounted high on the wall, aimed at the vault door.

"I can't even see the recordings. That goes to head office."

"In Denver, or Colorado, or one of those," Slater said.

Hernán gazed at a black fob on his key ring for a moment, then stepped over to the keypad on the vault door. Slater had seen those before—the fob generated a short-lived unlock code.

Glancing back at him, Hernán met his gaze. "Don't look." Shielding the keypad with his body, he punched in the numbers.

"Not that it matters. That combination is going to expire in two minutes."

"Actually ten minutes. How did you know that?"

He started cranking the handle, and Slater could hear the heavy mechanism rumbling inside the door. Once the bolts were retracted, Hernán heaved it open, and stepped in, and flicked on the light.

"This is it."

Slater stepped to the doorway. In the middle of the space a loose tarp was folded over a low square shape.

"You can go in," Hernán said, "but don't disturb anything."

"When you say that, it makes me want to." Slater squatted at the corner of the tarp and flipped it back.

Under it was a bare wooden pallet. He eyed Hernán. "Did you get jacked?"

"You know, there was a pickup on Thursday. I don't know why they didn't take the tarp. I guess there's not supposed to be anything in here."

Slater got to his feet. "Are you sure about that?"

"Of course I'm sure." He frowned. "I'm the only one who works here."

Once he'd stepped out, Hernán killed the light, then started to crank the door handle again. Watching him work, Slater couldn't quite figure him out yet. Hernán was either a birthright airhead or a calculating lowlife putting on a command performance.

Finished locking the door, Hernán turned toward him and smiled.

"Do you ever wave to Gary?" Slater said.

"What?"

He gestured to the camera. "In the head office."

Gazing up at it, his brow furrowed. "Do you think he's watching?"

"You could ask him."

Hernán led the way back into the hallway, and Slater paused at the door to the street.

"So what kind of places do you go to shake your booty?"

He chuckled. "Mostly downtown. There's a bar by the market, and then one over by Fort Ronnie."

"That one has food," Slater said. "Do you want to go? I haven't really eaten today."

His eyebrows shot up. "You're asking me on a date?"

"I'm not going to do couples yoga with you in Griffith Park, or wait in line for brunch for an hour, or buy matching chocolate labs, or whatever it is that people do on dates."

"So that means dinner, and …?"

Slater put his hands on his hips. "I'll fuck you, Hernán, if that's what you want."

"I can work with that." He laughed and swirled his palm at Slater. "I like all this. What you've got going on."

"Then it won't seem like work at all."

"Can I meet you there? I have to lock up."

Pushing his way out to the street, Slater walked over to his car. The golden light and long shadows of the end of the day ran through the neighborhood. As he climbed into the Thunderbird he wondered how Etta's taiko lesson had gone. He pulled out his phone and sent her a text:

Any luck?

Her reply came a moment later:

I'm close. Talk later.

It was a quick drive to the Historic Core, and he soon found a street space near the hulking state office building. Despite the pink granite facade, from the street it looked like a prison, and the desk jockeys who worked inside called it Fort Ronnie.

In the next block was that fun little pub, and he climbed the outdoor stairs, looking around for an open table. Hernán was already here, parked at a tall table by the windows, a bright orange drink in front of him.

As Slater pulled out the other stool, the server stepped up and eyed him. "What'll it be, hon?"

"A small of lager," Slater said, "and that thing you do with rice and vegan chorizo."

She nodded and took the menu. "Coming up."

"You must be a traffic savant," Slater said, eyeing Hernán.

"What are you talking about?"

"Just that you got here so fast. Is that a mai tai?"

"Yum, right? It's like liquid candy. You can't even tell there's booze in it. I didn't order for you because I don't know what you drink. But I got you a food menu." Hernán's brow furrowed. "You already knew what you wanted. And you're vegan."

"You sound like you don't believe it."

"No judgment. But you don't look like a vegan."

Slater waited while the server set down his beer glass and then hustled away.

"You're picturing a guy with long blond hair, tied back with a clip, wearing a billowy raw cotton shirt with no buttons on it."

Hernán laughed. "Exactly."

Hoisting his glass, he reached across to tap it on Hernán's cocktail. "He teaches my mindfulness class."

———·———

AFTER THEY'D EATEN, AND Slater paid, they walked down the stairs to the street.

"Regarding that other activity we discussed," Hernán said. "Do you live around here? I live with my parents, and my sister, and her boyfriend."

"The one who had her tubes tied."

"She actually had it reversed. She's got another kid now, if you can believe that. So the procedure worked."

"It sounds like it might be crowded there. I live alone, but you're not going to like it."

He frowned. "Why not?"

"It's old, and it's grungy."

"I can always bail, right? Is it far?"

"Westlake."

"That's closer than my place," Hernán said.

"Where's your ride? You can follow me."

They walked together into the next block, and Hernán stopped at a red Solara with the top down.

64

"This is me."

"I'm just a couple cars ahead," Slater said. "It's black, and it's easy to follow—it has very long brake lights."

Slater drove calmly, and watched in the rearview as the Solara followed him across the freeway, and into his alley. Pulling into his garage, he climbed out and waved Hernán closer.

"Park across my garage door," Slater told him. "You'll never find a street space at this hour."

Once he'd maneuvered the vehicle up tight to the doorway, he killed the engine.

"You should put the top up."

"There's nothing in it to steal," Hernán said.

"In this neighborhood someone will set up camp in it before you get back."

He spent a minute putting it up, and then followed Slater into the garage, and up the stairs.

"It's not that bad," Hernán said, looking around the apartment as Slater flipped the deadbolt. "I thought it was going to have wires and pipes sticking out of the walls, and I'd have to fight off the rats. Have you seen those brown rats? My uncle calls them roof rats. They're actually kind of cute. Like oversize mice. Not like those gray ones. Those look like the devil."

Slater snapped his fingers. "Hernán—focus."

"Right." He stood up straighter and met his gaze. Obviously he heard that a lot.

Slater stepped closer and put a hand on his neck, and leaned in to meet his mouth. Grabbing his belt, Hernán pulled him closer, until Slater could feel his woody, and then mouthed his neck. He ran a hand into Slater's hair.

"So what do you like to do?" Slater said, pulling back.

"In your sales pitch you mentioned that you wanted to fuck me."

Slater chuckled and led him to the bedroom as he

pulled off his shirt. Hernán reached for his belt and held his gaze as he deftly unbuckled it, then popped his fly, and groped his cock. Sliding his hands under Hernán's shirt, Slater pulled it over his head, then pushed him onto the futon. By the time he'd taken his boots off, Hernán was naked, waiting for him.

As he shifted closer, Hernán grabbed his cock, and stroked him until he was rock hard. Slater reached for the bedside table to grab a condom, and rolled it on, then pressed into Hernán with a lubed finger. Moving closer, he was soon inside him, moving slowly at first, then pounding him. Breathing hard, Hernán seemed to relish it, and met his eye. The look on his face was enough to send Slater over the edge, and he climaxed, straining deeper.

When he was spent, Slater flopped onto his side and grabbed Hernán's cock. "What are we going to do with this?"

"Do you want to ride me?"

Slater reached for a condom, and rolled it on him, then straddled his hips, wincing as he lowered himself onto Hernán. He didn't even have to do most of the work. Red-faced and panting, thrusting into him, Hernán grabbed his biceps, his face contorting as he came.

Waiting until he'd started to relax, Slater climbed off, and rolled onto his back, and folded his arm over his eyes. As he lay there dozing, he heard Hernán get up, and then water running. When he came back he draped an arm across Slater's waist.

Eventually Slater got up too, and found the bourbon bottle in the kitchen cupboard, and took a long pull. He rinsed his mouth from the tap and then climbed back onto the futon.

"Somebody had a little nightcap," Hernán said.

"You want one?"

"I don't. Can I stay?"

"Fine by me," Slater said, and shifted closer, luxuriating in the warmth of his body.

SEVEN

WHEN SLATER WOKE, DAYLIGHT was bright in the windows, and Hernán was getting dressed. He propped his head on his pillow to watch.

"You look weird," Hernán said, eyeing him.

"Thanks."

"Did I overstay my welcome?"

"I enjoyed your body. You're warm."

"So what did I do to make you look worried?"

Slater groaned. "It's not about you. I shouldn't be sleeping with a suspect in my case."

Hernán waved an arm and raised his voice. "What am I a suspect for?"

"It's just an expression." Slater sat up. "I meant that you're involved in my case."

"OK," he said evenly, adjusting his shirt collar. "I guess I'll see you again if you decide to arrest me."

"I can't do that. But I can put handcuffs on you, if you ask nicely."

Hernán chuckled. "We'll talk."

Slater heard the door close as he left, then grabbed his phone to check the time. It was still early. There'd been a text from Etta last night:

Developments.

Then an hour later:

Are you going to be in the office tomorrow?

Slater thumb-typed a reply:

On my way in.

Forcing himself out of bed, he made a mugful of powdered coffee, and slurped half of it down before he dumped the dregs in the sink and went to get dressed. A dark shirt and fresh jeans, he decided. Yesterday's had dirt on the knees from Doris's yard. This was the last clean pair, but Rosa was coming today to tidy up and do the laundry.

Once he'd left some cash for her on the counter, and trotted down to his garage, he climbed in the Thunderbird and drove to his office. Etta was already at the front desk when he walked in.

"You're here early," he said, pausing to flip the deadbolt.

"I went to first mass," she said, and leaned back in her chair. "I came straight here after."

"You still deal with those degenerates, even though they were going to shit-can you for having a girlfriend?"

She frowned. "It's my faith. I can't just turn my back on it."

"You should have some faith in yourself. Not those perverted control freaks."

"Have you heard that rule about the things you should never talk about? Politics, religion, and money."

He put his hands on his hips. "Did your priest tell you that?"

"You owe me money, by the way."

"How did it go with Rita?"

"It turns out your gaydar was calibrated correctly. I hardly had to flirt with her at all."

"Right on. Come and fill me in."

Etta rose and followed him into his office, sitting in front of his desk.

"After the drumming class we all went to a beer garden. I sat next to Rita, and she left her phone on the table while she went to get beer, so I was able to install your software."

"Nobody else in the group saw you do it?"

"I don't think so. I palmed the phone and took it over to the restroom, and managed to get it back to the table before Rita did. I could see the beer line was moving slow."

"Etta, you're a total badass."

She guffawed, throwing her head back. "Coming from you, that's a pretty big compliment."

"So you just banged on taiko drums and chatted her up?"

"There were only half a dozen of us, and it was pretty sociable. Part of it is that everyone goes out for a beer afterward. That made it easy. Drumming is actually kind of cathartic. Those things are freaking loud. I might go back."

"Did you get any sense that she's up to something?" Slater said. "The shipping delays could easily be her doing."

Etta shrugged. "Hard to say. I can imagine she could be a hard-ass about work. She's sharp, right, so if she's causing the delays, it's not because of incompetence."

"I'm going to get into her phone," Slater said. "Will you be here for a while?"

"I can be."

"Give me a few minutes."

As he woke his computer, his phone buzzed in his pants, and he pulled it out. Bender. Slater picked up and said, "Finally."

"You said you needed to talk to me."

"In person," Slater said. "Where are you? I'll come over there today."

"I can meet you out somewhere."

"I'll come to you. Are you at home?"

Bender heaved an audible sigh but then rattled off an address. "Do you know where MLK dead-ends at Central? It's not far from there."

Once he'd ended the call, Slater opened the tracking software he got from Svetlana and her brother Igor. They built audio bugs and surreptitious cameras and trackers, among other illicit electronics. It all had a clunky software interface, but the gear was robust, and Slater regularly attached their devices to vehicles or dropped them into handbags. It was so far from legal that Svetlana had trained him how to erase the software from his phone by punching in an alternate unlock code, in case he ever had to surrender the device to the cops.

Rita's phone was listed as a new device, first appearing yesterday—that meant Etta had installed the software correctly. But when he tried to connect to it, he kept getting an error message: a big red exclamation point with "нет соед." After he'd tried it a few times, and rebooted his phone, and reloaded the software, he dialed Svetlana's number, glad that she picked up.

"My favorite client," she said, with her lyrical Slavic accent. "You never telephone me. I am deeply honored."

Slater had to chuckle at that. "Your software always works so well."

"But you have telephoned me because you're having problems with it."

"I'm trying to get access to a cell phone. I installed the backdoor software, but I can't get in."

"Let me check," she said. "Can you stay on the line?"

He heard the clacking of a keyboard, then silence for a minute before she spoke.

"I see it. My software is functioning on the device, but sometimes the hardware maker's system updates interrupt the connectivity."

"So what can I do?"

"I can fix it. I will push an update to your phone, so you must open my app, and unlock the target phone, and tap them together. Then you will have access."

"When will the update come through?"

"Not long. Give me an hour."

Rising and tucking his phone into his jeans, Slater stood in his office doorway. Etta swiveled toward him and raised her eyebrows.

"We have to get Rita's phone again."

"Seriously?" she demanded. "The software didn't work?"

"It needs an update. We just need to tap my phone to hers for a second. Can you get her to meet you again?"

She waved a hand. "You're a very lucky man that I had the foresight to get her number."

"Can you set it up today?"

"I'll see what I can do. It'll cost you another hundred."

"It has to be my phone. Let me know if you can make it happen, and I'll come and give it to you."

Walking out, he went down to the street and hustled across to the parking lot. Firing up the Thunderbird, he headed south, toward the address Bender had given him. This neighborhood was dense and gritty, like where he lived, and in a few minutes he pulled up out front.

It was one of those ubiquitous 1950s four-up, four-down apartment buildings, with an external staircase and sunken parking under one side. He couldn't tell from here whether this one had undergone an earthquake retrofit. If not, when the shaking struck, it would collapse like a twink on GHB.

There was no security gate, and the first door past the mailboxes was unit 1. Bender was in unit 8—that had to be upstairs, at the back, the farthest from the street. Slater trotted up the stairs and strode the length of the open-air walkway. Pulling open the screen, he rapped on the inner door, then let the screen snap shut.

A woman opened it, peering out at him and raising an eyebrow. Her black hair was straightened and styled behind her ears.

"I'm looking for Bender," Slater said.

"He's not here."

It was hard to tell through the screen, but her expression looked hard.

"He told me he would be." Slater raised his voice. "If you're covering for him, I'll mess you both up."

She folded her arms. "Don't soft-soap it for me, *vato*. Just tell it like it is."

"Is he in there?"

"I just told you he wasn't. Are you hard of hearing, or just a little slow? Who are you, anyway? Are you from his old life?"

"You seem like you could handle yourself in a dust-up," Slater said. "Are you in the badger game with him?"

"He's not a con man," she said, her tone sharp.

A man appeared at the top of the stairs, his hair in knobby twists and a white plastic bag dangling from one hand. His brow furrowed in concern.

"You're Ibáñez?" He stepped to the screen door and pulled it open. "Come in."

"I'll let you navigate past the bouncer," Slater said, hanging back a moment before he followed him inside.

It was a pleasant space, a living room with big windows on two sides and overstuffed lounge furniture. Farther back was a dining room. The woman took the bag from Bender, and scowled at Slater, then walked into the hallway and disappeared.

"Have a seat," Bender said, and dropped into the

armchair. "That's my wife. I just went to get her lunch."

"I get the feeling she can take care of herself," Slater said, and sat on the adjacent sofa.

"So what do you need to know from me?"

"Why did she think I was from your old life?"

His brow furrowed. "She must have meant an old job. I've worked in a few places. You probably look like someone I used to work with."

"You're only with Seligman now?"

"Full-time."

"It's about the Elmer Mine. You always make the run up there?"

He nodded. "Me and Vitale."

"What exactly is the problem with that place?" Slater said. "All the delays."

"They call us out there when they're not really ready, and they make us wait. I think they do it so that it looks like they're making their quota even though they're not. Then they can blame us."

"Has anyone there mentioned a hairy creature?"

"I heard something like that," Bender said. "Bigfoot was messing with the miners at night. I don't see how that would impact the scheduling, though. It seems to me like that would be a separate problem."

"So you think the delays are because of human error, not bigfoot."

"I don't know why the delays happen. Human error or human stupidity or human skulduggery. It doesn't happen on other jobs. Only the Elmer Mine. It's rough to have screw-ups on that one because it's so far away and there's nothing around there."

"How long is the trip?"

"About eleven hours. I don't like to stop much in those little towns in the desert or in the Sierra. You don't see many black folks. We both pack food with us, and eat on the way, and piss at gas stations or on the side of the road."

"What's Seligman like to work for?"

Bender shrugged. "Same as any other place. The money isn't better or worse."

"Do you trust Rita?"

"She's my boss. Of course I don't trust her. I don't know her, or anything about her. With me she's all business."

"What about Vitale?"

"I know him a little more. All those hours on the road. We talk. Plus he's packing a heater, so I kind of have to trust him."

"Did you ever get into a situation where he needed to draw his weapon?"

"I know the cargo from the mine is really valuable, but we're mostly on desert highways, in an unmarked van. The only danger I've seen is trying not to fall asleep at the wheel."

"OK," Slater said, and stood up.

Bender followed him to the door, and spoke once he'd stepped out.

"Have you been out there?"

"To the Elmer Mine? I haven't." Slater peered at him through the screen, trying to read his expression.

"It's not what you think of when you hear 'mine.' Nobody's digging anything. It's more like a makeshift factory and a solar farm."

"I've been told they're using cutting-edge technology."

Bender shrugged. "You hear that a lot. I'm still waiting for my flying car."

As he climbed into the Thunderbird, Slater checked his phone. There was a text from Etta:

I'm meeting Rita at the central market, on the Broadway side.

Ten minutes later she'd texted again:

Hello?

Slater wrote back:

Meet me at the Hill Street side before you see her.
I'll be there soon.

A few minutes later he nosed the Thunderbird into the parking structure next to the market, and cruised up a few floors to find a space. The stairwell he stepped into led him down to the ground level, and he pushed open the crash door to find he was out on the sidewalk.

Slater looked over the dormant jacaranda as he walked past. It didn't really make sense to plant those here as street trees. That decision had been made long ago, as this one was mature, but it needed more light than it got with a northwest exposure next to a wall of tall buildings. It only had those showy purple flowers for a few weeks and then sat lifeless all winter, when it wasn't even cold.

"Idiots," he muttered, and walked toward the west side of the market hall.

Etta was standing near the coffee counter, and briefly met his gaze, but didn't acknowledge him, and looked away. She was smart to keep it on the down-low, in case Rita happened to walk by. Maybe Max had explained to her how to behave on a job like this, or maybe she really was a natural.

Stepping up to the counter, he ordered a double espresso. The clerk nodded and stepped away, and Etta appeared at his elbow.

"I'm glad she could meet you today," he said quietly, not looking at her. "What excuse did you use?"

"I just told her I wanted to see her," Etta said. "I'm sure it was hard for her to resist. As you're well aware I'm gorgeous and have a magnetic personality. I'm basically lesbian catnip."

"I'll take your word for it." Slater set his phone on the counter. "Where are you meeting her?"

"On the Broadway side."

"I'll hang out over here. Come find me after."

Etta palmed the device and stepped away.

Once he'd paid for his coffee, he took it over to a little table. With no phone to look at, he watched the people coming and going from Hill Street as he sipped the java. Some of them were tourists but mostly they were Angelenos. This city was a riotous array of ethnicities and social classes, and there weren't many places like this, where people mixed outside their own demographic.

A woman walked in from the street, dressed in jeans and a red blouse, her wild mane of dark hair pushed back. She was moving with determination, scanning the place. Why did she look so familiar? As she walked by she looked directly at him but didn't react.

Then it clicked. His heart started to pound. That was Safiya, Etta's girlfriend. Slater jumped up and strode after her. No way was he going to let her blow up this operation. When he caught up, just before the short set of steps down to the lower part of the market hall, he tapped her on the shoulder.

Safiya spun around, a scowl on her face.

"Remember me?"

Recognition sparked in her eyes. "Slater, right? What are you doing here?"

"I've got a better one for you. What are you doing here?"

"Etta came in." She turned to scan the lower section from their vantage at the top of the steps. "There she is," she hissed, and grabbed his forearm. "Who is that woman?"

Following her gaze, Slater could see them, Rita and Etta, at a little table near the Broadway entrance.

"Safiya." Slater raised his voice. "Focus. She's on a job."

"We'll see about that."

As she made to descend the steps, he grabbed her upper arm. "You can't interrupt them."

"Don't tell me what to do."

"Listen to me. She's not cheating on you. Etta's working for me right now."

Safiya scoffed and turned away. It left him no choice—he grabbed her around the waist, and lifted her onto his shoulder, and strode back toward Hill Street. She was light compared to some of the bruisers he'd had to deal with in middle school wrestling, but she was a lot squirmier.

"Put me down," she demanded, and pounded on the back of his belt with her fists. But the effort was half-hearted, and she soon went limp.

The market was crowded, as it always was, and people stepped out of the way, some eyeing them with alarm, some smiling at the spectacle. When he got close to the street entrance, a burly security guard stepped into Slater's path, his expression intent.

"What's going on?" he demanded.

"She fainted," Slater said. "It's too hot in there. She needs some air."

"There's a chair here," the guard said, pulling it out from a little table.

Slater crouched to set Safiya on her feet, and guided her into the chair. She was sobbing now, her mascara smeared around her eyes.

The guard squatted in front of her and looked into her face. "Ma'am, do you need assistance?"

"No," she said flatly, and waved him away.

The guy rose, and looked Slater over with that hard eye that cops used, then stepped a few feet away, standing with his hands on his belt. Slater took a deep breath. That could have gone very differently. The guard wasn't going to escalate now, but he wasn't going to leave them alone either.

Slater took the chair across from her and leaned in, speaking in a low voice. "You're going to get me arrested for domestic violence. Is that what you want?"

"I knew something was up," Safiya said, wiping at her eyes. It only made the dark streaks worse. "She wouldn't tell me where she was going."

"That woman is a target, not a date."

"Bullshit."

"Do you want a coffee?" he said. "Let's grab a coffee. They're selling it right over there. Etta is going to walk up here in a minute and explain everything."

She avoided his gaze but nodded. Slater stood, keeping the guard in his peripheral view, and held out his hand.

"Come on. Let's caffeinate."

She let him take her arm as they walked to the coffee counter, and Slater stayed close, not convinced she wouldn't try to make a break.

At the counter the clerk frowned at the sight of him. "You sure like your java."

"A double espresso," Slater said, "and whatever she's having."

"A latte," Safiya said, and once he'd paid for them, guided her to a different table, closer to the street and farther from the still watchful security guard.

Safiya sipped at her cup and then wiped the foam off her lip with her hand. "I hate that she works for you."

"She loves working for me," Slater said, "and she's really good at it. Etta has sangfroid. Very few people have that unless they've been driving an ambulance for a while, or a Humvee in a war zone."

"She teaches eighth-graders. That's basically the same thing."

Slater chuckled and folded his arms.

"I never know what she's up to," Safiya said. "It used to be easy—we'd eat out, and go for walks, and watch stupid television. Now she's a spy."

"You need to trust her more."

"How can I trust her when she doesn't tell me the truth?"

Walking up from the east side of the market, Etta appeared, her brow furrowing when she spotted them.

"What are you doing here, kitten?"

"Who was that woman?" Safiya shouted.

"Nobody. I had to interview her for a job." Etta spread her palms. "It doesn't mean anything."

"Where's your target?" Slater said. "I don't want her to see us together."

"She went the other way." Etta gestured into the market. "Her car was on Broadway."

"This gorilla picked me up and dragged me across the whole place," Safiya said, her tone hurt, like a whiny eight-year-old. "It was like *The Rape of Europa* in here."

"I didn't rape anybody," Slater snapped.

Etta frowned at him. "What's the big idea?"

He jutted his chin at Safiya. "She was going to blow your cover."

"So you manhandled her?"

"I was protecting the operation, and you're pissed at me?" Slater said, matching her tone. "I'm running back-up. Helping you out. How does that make me the asshole?"

"Slater, if you have to ask who's being the asshole, it's always you."

"Did you manage to do it?" he demanded.

Etta handed him his phone. "Affirmative."

Leaning back, he dug his wad of cash out of his front pocket, and riffled off four C-notes. He took a moment to fold them lengthwise before he handed them to Etta, and looked to Safiya, to make sure she saw them.

"Four hundred dollars?" Safiya said. "Just to make time with some woman?"

"It's worth her time, don't you think?" Slater said.

Etta held up a finger to him, and looked to Safiya. "It's complicated, kitten."

Safiya folded her arms and glared at Slater. "You're spreading money around like a sugar daddy."

"It's wages for labor," he said, and frowned. "There's no sugar."

"You can't get upset that she's upset," Etta said. "This has been traumatic for her."

"That's it." Slater flashed his palms and stood up. "I'm out."

EIGHT

S LATER COULD HAVE WALKED to Andy's from the market, but he wasn't sure when the parking lot closed, so he trotted up the stairs to his car and drove the few blocks to the surface lot behind Andy's building.

Upstairs, he knocked on his door.

"You're here early," Andy said when he pulled it open, grinning at him. "Eager beaver."

"I actually have a business ask," Slater said, and followed him inside.

"I was going to call you about those … guys you were looking into."

Andy got settled in his desk chair and pulled on his black plastic gauntlets. They looked like armor for some contact sport, but they were actually a computer input device that somehow overcame his lack of fine motor control.

"The one named Bender," Andy said, peering at his monitor. "Facial recognition linked him to … a different person. A guy named Lenny Dyer."

He pulled up a photo on the screen, and Slater stepped closer, leaning in to look.

"That's a DMV photo," Slater said.

"I didn't actually have to dig for it. It was released to the public because he's been incarcerated."

"He's got a little more mileage on him now, but that's Bender," Slater said. "Why did he get sent up?"

"He had a couple of penny-ante convictions, but then ... he went away for fraud along with two other guys. They all ... worked for the same company."

"What kind of fraud?"

"I didn't get the details, just the charge. I guess I could ... pull the court transcript, but then you'd have to read it. You know how ... much fun those are."

"Don't worry about that now," Slater said. "I'll talk to him again."

Andy raised his eyebrows. "And give him a tune-up?"

"If he needs one. What about Vitale?"

"I can't find much info on him besides the ... vital statistics."

"So there's no indication that he's tangled with John Law."

Andy shook his head. "What's the other thing you need?"

"It's about hacking."

"I don't ... do that."

"Of course not." Slater waved a hand. "What do we call it over here?"

"Deep research."

"That's what I meant. I have backdoor access to a cell phone, and I'm hoping there's something on the device that will give me access to the files at the company where the owner works."

"That sounds ... totally illegal."

Slater scoffed. "Like you care."

"What kind of access?"

He pulled out his phone and showed him Svetlana's app. Andy plugged it into a cable, and a mirror of Slater's screen came up on his monitor. Slater watched as he started to poke around on Rita's phone, and then watched Andy, lost in the task, his jaw set, his muscles undulating rhythmically, his hair perfectly tousled.

Such a beautiful man.

"I've never seen the Russians' … code before," Andy said. "It's really good."

"I think they outsource it to actual Russia. Nobody living here would use such broken English. It always works really well, though. Built ugly like a Soviet tank but functional like a Soviet tank."

"How did you get this … installed on her phone?"

"It's all about confidence." Slater stepped over to the window. "She trusted the wrong woman."

The last of the daylight was fading over the square, and the streetlights were already on. After a while Andy spoke.

"Her company is Seligman Trucking?"

"That's it."

"Rita's phone is linked to the company's … cloud drive. I can totally get access."

"How did you know her name?" Slater said.

"I'm basically the boss of her phone right now." Pulling his arms out of the gauntlets, he unplugged Slater's phone and handed it to him. "I've got direct access to … the cloud account. I don't need this anymore."

"Can you share that access with me?"

"Not easily. It would take longer … to show you how to do it than for me just to do it."

Slater whirled a finger in the air. "So let's go."

"In the morning." He grinned. "We have a plan, remember?"

"Of course. The guy with the twelve-hundred-dollar shoes is coming over to ruin perfectly good sex."

"You're just as … into it as he is."

Slater took a breath. More important, Andy was really, really into it. He wasn't going to mess that up for him.

There was a knock at the door, and Andy jumped as if he'd been shocked.

"Speak of the trust fund," Slater said.

He listened to them exchange a greeting at the door, and Kyle followed Andy inside. Kyle's mousy brown hair was in a natty style, and he had a great body, lithe and toned, shown off by his tan chinos. Kyle scowled at the sight of him.

"It's a golden twinkie made flesh," Slater said. "Kyle, you look as sweet as a whole bag of gumdrops."

"Great," Kyle said, looking to Andy. "You invited the booze hag." He turned to Slater. "You know, someone should teach you some manners."

"You and what army?" Slater demanded. "What do you weigh, like a buck fifty, and you're going to come at me?"

"I didn't say I wanted to do it personally. It would take an experienced specialist with a twelve-point action plan and an extreme detox weekend in Idyllwild after."

"I'm sure your trust fund would take care of the expense."

Kyle jabbed a finger at him. "You are an emotional wreck."

"I know that, Kyle. But did you know that I really, really want to punch you in the face?"

"Would both of you … shut up?" Andy said, raising his voice. "Just shut the fuck up. This is my place. I call … the shots."

Slater raised his eyebrows, watching him talk. He'd never seen him so loud and animated.

"I want something from both of you," Andy said.

Slater threw up his hands, a tacit *Name it.*

"Anything," Kyle said.

"More than just sex. It would be a total … turn-on to watch you two get tender with each other."

"That's the stupidest idea I've ever heard," Slater said.

"I'd need to get prescriptions first, sweet pea," Kyle

said. "Antibiotics and herpes medication."

"I'm not messing around," Andy said. "I want you two to treat … each other the way you both treat me. I don't care if you … don't mean it. Just for a little while."

Looking at Kyle, Slater's brow furrowed. This was going to be a challenge.

"Hop to it," Andy said. "Clothes off."

Slater huffed and unbuttoned his shirt, and Kyle, avoiding his gaze, started to get naked. Dropping into his computer chair, Andy tented his fingers and watched them.

"It needs to be verbal," he said.

Once he'd ditched his jeans, Slater climbed on the bed, and moved behind Kyle, and wrapped his arms around his chest. His pasty skin felt warmer than it looked.

"You're so beautiful," Slater said, and kissed his neck, and caressed his torso.

At first Kyle groaned, but then leaned back into him. "Those strong arms," he said. "They make me feel safe."

Andy was breathing hard, Slater saw, and watching them intently.

"Your body is perfect," Slater said. "Like Greek statuary."

Kyle was hard now, and Slater stroked him, running his other hand over his chest and his throat. Reaching up, Kyle grabbed the back of his neck and pulled him closer, meeting his mouth.

The guy was good at this, Slater thought, exploring his taught warm lips. That was part of why he found him so annoying. In the periphery he saw Andy stand up. He pulled away from Kyle when Andy loomed over them, then threw himself on top. Slater laughed and tumbled back. Andy was between them now, kissing them in turn, mouthing their skin, his hands grasping. Eventually he sat up.

"Fuck him like you'd fuck me," he said, eyeing Slater. "Does he even do that?"

Kyle frowned. "If you must."

He'd never fucked Andy, as his muscle spasms made it impractical. Reaching under the side of the bed, Slater grabbed a condom, and rolled it on, and shifted next to Kyle. With his arm around his chest, he penetrated him, starting slowly, gauging Kyle's reaction before he went deeper. He held Andy's gaze as he built up speed. It was a turn-on, looking into his eyes, and he pounded harder. But Kyle distracted Andy, caressing his face and his shoulder, and Andy leaned in to kiss him and grab his cock.

This was the part that he hated, seeing Andy get so into someone else. Pounding Kyle, he pulled tighter around his chest, then dug his nose into his hair, inhaling the scent of his sweat, and came.

Mouths together, Andy and Kyle stroked each other until they came, almost at the same time. Slater didn't want to watch, feeling like he was on the outside of it, but he couldn't look away.

Almost as soon as he'd climaxed, Kyle got up and went into the bathroom. Slater heard the water go on.

"He must be a germophobe," Slater said. "He always runs for the shower after."

Andy caressed his chest. "It might only be because of you."

He chuckled, and leaned in to kiss him, then sat up and found his shirt on the floor.

"You should hang out," Andy said.

"You two have stuff to do. The romance part of it."

"You can still stay."

Slater scoffed. "Broken people break people, man. You don't need that."

Walking around to the parking lot, he climbed in the

Thunderbird and drove through the sterile empty darkness of the Financial District. Maybe it worked for Slater too, in a way, hooking up with those two. He didn't feel as resentful of Kyle when they were with Andy at the same time. The guy was still irritating, but the sex took the sharp edge out of it.

Once he was up in his apartment, he pulled off his boots, and poured out his ration, frowning at the pittance in the bottom of the tumbler. He took a long pull on the bottle before he twisted the cap on. It had been a long day, he reasoned. A little extra didn't even count.

Music on the radio wasn't good on Sunday night. It was almost like they were preparing people for their return to office drudgery in the morning. Instead he turned on a podcast, and stretched out in the recliner, and sank into it. Half listening and sipping at his tumbler, he had to grin. This was the best part of the day.

NINE

T HE BUZZING OF HIS phone brought Slater to consciousness. He was in his own bed, he realized. It was a text from Andy:

We should do that computer work this morning. I'm going out later.

Swinging his feet onto the floor, he washed up and pulled open the icebox to look for food. A foil-wrapped lump sat on the top shelf. An ancient forgotten taco, he saw when he peeled it open. No longer edible. He tossed it in the trash, and got dressed, and drove to Andy's.

Instead of going up to his loft, Slater detoured a block up Broadway to a coffee joint to buy a dry bagel and a soy latte for himself and a Greek coffee for Andy. He munched on the bagel on the walk back, and slammed his latte, dropping the paper cup into a street trash can before he went up.

Andy pulled the door open and raised his eyebrows. "You should have just stayed over."

"If I had, you wouldn't have a java delivery." Slater followed him inside and set the cup on his computer desk. "Interesting that dirtbag Kyle is gone already. He doesn't seem like the fuck-'em-and-forget-'em type."

"He's not," Andy said, dropping into his desk chair. "That's you. Kyle left for … work hours ago."

"That guy has a job?"

"Why wouldn't he?"

Slater put his hands on his hips. "I don't think polo practice counts as work."

"You don't know anything about him."

"I know you care about him. That's the only reason I've never punched him in the face."

"Just stop talking," Andy said, and turned to his computer, and pulled on his gauntlets. "I got a list of the ... folders in the transport company's cloud drive."

Slater pulled a chair over beside him and leaned in. He wanted to grab the mouse, but there wasn't one. "Scroll up ... Click on the one called 'accounts.'"

A lone spreadsheet occupied the folder. When Andy opened it, he saw the column headings were SITE and USER NAME and PASSWORD.

"Is that all their logins?" Slater said. "Fuck me—you could drain all their bank accounts."

"Let's not do that." Andy clicked it closed. "There's so much stuff here. Can you be ... specific about what you need to look at?"

"Anything to do with a company called Mott Minerals, or the Elmer Mine."

"I can search for those." Once he'd done that, a list of files filled the screen. "It's all different ... formats—documents, spreadsheets, images."

"Can you copy those for me?"

"I'll share them." Andy spent a minute working on it, then sat back.

"What do I owe you for this," Slater said, "and for looking into those knuckleheads?"

"Will you get angry if I said five?"

He frowned. "That does seem excessive."

"Could anyone else you know do ... this stuff for you?"

"Not a chance."

"So it's worth it," Andy said flatly.

Slater dug out his wad of cash, and counted out five C-notes, and folded them lengthwise before he set them on the desk.

"Do you want me to smoke you before I go?"

"Tempting," Andy said, "but I think I'm still sated from last night."

"When a man is tired of blow jobs, he's tired of life."

He chuckled. "I'm not tired of them. I just need to … get some work done today. Kyle says you're not a slut—I have to frame it that you … have a high sex drive."

"If Kyle said I'm not a slut, that means you think I am a slut."

"I think you're an addict."

"Says the guy who hosts a regular three-way, complete with stage direction." He waved a hand. "So I like sex. I work and I work till I'm half dead, and I'm not allowed to drink anymore. Sex is pretty much all I've got."

"That makes you … sound depressed."

"All through my youth I had a parade of shrinks telling me what's wrong with me. I do not need to hear it from you too."

"I'm not judging you."

"So what else is there?" Slater demanded. "I'm supposed to get a hobby? Bake bread or knit sweaters or fix up old cars?"

"Other people, Slater. There's … relationships with other people."

He took a breath, then leaned in and kissed him. "Bye, beautiful."

Out in the hallway, walking to the elevator, he muttered, "Other people." What a world that guy lived in.

Climbing into the Thunderbird, he checked the tracking software for his idiot ex-boyfriend Conrad. He'd put a stealthy tracker on his phone when they'd been together, and it was still useful because Conrad was a cop, and that meant he had access to information that most people didn't. Technically he didn't know Slater could track him, but it was his own fault—you'd think a cop would have been more security-conscious.

The map in Svetlana's app showed that Conrad was at his station. Of course he was, the moron. Since he'd been bumped up to detective he almost always worked the day shift.

Pulling out of the parking lot, Slater drove west, back across the freeway to Rampart, and parked outside the station. When he dialed Conrad's cell, he picked up.

"You know I'm working, right?"

"I just need a minute of your time. Put your dick away, and zip up your fly, and come outside."

Conrad huffed, and the call disconnected. Climbing out of the Thunderbird, Slater waited on the sidewalk, looking over the plantings in the adjoining little park. Whoever they'd hired had done a good job with the native plants. The *Salvia* and *Verbena* were thriving, and even the asters they'd put in as ground cover had taken off.

Conrad strode out of the building, his brow furrowed. He was wearing civvies, but it was a distorted version—a plaid jacket and tie, with a weapon on one hip and his badge on the other, barrel-chested and with that familiar bulge in his pants. Slater watched him approach. Even dressed like that he was such a beautiful man.

"That suit is making my skin crawl," Slater said. "Is there some cop manual that says you have to dress that way, or did you just ask the saddest guy in the office where he buys his threads?"

"Always a pleasure to see you too." He frowned. "And you wouldn't know style if it bit you in the ass."

"At least the shoes aren't painful to look at."

Conrad waved impatiently. "What do you need, Slater?"

"This guy came up in my case. He went up for fraud. I wanted details on the conviction."

"Text me the name. I'll see what I can find out."

Slater pulled out his phone and tapped at it.

"You know, with my new rank comes greater accountability," Conrad said. "It's getting harder to poke around for you and call it a gray area."

"Getting harder, or getting easier?" Slater raised his eyebrows. "They're paying you more now, aren't they? You need to sort out your priorities."

He laughed. "And I should prioritize you."

"You still owe me for Galliform."

"The feds compensated you extremely well on that one. I don't owe you anything."

Slater held his gaze. "Don't forget that I could burn you to the ground."

"I know you don't have anything on me, Slater. Even if you did, I know you better than that. You're not a cheap blackmailer. Somewhere in there you're a decent person."

Leaning in, he jabbed a finger toward his chest. "Keep telling yourself that," he said through clenched teeth, then walked toward his car.

Idiot dick-smack Conrad. Climbing in behind the wheel, he started the engine and watched him stroll back inside. Of course he wouldn't blackmail the guy. But he needed Conrad to take him seriously.

TEN

BACK AT HIS OFFICE, Slater saw that the statue of Rey Pascual was facing the opposite way now, his bony empty eye sockets surveilling the front door. Etta must adjust him when she comes and goes. Maybe she wanted him to watch the place when she wasn't here.

When he stepped into his own office he found a shipping box sitting on his desk. It wasn't that heavy when he picked it up, and it had stamps on it, so it had come through the mail. There was a return address in Albuquerque.

The only person he knew out there was Pike—they'd worked together to take down Galliform. Stepping back to Etta's desk, he pulled open the top drawer and dug around until he found a box cutter. Of course she'd have one of these. Like Doris, she was well organized, the quintessential teacher.

Once he'd cut through the packing tape, he dug into the foam peanuts, and pulled out a little statue. Similar to Rey Pascual, it was just a few inches tall, and made of white plaster. It depicted a naked guy, one knee slightly bent, standing with a horse. He had great hair. Along the base it was inscribed POLLUX.

Things had gotten a little personal with Pike, and they'd had some freaking great sex, but he didn't need to be getting gifts from him. Dropping into his desk chair, he pulled out his phone, and found Pike's number, and dialed.

"Who's Pollux?" Slater said when he picked up.

"I'm glad you got it. He reminded me of you."

Reaching for the statue on his desk, Slater rotated it, looking it over. "This little guy has better hair than I've ever had, but I've got a much bigger dick than he does."

Pike laughed. "I was reading the story of Jason and the Argonauts. He's one of them. From classical Greek mythology."

"This guy is the god of horses?"

"Of horse people, I think," Pike said. "He reminded me of you, stealing that horse to track down Galliform."

"Technically I rented that horse."

"When he was with the Argonauts, Pollux was happy to throw punches. He got into some serious fistfights."

"That does sound like me."

"How are you?"

"OK," Slater said. "Working. You know."

The line was silent for a while.

"Maybe I'll see you again," Pike said finally.

"Everybody floats through LA at some point, right? Hit me up," Slater said, and ended the call.

He dumped the packing peanuts into the trash, then folded up the box and tucked it in next to them, then studied the statue. "You can stay," he said finally, and positioned it at the base of his computer monitor.

Swinging his boots up onto the desk, he grabbed the keyboard and pulled it into his lap, then started going through the documents Andy had retrieved.

Most of it seemed to be records of payment transactions. Shipping that metal from the far end of nowhere was not cheap. Another document that came up was on Mott Minerals letterhead, a scan of a bill of lading. Slater had to look up what that was—basically a legal document that listed the cargo loaded onto a vessel, in this case those stealthy armored vans.

The cargo was named as palladium, but it seemed

odd that it was enumerated in kilograms—"1,368 kg." In the browser he did a quick conversion. That was just over three thousand pounds. It wouldn't strain that reinforced van, but it was a full load.

There had been something like this in the files from Della, he remembered, and spent a minute clicking through the folders. It wasn't a manifest, he saw when it came up, but a bill of sale for product that had been delivered to Della's client. This document listed the palladium in pounds. That made more sense, as all the players were U.S. companies.

The weight was a little different, just under three thousand pounds, but then this was a different shipment; the date was months earlier. Eventually he found the bill of sale for what had to be the same shipment, as it was dated just two days later. The weight in pounds was the same, just under three thousand. Looking at the bill of lading again, he converted the metric weight, but it was over three thousand pounds.

He sat back in his chair. Was he doing it wrong? Reading on the Web about the relationship between kilograms and pounds, there was no ambiguity in it, and the conversion was straightforward. He ran the numbers again, but the result was the same—the shipment was 52.9 pounds lighter when it was sold than when it was loaded on the van.

Looking over the bill of lading, he saw that it was signed by Mo. He'd heard that name before. She worked at the mine. But maybe something else was going on. Maybe Mott removed that much of their product at the depot before it was sold.

Digging through the rest of the documents Andy had copied, it seemed like there were only a few deliveries a year. When he matched the dates to the sales data Della had sent from her client, he wound up with four bills of lading that lined up with bills of sale. Every time the sale was lighter—52.9 pounds in three cases, and 79.4 pounds in the other. Playing with those numbers, both were tidy round numbers when they were converted to metric: 24 kilograms and 36 kilograms. Both multiples of 12. That had to mean something.

When he looked up the price of palladium, that discrepancy would be worth around two hundred grand. If someone was stealing from the shipments, it was pretty lucrative. But someone else would have noticed that. Maybe Mott kept some of the product in LA. He needed to talk to Hernán.

When Slater dialed his cell, it went to voice mail. "I was thinking about you today," he told the machine. "We should talk."

It was a little devious, framing it that way, but if Hernán thought it was about a hookup, he'd be more likely to call back. Next he texted Della:

Can I come talk to you?

Her response came a moment later:

Always.

Locking his computer with a keystroke, he stood up, and eyed the statue of Pollux. What a weird gift. On the way out he flicked off the lights, then headed down to his car.

Once he'd parked under Della's building, he rode up to her floor. No one was on the front desk, so he walked toward her office. The sound of voices came from inside. He rapped on the half-open door and stepped in. Crystal was seated across from her, wearing a dark jacket, with a tablet in her lap.

Della beamed as she greeted him and waved him to the other chair.

"It seems your frontwoman abandoned her post," Slater said.

"Crystal is going to sit in again."

He scowled at Crystal as he sat down. "You'd better not be planning to steal my gig work."

She laughed. "How could I do what you do? I'm not a thug."

"You know she means no disrespect," Della said.

Crystal raised her eyebrows. "I wouldn't say that's necessarily true."

"Slater actually respects you too, believe it or not. He once told me that if you two got locked in a shipping container, he wasn't sure which one of you would make it out alive."

"In a boxcar," Slater said. "Not a shipping container."

"That's the only way it would make sense," Crystal said. "A boxcar would have ventilation."

Della sat up and shifted closer to her desk. "So what have you learned?"

"I'm not completely sure what's going on with the delays yet. Everybody blames someone else. None of the stories quite wash."

"Everyone has something to sell," Crystal said.

He raised his eyebrows. "Exactly. If you're not the chiseler, you're the mark."

"You probably don't want to hear this," Della said, "But you two really are cut from the same cloth."

Slater scoffed. "Did you notice the discrepancy between what the mine says they're shipping and what your client says they're buying? The shipment is fifty to eighty pounds lighter each time."

"Maybe bigfoot is taking it," Crystal said. "Like a tax."

"It must be intentional," Della said. "Mott is reserving part of the shipments for some other purpose. Otherwise I can't believe no one would have noticed."

Slater nodded. "That sounds most likely."

"I've been through the file," Crystal said. "I didn't see any specific documentation about what left the mine."

"It's Seligman's paperwork," he said. "I've seen the bills of lading for the last few trips. Seligman uses the documents, but the Mott staff at the mine prepares them."

Crystal frowned. "How did you get access to that?"

"You don't want to know. But they're solid."

"Have you talked to Hernán?" Della said.

"I'll interview him again about this. The guy is an airhead."

Della nodded. "I've spoken to him, and I have to agree. But he doesn't seem disingenuous."

"I don't think he's smart enough to be stealing anything," Slater said. "At least not in a way that nobody noticed."

"The part that's costing us money is the delivery delay," Della said. "Not the shrinkage. The actuaries downstairs are talking about how to address that."

"Can't you make Seligman pay you for the holdups?"

"It's a lot of work to go after them legally." Her brow furrowed. "You said 'Seligman' the right way. Did Rita school you in the proper pronunciation?"

"It felt like being in third grade." He waved a hand. "Seligman blames the mining company. I want to go to this mine and talk to the workers. I'd be able to figure out if they're responsible."

"The idea was floated downstairs to fly a cargo plane up there to transfer the currently pending shipment," Della said.

Crystal frowned. "That sounds extreme."

"The cost isn't actually that much more than trucking it. We could avoid another payout if the shipment was delivered in a timely manner, and we could make sure of timely delivery if it was accompanied by our own people." She eyed Slater. "That could be you. If you went to the mine, you could confirm that the product was actually ready to go, and you could ascertain what the snags might be. Do you want to ride up on that plane?"

"That's a lot more palatable than a twelve-hour drive."

Della nodded. "And Crystal can go as your backup."

"Hold on," Crystal said. "I don't do field work."

"But you're capable of it."

Slater sat up. "It's moot anyway. I work alone."

"In a situation like this," Della said, "you need two heads, two sets of eyes. The plane won't be on the ground all that long."

"Did the bean counters decide that too?" he said.

"They're really good at things like this. They call it tactical planning."

He flashed his palms. "So send them to the mine."

"Are you worried about Crystal's capabilities?"

"It's not that." Slater eyed Crystal. "I don't know you."

"But you know me," Della said. "Do you trust me?"

He stifled a sigh. "Mostly."

"I'm telling you she's OK. She has the chops to help you."

"I don't know you either," Crystal said. "I do know you're crass and have zero social skills."

"That's common knowledge," Slater said. "So what?"

"I'm saying I'm not afraid to work with you. But I can't work in a field setting with someone I don't trust."

"Ditto." He frowned. "Let me see if I can get one of my operatives to go."

"That sounds like a much better option," Crystal said.

"I guess you two have sorted that out." Della sat back. "I'll try to make the cargo plane happen."

Slater stood up. "I'm ready whenever."

———·———

ONCE HE WAS IN his car, he nosed it up the ramp to the street and pulled into the traffic. He didn't need to check the address, as he remembered exactly where he was going in South Park.

It took a minute to find parking, like it usually did in these dense neighborhoods. When he finally found a street space, up the block in front of another apartment building, he climbed out and stretched in the bright sun. It felt warm despite the autumn air.

Someone had planted a chalk *Dudleya* in a big pot out front, and he paused to look over its showy pale-green rosettes. It wasn't native to the basin, but it grew wild in the foothills not far from here, so it wasn't really an interloper. The bees and the hummingbirds were going to love this when it bloomed in a few months.

Walking back to Bender's building, Slater trotted up the stairs and pulled open the screen, then pounded on Bender's door with the heel of his fist.

It opened a crack, and Bender peered out at him. "What do you want?"

"Hey, Lenny," Slater said. "We need to talk."

He tried to push the door closed, but Slater had shifted his boot into the gap, and heaved it open. Bender lost hold of it and took a step back.

"I don't have to talk to you."

Stepping close, Slater slapped him hard, left and then right, a firm kovac. "I've had enough of your guff."

Attempting to throw a punch, Bender swung with his right in a wide looping arc. He didn't really know how to do it, and Slater easily blocked him, and delivered another slap.

"Why do you make me do this to you?" Slater shouted.

"Get your hands off me," Bender said, shoving him away.

He was almost at the sofa, and Slater pushed his shoulder, and he tumbled onto it.

"Sit still," Slater barked, looming over him. "Is your wife around?"

"It's just me." Bender took a breath. "You're a damn bully."

"And you're a liar."

"How did you find out about Lenny?"

"Why did you change your name?"

His mouth a taut line, Bender folded his arms.

Slater raised his voice. "Sing, brother."

"I got into some trouble. I went on a retreat upstate."

"How long were you in?"

Bender looked away. "Four years."

"That sounds like serious trouble."

"I did my time," he snapped, glaring at him. "But employers tend not to think of that as a clean slate."

"What do you know about the trucking delays from the Elmer Mine?" Slater said.

"Exactly what I told you yesterday. It's the people at the mine jerking us around."

"What about the stuff that goes missing from those shipments?"

His eyebrows shot up. "I don't know anything about that."

"You can understand my problem," Slater said, resting his hands on his hips. "It's so hard to take that at face value, coming from an ex-con."

"If someone's mopping from those shipments," Bender said, raising his voice, "it's nothing to do with me. I'm staying straight."

Slater studied his face. His indignation seemed genuine. But you never knew with these birds. Part of running a successful con was being a good actor.

"You should look at Vitale," Bender said. "Did you

know he has a house in the Hollywood Hills? How do you suppose he manages that when he's an armed guard making minimum wage?"

"Vitale owns a house up there?"

"Hard to fathom, right?"

"Does he have the opportunity to mess with the shipments?"

"I've never seen him do that. We take turns driving and sleeping. Mott loads the pallet in the van, and Mott unloads it at the other end. If those shipments are coming in light, you should look at that guy from Mott."

Slater frowned. "What guy?"

"The one at the LA depot. His name is Hernán, and he's a fucking moron. I watched him drive a forklift through a half-open steel garage door. If the forklift didn't have a roll cage, it would have taken his head off."

"He did that at his office?"

"There's a delivery space next door to it," Bender said. "A big garage bay and a vault. That guy easily could have misplaced an ingot of palladium. That's the level he's operating on."

"Do you know where Vitale's house is?"

"All I heard was that it was in the hills. I've never been there. It might just be office gossip." He threw up his hands. "So I guess I'm out of a job, once you tell Seligman about my past."

Slater scoffed. "Why do you think I'd do that?"

"So you want cash?" Bender said, and scowled. "Look around. Does it look like I'm flush? I'm not exactly in a position to be one of your income streams."

"I'm not going to chisel you," Slater snapped. "I don't give a damn about you changing your name. I know exactly why you had to. If you're done with parole, that means you've paid your debt. Nobody's beyond redemption."

"OK," he said quietly, and took a breath.
"But if you've lied to me, and you're involved in this horseshit at the Elmer Mine, I'm coming for you."
Bender held his gaze. "Got it."

ELEVEN

S LATER WALKED OUT, LETTING the screen door bang closed behind him. As he climbed into the Thunderbird, he dug out his phone and texted Andy:

One of the guys you researched for me. Vitale. Can you find out if he owns a house in the hills, and how he acquired it?

There was a text from Della, he saw:

Cargo plane booked for Wednesday first thing. Come talk to me in the morning.

Firing up the engine, Slater drove back downtown, and parked across from his office, and weaved through the day laborers hanging around the lobby. The lights were on when he stepped in, and he found Max in his office, wearing his gray checked suit with his necktie loose at the collar, peering at his computer.

"Have you got a minute?" Slater said, standing in his doorway.

"Sure," Max said, his tone affable, and swiveled away from his screen.

That was the best thing about this guy—he was a bruiser, and Slater regularly wanted to punch him in the face, but he was usually pretty relaxed.

"I need backup on a run to a mining camp in Nevada," Slater said, dropping into the chair. "Cudahy Mutual rented a plane. I'm going to fly in, knock some heads together, and fly back, hopefully the same day."

"When is this?"

"Wednesday."

Max slowly shook his head. "I can't. I'm up to my armpits in this window-shade job. Wednesday is the wife's day off—I have to tail her."

"She's the alleged cheater?"

He told him a little about his case, then said, "What about Etta?"

"Do you think she's ready for out of town?" Slater said.

"You know her as well as I do. I think she has good instincts."

"And sangfroid."

Max nodded. "That counts for a lot."

Once he was at his own desk, he dialed Etta.

"I need you for an out-of-town operation," Slater said when she picked up.

"Yeah, baby," she said, so loud that Slater had to pull the phone away from his ear. "I'm just leaving school. Are you at the office? I'll swing by."

Tucking his phone away, he had to grin at her enthusiasm. He sat for a minute, staring absently at the little white statue of Pollux and his horse, and thought it through. For the trip to the mine, he was going to need gear. Wheeling his desk chair over to the safe, he dialed in the combination, and pulled open the door, then took out a rack and split it in half. Once he'd stuffed the wad of bills in his pants pocket, and tossed the other half back in, he wrote "Slater: –5G" on the accounting envelope and locked the safe again.

Back at his desk, he dug through more of the documentation Andy had pilfered from Seligman's files, but nothing stood out as especially informative. Eventually he heard the front door open, and Etta's voice greeting

Max. He locked his computer and sat up.

As she stepped into his office, Etta picked up the statue of Pollux, and studied it as she sat across from him.

"This is new," she said, setting it down again.

"It was a gift. I'm not sure how many tchotchkes we need in here. Does it clash with your decorating job? I kept him because he's got great hair."

"Where's Castor?"

"Who's she?"

Etta chuckled. "Castor is a he. Pollux's twin. They kind of go together. Castor and Pollux."

"That's a very good question, Etta. I'll look into it."

"So what's the out-of-town job?"

"You'll need to work independently," Slater said, "but we'll also collaborate. The actuaries at the insurance company decided that it's a two-person job."

"Where are we going, and for how long?"

He explained Della's idea to fly the shipment back from the Elmer Mine in a cargo plane.

"So we'll be back the same day?" Etta said.

"That's the plan. Do you need to be in town Thursday?"

"It's actually good timing. I have a couple of professional development days this week. Technically I'm supposed to be at school, but I'm told lots of people just skip out and make it a five-day weekend."

"My tax dollars at work," Slater said flatly.

"Do you even pay taxes?"

"What are you going to tell Safiya?"

Etta frowned. "You leave that to me."

"We're going to need some stuff for the desert. Do you have any night-vision gear?"

"There's not much call for that in middle school. Why will we need that?"

"I'm assuming they have night in Nevada. And beyond

the ass end of nowhere I'm thinking there won't be any streetlights."

"You just said we're coming back the same day," Etta said. "We won't be there after dark."

"Every time the transport company goes to the mine, there's a delay. I'd bet cash money that's going to happen to us too."

"So it's the miners who are causing the delays? Don't you think they'll get their act together because they're sending an airplane?"

Slater shrugged. "Why would they care how the shipment happens? The plane is about the insurance company." His phone buzzed, and he picked it up to check—Andy. He eyed Etta. "Have you got enough info for now? I should take this."

Etta rose. "You know where to find me."

"So your guy does own a … house," Andy said when he picked up the call. "It's in a tony part of the hills, but it … feels a little hinky. A trust owns the property, and Vitale … is the only trustee. The place is worth about three million."

"Can you tell where the money came from?"

"No idea. The trust didn't exist before about … eight months ago. That's when it bought the place. it was a … listed sale."

"What does that mean?"

"It wasn't an inheritance or a private transaction. It was … listed with the real estate people. Anyone could have bought it."

"Text me the address."

"I'll do that now," Andy said. "And you're welcome."

"If you're fishing for accolades, you'll get them in the form of greenbacks after you submit your invoice," Slater said, and ended the call.

Etta was in Max's office chatting with him, he saw as

he walked out. On the way down to his car the address came from Andy, and when he plugged it into his navigation app, it told him to take the 101 to Hollywood.

The freeway was stop-and-go in the late afternoon, a frustrating sea of red taillights. He was almost at his exit when his phone buzzed—Hernán.

"I want to see you again," Slater said when he picked up. "Where can I meet you?"

"I'm working right now, but I'm around this evening," Hernán said. "Do you know that town that's all Danish? It's on the way to San Luis Obispo."

"I'm not driving to another county tonight."

"I'm not asking you to. They do a whole Oktoberfest thing."

"Isn't that German?" Slater said. "Why would a Danish town have a German festival?"

"I'm sure it's about making money. Dollar, dollar bill, y'all."

"I'm still not driving up there."

"Neither am I," Hernán said. "Didn't the Germans take over Denmark at one point? You'd think they would have had enough of them."

"So you're not going to the festival?" Slater said, struggling not to shout at him. He veered onto the exit ramp and braked for the stoplight at the top.

"My parents and my sister and her dimwit boyfriend and their kid all drove up there, and they're staying over."

"So you have the house to yourself. Is that the take-away?"

"Exactly. They all piled in my pop's car. Three people in the backseat. I'd be ready to throttle someone after a few hours in an enclosed space like that. But I guess they're a couple, and it's their kid."

"Hernán," he said intently. "Do you want me to come over later?"

"That's what I'm saying, dog."

"Text me the address," Slater said, and ended the call.

Traffic on the surface streets through Hollywood was mostly inching along, but eventually he turned onto Fairfax, and drove up into the hills, and onto a smaller winding side street. This was the right address, he saw, comparing Andy's text to the numbers painted on the curb.

He climbed out and stepped around the car to look over the house. The gate across the driveway was rolled open, and the lot was on a hillside, sloping upward, placing the structure in prominent view above the hedge. With three stories and a silly turret at the front corner, it was a modern riff on a Victorian.

The hedge was some kind of evergreen *Ficus*, probably a *benjamina*. It hadn't been here long. What a stupid thing to plant for privacy. In a couple of years the roots were going to bust up the concrete and the asphalt.

A guy with gray hair and a bowling shirt was standing in the driveway near the house. Eyeing Slater, he walked down toward the street.

"Can I help you?" he called.

"Is Vitale around?"

"You mean my landlord?"

"Does he live here?" Slater demanded.

"I live here. I don't know where Vitale lives."

"How long have you been here?"

He frowned. "Why are you asking?"

"I'm an insurance investigator. I need to determine whether what Vitale told us about this place is true."

"I've been here three years. I don't know anything about his insurance." He waved his arm. "When he bought the place I thought he'd throw me out, but he said he didn't need the house for himself yet."

"My records show that he bought it in February," Slater said.

"Well, I heard about it in March."

"Does he take care of the place?"

"I never see the guy. He sent a handyman when the air-conditioning went out, and he takes my money."

"All right." Slater looked over the house again. The guy was still standing there, watching him, so he added, "Keep your nose clean."

Back behind the wheel, he saw a text from Hernán, and copied the address into his navigation app. It was just over the hill in the Valley, but at this time of day it was going to take a while to get there. The app took him on side streets to Laurel Canyon, and then a slow crawl over the hill. Eventually it put him on the freeway for a few minutes, with the traffic actually moving, before he exited into Hernán's neighborhood.

The street was lined with big houses. It wasn't an obnoxious display of wealth, like where he'd just been, but there was definitely money here. At Hernán's address there was a brick fence with lampposts fronting the expanse of uniform green turf. The iron gate across the driveway was propped open, and Slater nosed in and parked in front of the garage doors, next to the familiar red Solara. It was hard to believe Hernán commuted on the freeway with the top down like that.

When he rang the doorbell, Hernán soon pulled it open.

"Great timing," he said, beaming at him. "I just got home."

He led the way through to the kitchen, with a big island and oversize appliances. A sliding door had a view onto a pool deck backed by a tight row of greenery. Some cultivar of a *chinensis* juniper, it looked like.

"I can see why you live with your parents," Slater said. "You'd never have to look at them."

Hernán braced his hands on the kitchen island. "It's a

nice house, but it's not that big."

"Your parents must work a lot."

"I guess so. They're middle-class. I think buying this house was a stretch."

"I'm amazed the neighbors let that happen. Brown people moving into a neighborhood like this."

"They pushed back for three years, my pop said. Then they gave up. By the time I remember it, they just ignored us."

"So you grew up here. What is this, North Hollywood?"

"Toluca Lake. My parents wanted room for a family."

"Including your sister," Slater said. "The one who had her tubes tied."

"That's the only sister I have." Hernán grinned. "She had it reversed so she could have another kid. Can you believe they can undo something like that? I think it was even an outpatient procedure."

Slater put his hands on his hips. "I think you may have told me about that already."

"Have you eaten? I was going to order Thai."

He watched Hernán tap at his phone, and waited until he set it down.

"When you unload the shipments from the Elmer Mine," Slater said, "is any of the palladium set aside, or sent somewhere else?"

"I don't do anything like that. What comes in is what goes out, all in one load."

"And you're the one who loads the shipment onto the buyer's truck."

"Me and my little forklift."

"Does anyone else have access to it between the delivery from the mine and when the buyer picks it up?" Slater said. "To inspect it, or count it, or rearrange it?"

"It doesn't sit there very long. Buyer pickup is usually the next day. Why are you asking?"

"What do you know about the bill of lading for the shipments from the Elmer Mine?"

"Does the transport company make those? I know 'lading' means it's for the truck."

"Mo prepares it at the mine," Slater said. "Letting Seligman prepare the bill of lading would be like letting your banker keep track of your money. They have an incentive to skim."

Hernán frowned. "Do banks do that?"

"Do you work with the bill of lading?"

He pursed his lips, considering that. "I think they give me a copy of it," he said finally. "When they drop off the shipment. It's in with the paperwork. Usually I just run it through the scanner and file it. I guess I could check who prepares it. It's probably written on the document, right?"

"I already know who prepares it," Slater said. "When a shipment gets to your depot, do you write up the bill of sale?"

"That's definitely done at head office."

"In Denver, or Colorado, or one of those."

Hernán nodded. "I'm pretty sure it's in Denver."

"Do you even see the bill of sale?"

"I print it out, and I'm supposed to get the people who pick up the product to sign it. I scan it and send it back to head office. It's the same for every shipment. Not just the Elmer."

"Do you ever compare the bill of lading with the bill of sale?" Slater said.

"Why would I do that?" Hernán furrowed his brow. "And why are you so curious?"

"I'm still running an investigation here. I just need some background."

"I can take a look at both those papers, if you want. I have my laptop. It has access to all my work files."

Slater waved a hand. "Let's do it before the food gets here."

He walked out, toward the front of the house, and returned a moment later to set the laptop on the kitchen island and climb onto a stool. Slater moved next to him, one hand on the edge of the counter, and watched the screen. Clicking through the folders, Hernán pulled up the bill of lading for the most recent shipment. He'd already seen this today. The number for the weight of the shipment matched the version in Rita's files—this was the same document.

"It's Mo," Hernán said, pointing to the signature at the bottom. "She works at the Elmer."

Slater eyed him sidelong. Was he really this dumb? "I just told you it was Mo."

"I always thought it was strange that they do it in 'k-g.' That means kilograms." Hernán turned to meet his gaze. "It's what they use in Europe instead of gallons and pounds."

"Who knew?" Slater said flatly. "So you scan this, and send it to Gary at head office?"

"Well, I file it. I don't know if Gary actually looks at it or not. I guess anybody up there could. Gary had this weird experience where he was dating a woman he met on an app, and it turned out they were kind of related."

"I thought you didn't know Gary."

"I never met him," Hernán said, swiveling the stool to face him, his hands dropping into his lap. "But we chat sometimes. The woman was talking to her mother, and she recognized Gary's name. She said, 'Girl, that's going to be your cousin.' I think they were both freaked out. Her and Gary, I mean. Probably the mother was too. As it turns out, it's not actually illegal to sleep with your cousin in that state."

Slater took a breath and ran his hand through his

hair. "Hernán, you need to focus."

"Right. Of course." He nodded to the screen. "So I don't know if Gary actually sees these. There's a woman in the office, and he says he wants to ask her out. But there's always a risk to that, right? If you break up, you still have to see each other every day. I'd never do it. But then it's easy for me to say that. I work alone."

Slater wanted to resist the urge, but he just couldn't help himself. He slapped him, left and right.

"What the hell?" Hernán shouted, recoiling and then touching his palm to his face. "You come into my house and slap me around?"

"It's called a kovac," Slater said. "The point is to sharpen your focus."

"I don't care what you call it. You're an asshole."

"I know that," he said. "It's nothing personal."

Hernán huffed, and glared at him, his face contorted with anger. "You even look like the guys who used to push me around in high school. I think that's why I'm attracted to you. Because you don't respect me. Is that pathetic or what?"

"It's not about disrespect. I just need you to try to think clearly."

"About what?" he shouted.

"Do you weigh the product when it comes into your office?"

"Did you see a scale? I unload it, and I lock it up, and I load it on the next truck, and I file all the paperwork. Boom, done. How many times can I explain it to you?"

"That's all I need to know." Slater could see he was breathing hard. "You look steamed."

"Because you hit me."

He stepped closer. "Maybe I can make it up to you. Do you want to hit me back?"

"What is wrong with you?" he demanded.

"I get asked that a lot."

The doorbell rang, and Hernán slid off his stool.

"After dinner," Hernán said, holding his gaze, "I'm going to make you scream."

TWELVE

After they'd eaten, perched on stools at the kitchen island, Hernán dumped the containers in the trash.

Slater swiveled on his stool to face him. "So what is it exactly that you want to do to me?"

"I think you already know that," Hernán said. "Sex and stuff."

"There's more to it. The red mist."

"What's that?"

"Rage. Everyone has it. You need to embrace it once in a while."

Hernán folded his arms. "I'm not really that guy."

Sliding off the stool, Slater stepped closer and massaged his biceps. "I think you might be. You want to take a poke at me?"

"Why would I do that?"

"It could be gratifying. You were pretty pissed when I slapped you."

"It's not really my thing."

"So step out of your comfort zone," Slater said. "Come on—give me your best shot. Imagine I'm one of those chumps in high school who couldn't see how hot you are."

"I'm not going to punch you," he said flatly.

"A slap, then. Or a kovac. I'm not sure you could pull it off, though. It requires a degree of finesse."

Lightning fast, before he was ready for it, Hernán

slapped him, hard enough to turn his head. Slater could feel his heart pounding, and he narrowed his eyes.

"Too much?" Hernán said, and bit his lip.

"I can handle it." He jutted his chin. "Again."

"Your cheek is red."

"It doesn't matter. Hit me again."

"You can't hit me back," Hernán said.

"Deal."

With his other hand Hernán struck the other side of his face.

"Yeah," Slater roared.

"It does feel kind of cathartic."

Slater grabbed his waist and pulled him close. He could feel his woody in his pants.

"It's more than cathartic," he murmured, mouthing his neck. "It gave you a stiffy."

"Come upstairs."

Hernán briefly tugged his arm and walked into the foyer, and up the stairs, and to the end of the hall. His bedroom was bigger than Slater's entire apartment, with windows that looked over the pool deck.

The bed was narrow, set in a frame built to look like a Formula One car, complete with a spoiler on the headboard and wheels painted on the sides.

"Vroom-vroom," Slater said.

"Is it tacky? I guess I should update it. I just thought I'd eventually move out, and get a grown-up bed at that point."

"It's actually kind of cool. I've never fucked anyone in a race-car bed before."

Hernán frowned. "I thought I was going to fuck you."

He spread his palms. "Bring it on."

"So let's get naked, son."

Slater curled his lip into a sneer. "Make me."

"Seriously?"

He raised his eyebrows in a tacit challenge, and Hernán slapped him, way too hard, spinning his head. Slater pushed his hands away, and leaned in to meet his mouth, and spent a minute in it. Eventually he pulled back, and stooped to untie his boots, and got undressed.

Hernán was quickly out of his clothes, revealing his raging woody, and guided him onto the bed. Climbing up and straddling Slater, he ground his cock into his belly.

"You're so beautiful."

"And you're going to need a condom," Slater said.

He dug in the bedside table, then rolled it on himself, and found a squeeze bottle of lube. Shoving Slater's knees up, he was soon pressing into him, breathing hard, his face close to Slater's.

Wincing at first with the intensity of it, Slater slapped him.

"Fuck, man," Hernán snapped.

Slater grabbed his waist and pulled him closer. "Who's the boss?"

"I am."

"Show me," Slater demanded.

Hernán pounded him, building up speed. Slater slapped him again.

"Fuck," he roared, and slapped Slater, too hard, and then struck him again. Straining into him, he yelped as he climaxed, and then collapsed.

Eventually Hernán pulled back and grabbed Slater's cock, stroking it. "What do you want me to do?"

"You tell me. You're the boss."

Mouthing his neck, then pulling back and holding his gaze, Hernán stroked him. He wasn't very bright about a lot of things, but he was intuitive about this. Pulling him closer and meeting his mouth, Slater thrust until he came.

Pulling away, he rolled onto his back, and caught his breath, and folded his arm over his eyes. Hernán's heavy breathing gradually slowed.

"Do you want to shower with me?" Hernán said finally.

Slater lifted his arm to look at him. "I want to get in that pool. Is it heated?"

"It is, but we can't. There's a camera."

"Can you turn it off?"

"My pop is in charge of it."

"There's just one? Show me where it is."

"You can't break it," Hernán said, then got up and led the way downstairs, still naked.

Standing at the sliding door to the pool deck, he pointed outside to the camera mounted just above, on the eaves, aimed at the water.

"It's right there," Hernán said. "If you step out, it'll record you."

Slater unlocked the slider and dragged it open.

"What's that?" Hernán said, gesturing to the wad of fabric in his hand.

"My socks."

Stepping outside, Slater positioned himself directly under the camera, then reached up and stretched a sock over it, and then the second one on top of it.

Hernán stood in the doorway and wrinkled his nose. "Gross."

"Are you coming in?" Slater stepped over to the pool, its blue depths lit from below. It was deep here, he saw, and dove in.

The water wasn't that warm, and it hit him like a shock. He took a big gasp of air when he surfaced. Hernán's father must be a skinflint if that's what he considered heated. At least it wasn't heavily chlorinated. Digging into the water, he swam to the other end. When he turned back he saw that Hernán was in now, his hair wet, plastered to his scalp.

"I've never gone naked in this pool," he said, paddling up to him.

"Time to live a little."

Hernán wrapped his legs around Slater's waist, his arms around his neck, and kissed him. Slater could taste the astringent pool water.

Hernán pulled back. "Want to go again?"

"You're too much for me, boss."

"That's no fun." He chuckled, and heaved himself backward, and swam away.

Eventually they climbed out, shivering in the chill night air. Hernán pulled some towels out of a cabinet near the kitchen slider. Once he'd dried off, Slater stood under the camera to retrieve his socks. He followed Hernán upstairs, and found his clothes on the bedroom floor, and started to pull on his jeans.

"You don't have to go," he said. "My parents won't be home until tomorrow sometime."

"Would we both fit in the race car?"

Hernán looked at the bed. "Good point."

Once he'd tied his boots he followed Hernán down the stairs.

"The pool was fun," Hernán said. "I had to clean it when I was growing up. That was one of my jobs. It's not as hard as you'd think. My pop does the chlorine, though."

Slater pulled the front door open, interrupting his monologue. "Bye, hot stuff."

Walking out to the Thunderbird, he wondered if so much chatter could damage his hearing.

The freeway back to the city was moving at this hour, and he soon pulled into his garage. When he got upstairs he ditched his boots, and poured out his nightly ration from the fifth, then stretched out in his recliner and scowled at the tiny volume in the tumbler.

Hernán had an extremely short attention span, even for a city where that was the norm. Maybe he had some kind of disability, or a neurological problem, or brain damage from a bad drug trip. He said he wasn't removing any part of the palladium shipments. Slater believed him, he decided. If he'd been lying about it, he wasn't the kind of person who'd be able to keep his story straight for very long. The details he'd repeated had never wavered.

Hanging out with that guy felt like being in a whirlwind. He'd seen those before, in the summer, in the Central Valley and out in the Mojave. A column of dust just a few feet across, if it swept over you, you wound up covered with dirt and twigs and debris, and it moved on before you'd even figured out what the hell was happening.

Not the kind of guy he should be spending time with. He knew that. Hernán was exhausting compared to Andy, or that G-man in Albuquerque. He thought about that funny little statue of the naked horseman. Pollux. He remembered what Etta had said about him, that he had a twin. Pulling out his phone, he looked up Castor and Pollux, and read about the mythology.

They were only half-brothers, it turned out, and when they sailed with the Argonauts they didn't shy away from the rough stuff. Pollux defeated a king in a fistfight, resulting in the overthrow of the kingdom. The pair helped destroy entire cities, and after their time on the *Argo*, they managed to help set in motion the Trojan War.

It was later in Albuquerque, but not that late. Peering at the screen, he thumb-typed a text to Pike:

Where's Castor?

He set the phone face-down on his belly, lifting it again a moment later when it buzzed with Pike's reply:

On my desk.

Staring at the little word bubble, Slater could feel his heart beating. He knew what the guy was trying to say. They were similar, and they were connected. He set the phone on the carpet.

Why did people have to get sticky? It made things so complicated. He slammed the last dribble of bourbon and stared at the empty glass. Fuck it, he decided, and got up, and poured from the bottle until the tumbler was half full. Slurping at it, he went back to the chair, relishing the delicious burn, the fumes in his nose.

This was more like it. The world would start to slow down, and retreat, and let go of him for a little while.

THIRTEEN

T HE SOUND OF SLATER'S phone buzzing woke him. This was his own bed. His mouth was dry. As he sat up, a wave of nausea rolled over him, and his head throbbed.

"Damn it," he muttered. It felt like he'd been beaten unconscious. At least the room wasn't spinning. It might not be too bad.

Standing up, he had to take a deep breath and pause to steady himself. At the kitchen sink he slammed a glass of water, and noticed the fifth on the counter, almost empty now. Had he drunk that much on his own? Treading over to the bathroom, he splashed water on his face. In the mirror he looked haggard, with dark blotches under his bloodshot eyes.

"Idiot," he said sharply, glaring at his reflection.

When he climbed back into bed, he looked at his phone. It was a text from Conrad:

Meet me for breakfast at that place on Vermont? I've got info on your query.

Idiot dick-smack Conrad. He texted back:

I'll be there in 20.

Tapping at his phone, he checked for overnight outgoing calls. Thankfully he hadn't drunk-dialed anyone. There was a text, though, sent to Pike in Albuquerque, half an hour after he'd asked about Castor:

I guess we're connected now.

Why couldn't he remember sending this? Pike hadn't answered it, not yet. He must have gone to sleep.

Rising again, he paused for a minute, until he felt steady on his feet. His head was pounding. Eventually he stepped over to the closet and got dressed, then went down to his garage.

The diner they used to go to was in a strip mall, just a few blocks' drive. When he pulled into the lot he spotted Conrad, already inside, at a table by the window. Breathing deeply to steel himself, he walked inside.

Conrad's suit jacket hung on a hook next to the booth. He was wearing a powder-blue shirt with a necktie, his hands wrapped around a coffee mug.

"You look terrible," Conrad said, his brow furrowing.

Slater slid onto the bench across from him. "Fuck you."

"I thought you had a handle on the sauce."

"I'm not a wastoid," he said intently. "I've got a system. It's mostly under control."

"All evidence to the contrary," Conrad said.

"Just—fuck you, OK?" He ran a hand through his hair, ignoring the woman at the next table who was openly staring at him.

"Too late for that."

The server stepped up and said, "Boys?"

As Conrad ordered breakfast, Slater looked her over. She wore her mass of wild hair loosely tied back, and even though she'd tried to conceal it with makeup, the skin around one eye was bruised and puffy. He asked for hash browns and a coffee, and she nodded and stepped away.

"I'm not trying to be a dick here," Conrad said, "but I'm curious as to whether you plan on always being the hot mess you are today?"

Looking out the window, at the cars lined up in the little lot, he could feel a lump in his throat. "Probably," he said quietly. "It's always where I seem to be at."

"It doesn't have to be that way. That empty space you feel inside—you can't fill it with booze."

The server set a mug in front of him, and he took hold of it, and sipped at the acrid java, willing himself not to react.

"Tell me about Lenny Dyer."

Conrad leaned back. "I'd say he's a knucklehead, but he's not really dangerous. He actually has a college degree."

"How did he go from that to becoming a lowlife?"

"There were three of them that got sent up together on a big-dollar bunco racket. They set up a company to take investments on a golf course project in the Palisades."

"I've never heard of a golf course up there."

"Exactly. There's no room for one. These yahoos told people it was going to be built on public land."

"So it was just believable enough," Slater said.

"Several investors believed it, at least. It was a whole thing. The woman I talked to said Lenny Dyer was the muscle and the other two were the brains."

"She investigated it?"

Conrad nodded. "The other guys ran a string of shady businesses over the years, and got sued a dozen times. Lenny claimed he wasn't in on the planning part of the golf course grift, but his paw prints were all over it, so he went down with them. What's your interest in Lenny Dyer?"

"He came up in a case."

"Well, he hasn't been in trouble since he got out of the hoosegow. Not with us, anyway."

The plates of food started to arrive, and Conrad dug in. Slater felt a little better after he'd eaten the greasy hash browns. When he'd finished, Conrad pushed his plate away.

"I should get to work. Are you going to be all right?"

Slater scowled. "I'm always all right." He dug out his wad of cash and peeled off a fifty.

"You're buying me breakfast?"

"It's not a bribe, officer," he said, and stood up.

"No way is it going to cost that much," Conrad said. "You're not going to wait for your change?"

"Did you see our server's shiner?"

"I did notice that, actually."

"Maybe a few extra clams will subsidize making a break from whoever's pounding on her."

Conrad pulled on his jacket and followed him out to the parking lot. Before they parted, Slater stopped to look him over: the officious suit, the sidearm and the tin, his thick dark hair.

"It suits you, all this." Slater gestured toward his torso.

"Thanks, Slater," he said, with a sad smile, and walked toward his SUV.

That lump in his throat was there again as he climbed into the Thunderbird. It made no freaking sense. Maybe it was just the hangover. There was no reason to be getting emotional about that dickwad. Not after that breakup, the way he'd ripped his heart out and kicked him to the gutter.

Nosing into the traffic on Vermont, he drove downtown, into the Financial District, and pulled into the garage under Della's office tower. Upstairs, Crystal was on the front desk, and scowled as he walked in.

"Finally."

"Have you been waiting for me, princess?" Slater said. "I'm flattered."

Her tablet in hand, she rose and walked toward Della's office.

"Are you spying on our meeting again?" he said, following her.

Ignoring that, she pushed open Della's door.

Della sat back in her chair and gave him the once-over. "Rough night?"

"Why would you say that?" he demanded.

Crystal scoffed as she sat down. "You look like you got run over by a cement truck."

His eyes narrowed. "And you look especially lovely today."

"You're the only person I know who could make that sound like an insult," Della said.

He dropped into the other chair. "You know me, Della. I like to keep it strictly professional."

"So we got the plane set up," she said, "but it's not going to happen the way I'd planned. Seligman is still involved."

"In what way?"

"Legally they hold the contract for transporting the cargo. Seligman insists their security guard be on the flight to accompany the shipment."

"Vitale?" Slater said. "The guy seems a little thick. It probably won't matter. Although I don't love the idea of being on an airplane with an armed yahoo."

"You don't have a choice," Crystal said.

"Does the mining company know about me?"

"I told the staff at the mine that you'd be on the plane, and that you're an investigator," Della said.

"That should grease the wheels. If they expect to be interviewed, they'll be more likely to talk."

"Have you found a second to go with you?" Della said.

"My operative Etta. Do you need her details?"

"You're paying her, not me, so no. All the company needs is someone to go out there with you."

"Did any of those eggheads ever explain why? I mean, beyond 'two heads are better than one'?"

"It's probably something about reducing the risk and the associated liability. That's what they do down there all day—assess risk. With two agents it's less likely that something will go wrong."

"Actuaries work in mysterious ways," Crystal said.

They talked about the details, and the departure airport, and the time frame, and half an hour later, Slater walked out. In the elevator on the way down, he texted Svetlana:

Can I visit you today?

Her reply came as he was climbing into his car:

I am always here for you.

Once he was up on the street he navigated onto the freeway and drove to Glendale. Svetlana's workshop wasn't in the spiffy renovated part of town but on a grimy commercial backstreet, in a long low building with a sagging roofline.

He parked in front and climbed out, looking over the ivy the landscaper had planted in the narrow beds along the sidewalk. Svetlana had asked Slater to do it, but instead he'd recommended a woman who'd been in the horticulture program at the same time he had. She was the right choice—the ivy had grown to cover most of the wall, almost to the roof, and the cedar hedge in front of it was still young but looked healthy. It had recently been trimmed into neat even shapes. It was a cheap way to make the place look sharp, and it should be enough to get the city to back off from bugging Svetlana about the run-down vibe.

The way in was around back, and Slater walked to the side street and into the alley, and rang the bell, and looked up into the security camera. When the door buzzed open, he stood in the dark anteroom, waiting while the scanner did its thing. It didn't make any noise but he could see the wiring and electronic components in the corners overhead. After a minute the inner door buzzed open, and he walked inside.

Workbenches lined the walls, littered with electronics and spools of wire and tools. In her fifties, Svetlana was here alone today, perched on a stool in front of a computer monitor, wearing a wild orange and yellow print dress cut low to show her ample cleavage. The fabric looked too light for the fall weather, but it suited the workshop—it was warm in here.

Svetlana swiveled to face him, and on the screen behind her he could see the image of a human form, gray with white spots at either hip where his phone and his keys were.

"It always freaks me out a little to see a scan of my own body," he said.

"I can't see inside it," Svetlana said, with the flat vowels of her Slavic accent, "so it's not really a violation of your privacy."

"I'm not worried about that."

Her brow furrowed as she studied his face. "You've been fighting."

"Worse. Drinking."

She nodded. "Almost the same effects. I wish I could offer you some pickled cucumbers. It's an effective hangover cure. But I don't have any here."

"I'm not suffering too much," he said, and shifted on his feet. "I'm going to a site out in the desert tomorrow. There's no cell service, so I'll need a satellite phone."

"I can do better than that. Satellite internet. A portable modem with the antenna built in. It works better than a satellite phone because it's a data connection.

You can use your own phone."

"Is it reliable? I don't want to have to wait ten minutes for it to connect."

Svetlana spread her palms toward the ceiling. "Lots of satellites up there now. There is higher data speeds in isolated areas because not so many users."

Sliding off the stool, she walked over to the corner, and pulled a black plastic box off the shelf, and handed it to him. Just a few inches square, like a deck of cards, it had a metal clip on one side.

"It will get online in just a few seconds," she said. "But I can't demonstrate the connectivity in here."

"That makes sense. No satellite access through the roof."

"Also this workshop is isolated from radio waves. For security. The modem needs to have a view of the sky. That will be easy in the desert. The clip is to attach it to your backpack straps." She tapped her shoulder. "You have to charge it every day."

"I'll need some way to do that," Slater said. "Can you sell me a battery pack or something?"

She pursed her lips. "The desert has no water but lots of sunshine. You should buy a backpack with a water bag. I can attach solar panels to the backpack, and place a battery pack inside. It won't be too heavy. Just leave it in sunlight a few hours each day to charge, and the battery pack will recharge the modem and your telephone."

"Svetlana, you're a genius." Slater handed her the device. "I'll actually need two of these. Where can I get a water-bag backpack?"

"Go to a camping store. The brand doesn't matter. I can put the solar panels on any of them. If you need them before tomorrow, I can do a rush job for a small extra charge."

"What about night-vision goggles?" Slater said. "I also

need two sets of those."

"Portable is most important, I'm thinking?"

"What's the other option?"

"I have a few models. Some are very portable, and some have a wide field of view. Wait one minute."

She stepped over to a door and waved her wrist at the reader mounted on the wall beside it. It seemed a little extreme, but Svetlana had told him she and her staff had had RFID chips implanted so they wouldn't need to bother with keys. The lock snapped open, and she stepped into the next room, pulling it closed behind her.

Looking around at the workbench and the shelves, there was a lot of stuff in here. He wondered how many customers Svetlana had, and whether all of them were cash-only down-low types like Slater. Her brother had been overseas for a while, but he'd seen at least half a dozen other people here, working on stuff, guarding the place, making deliveries.

When Svetlana came back, she had two sets of black goggles in hand, each with an elastic headband and barely bigger than a pair of ski goggles.

"The batteries should last for a whole night," she said, and handed him a pair.

Turning them over in his hands, he saw the power switch, and clicked it on.

"Let me kill the lights," she said, and stepped over to the wall switch.

The room plunged into darkness, and Slater pulled the goggles on, his eyes soon adjusting to the screens. He could see the room in shades of red, like a black-and-white photo seen through a red filter. When he turned to look at Svetlana, the print of her blouse was all in red tones, and her eyes had an eerie glow to them.

"These work great," he said, and pulled them off.

"Like mine, your business is about discretion, yes?"

she said, flicking the room lights on again. "These glass-es require extra discretion. They're supposed to be limit-ed to military use."

"Got it," Slater said, and furrowed his brow. "The U.S. military?"

"No." She met his gaze and handed him the other set. "Both pairs are fully charged."

"What do I owe you?"

"Five dollars for the glasses, and four dollars for the satellite internet box. Let's say three for the solar panels and the battery."

Digging out his wad of cash, Slater riffled through to count out the C-notes. "Is there a fee for the satellite access?"

Svetlana waved dismissively. "Included in your sub-scription."

Taking the sheaf of bills, she stepped to the work-bench near her computer, and spent a moment folding them flat, then dropped them in the top of a little device with white plastic housing. A cash-counting machine, Slater realized. It quickly flipped through the bills, with the mechanical sound of shuffling paper, leaving the red digits on the front to read 2400.

Heaving herself up onto her stool, Svetlana scanned the bar-code label on each of the little modem boxes with a pen-shaped wand, glowing red at one end and wired into her computer at the other. She tapped at her keyboard for a moment, peering at the screen, then peeled the labels off each of the devices.

"Modems are active now," she said. "I'll keep them to sew into the backpacks. Give me the glasses."

Slater handed over the night-vision goggles, and she tucked them into a brown paper grocery bag, and swiv-eled around to hand it to him. "See you later today, yes?"

"I'll be back soon."

FOURTEEN

S LATER WENT TO THE door and waited for her to buzz it open, then stepped into the anteroom. The outer door had a crash bar, and he pushed his way into the alley, then walked around to the Thunderbird and stowed the paper bag in the trunk.

Once he was behind the wheel, he called Etta, glad that she picked up.

"Do you have one of those backpacks with a water bag inside?"

"Isn't that for trail running?" she said. "I don't do that. Why would I have one of those?"

"You have to come to the camping store with me. Like, now."

"If you get here soon, we can do it on my lunch break. There's one near here."

"Where's your school, again?" Slater said.

"East LA." Etta rattled off the address. "Pull up where it says 'buses only.' I'll come out."

It wasn't that far at freeway speed, once Slater got on the 5, and a few minutes later he pulled up at her school. He sent Etta a text:

Here.

Farther up the block a woman in a crossing-guard vest was eyeing him, and eventually she started to wander over. But Slater didn't need to engage her, as Etta hustled out of the building and climbed in the passenger seat.

"You look like hell," she said, peering at him and frowning.

"Thank you so much. I deeply treasure your candor, Etta." He dropped the transmission into gear and made a U-turn. "Where's the damn camping store?"

"Right down the 5," she said. "At that outlet mall."

Slater braked to make the turn onto the boulevard, then headed back toward the freeway.

"So why do we need water backpacks?" Etta said. "And why do you need me with you?"

He explained Svetlana's reasoning and the tech he'd bought from her. "I can't just buy you any old backpack," he said. "You have that mysterious female anatomy."

"You mean I have breasts. In my experience backpacks work fine with those."

"I still wouldn't know what to buy."

"You could just tell the sales clerk you're buying it for a woman."

"But then they'd want all the details about your contours, and your dress size, and your bra size. I don't know anything about that."

Etta chuckled. "Have you never seen a female body before?"

"Sure. In textbooks."

"You've never slept with a woman?"

"That depends on how you define that term," Slater said. "It's a spectrum, isn't it? I've slept with femmie guys, and trans men. That's a trip. Like, where's the money? And then it's like, oh, OK, it's made of silicone."

"He didn't tell you up front that he was trans?"

"I'm sure it was mentioned, but I wasn't focused on it. A man's a man. You'd sleep with a woman who had a prosthetic arm, wouldn't you? A prosthetic weenie is the same deal. It would just be racist to reject someone because of that."

"I'm not sure *racist* is the right word," Etta said, raising her voice over the roar of the engine as he accelerated up the ramp onto the 5. "I also can't imagine you with a femmie guy."

"Femmie guys are fun."

"Dare I ask?"

"They're more attentive, maybe. More focused. So what's the deal with Safiya?"

"There's no deal. She's just a little emotional."

"She almost blew up an operation," Slater said. "That's a deal."

"There wouldn't have been an operation if your software had worked right the first time."

"It worked perfectly. It just needed a little update."

"I just figured it out." Etta looked at him. "You're a Svetlana stan."

"What are you talking about?"

"It's like those people who adore their cell phones, or their electric cars. The tech companies can do no wrong. That's your relationship to the Russian—you love her. She's like your religion."

"She makes good stuff," Slater said, "but it's a transactional relationship. If I didn't pay her, she could blow up my life."

"Do you ever find yourself daydreaming about her, like when you're driving, or in the shower?"

"Listen—Svetlana is not the point. Your girlfriend is. What happens next time, when you're undercover, and Safiya shows up shouting at you?"

Her expression sobered. "I'm going to work on that. I think it's about getting her to trust me."

"Or hiding her car keys so she can't follow you."

"I'll figure it out." Etta took a breath. "If not, there's more where she came from."

"Really." He glanced at her sidelong. "So this isn't the

greatest love of all."

"Like you said, she almost blew up an operation. I can't be with someone who's going to sabotage my professional life."

That, Slater thought, was very good news. He pulled into the mall parking lot and found a space, and they climbed out, and walked into the camping store.

Near the wall of backpacks, arranged from oversize trekking bags to minimalist day packs, they found a clerk. Dressed like he'd just been camping, in a plaid shirt and jeans, the guy had wild snowy hair and sun-lined skin.

"I need one of those day packs with a water bag in it," Slater told him.

"That's called a hydration pack."

The clerk stepped over to the wall and pulled down a slender blue one with black straps. It was unbelievably light, Slater realized, taking it from him. He handed it to Etta.

"How do you drink out of it?"

"Here's the tube," the clerk said, pointing it out. "You just suck on the nozzle."

"Svetlana never mentioned that part."

"This is actually cool," Etta said, zipping it open to look at the water bladder. She slung it over her shoulders and adjusted the straps. "It fits fine, even with breasts."

It was designed to work around them, Slater saw, watching her adjust the straps. Even on her bulky frame it looked comfortable.

He eyed the clerk. "I suppose the other option is just to get a regular day pack and carry water bottles."

"Trust me," the clerk said. "You'll be happier sucking on the hose."

Etta pulled off the bag and handed it to the clerk. "I vote yes."

"It holds three liters," the clerk said. "Enough for the whole day."

"Three liters is three quarts?" Etta said.

"Right, but liters are the international standard. Saying that makes you sound high-brow." He gestured with the bag. "You know, Euro."

"We'll need two of them," Slater said.

As the clerk walked into the back, Etta said, "You could almost pass for Euro."

"Especially if I drink my water in liters."

"It might take some getting used to. The sippy hose, I mean."

"Suck it up," Slater said intently.

She laughed at that, and after Slater had paid for the bags, they walked out to the parking lot, and he drove back to Etta's school.

"Come by the office tonight, and we'll go through the gear," he said, watching her climb out.

———•———

BACK AT SVETLANA'S WORKSHOP in Glendale, Slater handed over the backpacks. There was a gloomy-looking woman here now, with voluminous blond hair, standing back and watching them talk, her arms folded.

"My seamstress," Svetlana explained. "She will have them ready in a few hours. One of my people can drop them at your office. He's driving through downtown any-way."

"That works."

"I'll text you with his ETA."

Exiting through the antechamber, he walked around to his car. Svetlana didn't need to ask where his office was because she already knew, although he'd never told her. Undoubtedly she collected a lot of information about him. He would too, he had to admit, if he was selling such illicit stuff. She was protecting her operation.

Traffic was sluggish on the way back downtown, and once he'd parked in the surface lot across from his building, he grabbed the bag with the night-vision goggles and hustled across the street. Nobody was here, he saw, flipping on the lights and sticking his head into Max's office to make sure. At his own desk he put his feet up and studied the statue of Pollux.

His plan had been to read through more of the paperwork Della had given him, and the documents Andy had obtained, but once he had his feet up on his desk, exhaustion from his overindulgence started to weigh on his eyelids. Why did he do this to himself? The smell of his own skin right now was nauseating. It was the same cloying tang that dive bars had, the products of alcohol broken down and seeping through his pores.

Slater started awake sometime later when a knock came at the door. Pulling it open, he found a skinny guy with jet-black hair holding the two backpacks, studded now with shiny black panels the size of dominoes.

"I thought you'd text first."

"Sveta said you'd be in your office," he said, with a slighter version of Svetlana's accent.

That probably meant she was tracking him, the same way he tracked lowlifes, through her software on his phone. It made him feel a little queasy, but today at least she had a legitimate reason to do it.

"The battery and charging cables are in the outside pouch," he said, and zipped it open to show him. "Modem is in the top pouch."

"I see," Slater said, and took the bags. "Am I supposed to tip you or something?"

He laughed. "Of course not. But do you need me to explain anything about the technology?"

"Sveta already covered it."

"Good night, then," he said, and walked toward the elevator.

Back in his office, Slater set the bags on his desk to look them over. The little solar cells were shiny, and thin, like ceramic tiles. Individually they were solid and hard, but overall the bag was still flexible, and with its inherent curved shape it looked a little like a polished black tortoise shell.

Dropping into his chair, he moved the bags so that he could see Pollux. Of course he was going to think about Pike every time he saw it, and how Pike was looking at its twin in a different time zone. The guy was supremely hot. But why would he get involved with him? Pike was another damn cop, and he lived so far away.

A while later he heard Etta come in, and call out a greeting, and flip the deadbolt. Stepping into his office, she picked up one of the backpacks.

"Your Russian girlfriend bedazzled them."

"Those are the solar panels."

"I figured. Where's the charging cable?"

"Zip it open."

Etta dug into the various pockets. "The battery pack sits higher than the water bladder. That's smart. If the water leaks, it won't get fried." Zipping open the top pouch, she pulled out the little black box.

"That's the satellite modem," Slater said.

"She hardwired it to the battery, but you can disconnect it if you need to. It's in the pocket that's right at the top, so when you're wearing it, you can just leave it there, and it'll always have a view of the sky."

"Svetlana has a lot of experience with this stuff."

"It's really well planned," Etta said. "I want to meet this woman."

"It sounds like you're becoming a Svetlana stan too." He handed her a pair of the goggles. "Night vision. Want to try them out?"

She pulled them on, adjusting the strap behind her head, and toggled the power switch. "All I see is red."

"There's too much light." Slater stood up and clicked off the room light.

"That's better," Etta said. "Ooh, weird—your eyes are glowing. Red like the devil."

"It's totally dark in here, but you can see?"

"Like daytime if I was wearing red-tinted glasses. It's pretty high resolution too."

Once he'd turned the lights on again, they stowed the goggles in their packs.

"So what else do I need to bring?" Etta said.

"A jacket. It's cold out there right now. A change of clothes, if you need it."

"Because you think we're going to get stuck overnight."

"I should give you some dough," Slater said.

"What for?"

"In case something comes up." He dropped to one knee in front of the safe and twisted the combination on the dial. "Folding money works better than plastic lots of times, and it doesn't reveal your identity." Pulling open the door, he took out the rest of the rack he'd split yesterday. "How does two G sound? Maybe three G. We're going way out of town."

"That sounds like a hella lot of dough."

"Think of all the contingencies. You might get stranded somewhere. You need to be able to hire a driver or book a flight." Slater counted out the cash and handed it to her. "If you don't use it, you'll bring it back."

He pocketed the rest of the rack for himself, and then noted it on the back of the accounting envelope, and locked up the safe.

They rode the elevator down together and walked out

of the lobby. It was dark out now, and the air felt cold. Once they were in the parking lot, Etta spoke.

"There's open sky here. Should we make sure the space modem works?"

Slater waved a hand. "Have at it."

Etta zipped open the backpack, and clicked on the device, then slung it back on her shoulder. Digging out her phone, she tapped at it, the blue glow of the screen illuminating her features.

"Oh, weird. I've never seen that before."

"What are you seeing?" Slater said.

"A very strong open Wi-Fi point with Russian letters."

"Is it working?"

"I'm online. It seems like excellent speed."

"So we're good to go." He opened the trunk of the Thunderbird and set his backpack inside. "Do you want me to pick you up in the morning?"

"That would be great." Etta pulled off her backpack and set it next to his.

"Wheels up is six thirty, so I'll be at your door at five thirty."

He watched her climb into her little red Prius, then started his engine and followed her into the street. Once he was at his apartment, he carried one of the backpacks upstairs. The essentials would fit in this, even when the water bladder was full. He tucked in a pair of socks, and underpants, and condoms. In the kitchen cupboard he found a metal hip flask, and filled it from the bourbon bottle, and zipped it into the bag. It still felt light. He could wear his jacket, but what else would he need?

Trackers. A couple of those might be useful. With the backpack and his jacket in hand, he went down the stairs to his garage. Just past the nose of the Thunderbird was his armored cabinet. It looked like a sheet-metal box from an office-supply store, but that was so it could hide in plain sight. In reality it was reinforced like a safe. His gardening tools hung on the garage walls, but the sensitive stuff, Svetlana's gear, was kept in here.

Once he'd unlocked it, he grabbed a magnetic vehicle tracker, and then a couple of smaller ones, disguised as little calculators, to slip into jacket pockets or handbags. He tucked them into the bottom of the backpack and then left it in the trunk of the Thunderbird.

Upstairs again, he poured out his ration. No way was he going to overdo it tonight, not when he was still feeling the effects of last night's bender. Settling into the recliner, he looked at his phone, and hesitated, but then opened the hookup app. As he swiped through the torsos and dick picks and head shots, his eyelids started to droop, and eventually he shut it down. He had to get up so damn early. He could take a night off.

FIFTEEN

W AKING TO HIS ALARM, Slater slapped it off and sat up so that he wouldn't drift off again. He rubbed his eyes and took a breath. What a relief to be clear-headed.

After he'd made a mug of powdered coffee in the microwave, he slurped at it and then hustled down to his garage. Merging onto the 110, it was just a few exits to Highland Park, and this early in the morning the traffic was moving fast. Where were all these idiots going so long before daybreak?

When he pulled up at Etta's apartment house he left the engine running and texted her:

I'm out front.

A minute later he saw her exit the building, carrying a rolled-up plastic bag the size of a wine bottle. If everything she needed for an overnight trip fit in that, she was showing impressive restraint.

"Hello, gorgeous," she said as she climbed in.

Slater shot her a look as he pulled into the street. "You're a morning person. I never knew that."

"I guess I am. I'm usually pretty energized at this time of day."

"Great," he said flatly.

She laughed at that. "What airport are we leaving from?"

"Van Nuys."

"The 818 be where I holla from / I be reppin' Pacoima, son."

"What the hell are you talking about?" Slater demanded.

"It's a song," Etta said. "All my kids are blasting it right now."

"It sounds like a barn burner. Did you realize it doesn't even rhyme?"

"You need to get out more, son."

His navigation app sent him on surface streets to the 134, and soon they were looping up the ramp, and accelerating onto the freeway.

"So what do we do when we get to the Elmer Mine?" Etta said.

"I'm sure the company weasels will try to waste our time. We can split up and interview people."

"Just anybody?"

"Focus on the administrators," Slater said, "but talk to anyone who seems jumpy."

"I guess the question that comes to mind is, why would they talk to us?"

"They know we're coming, and they know we're conducting an investigation. You have to act like you have the authority to be questioning them. Most civilians respond to that with compliance. They'll tell you whatever you ask, especially if they think their employer requires it. But that doesn't mean they'll tell you the truth."

"How do you project authority?" Etta said.

"It's that thing that cops do. They call it command presence. They have to learn it, but as a lesbian it's kind of your birthright. You probably call it something different. Like 'ordering lunch.'"

"Not that we're stereotyping or anything."

"Don't try to tell me you don't know what I'm talking about," Slater said. "Just be the woman in charge."

"What if they ask to see a badge?"

"That means they're not buying your authority, so you switch gears. Tell them you need their help, that they might have critical information, and it's the right thing to do. That approach won't sway a lowlife, but it works with lots of normies."

They talked for a while about what questions to ask, and finally Etta said, "I get the satellite modem and the hydration pack, but what will we use the night vision for?"

"People keep saying an oversize hairy biped is stalking the Elmer Mine at night," Slater said. "We're going to look for bigfoot."

———————

WHEN SLATER FOUND THE address that Della had given him, he parked nose-in amid a row of cars along a chain-link fence topped by loops of razor wire. On the other side was a low white building, unmarked except for the street number, its bulk visible in the growing twilight. Slater opened the trunk, and grabbed his backpack, and Etta stuffed her plastic bag into hers.

There was a gate in the fence next to the building, and they walked over to find a window with a uniformed guard in a little office.

"IDs?" he said, and once they'd both handed them over, he checked a computer screen. Eventually he gave them their cards back, and the lock on the gate clicked open, and he waved them through.

Inside, they walked the length of the building.

"Dude," Etta said. "We're on the actual tarmac."

"That looks like our ride." A squat boxy aircraft was parked nearby. Pulling out his phone, he snapped a picture of it.

"Is that for your social media feed?" Etta said. "You

should have brought a bunch of gold necklaces and a champagne bottle as props."

He scoffed. "I took a photo of the registration number. I'm going to text it to Max. That way if you and I go missing, somebody knows what aircraft we got on."

The plane's wings were at the top of the fuselage, with a lone propeller engine mounted on each. At the far end, the nose looked like it was drooping toward the ground. Three men were standing there, two in blue flight suits and one in black—Vitale.

As they approached the aircraft, Slater looked it over. Boxy vertical fins framed either side of the tail, and below that the rear end was one big cargo gate, lowered to the tarmac to form a ramp. The floor inside was open, about the size of a box truck, and right up front, behind the cockpit, two sets of seats were bolted to the floor, like the ones on a commercial airliner.

Vitale spotted them and walked toward the back, briefly touching the strut under the wing as he passed.

"That's Vitale," Slater said quietly.

"He's definitely dressed like security."

Or a bouncer, Slater thought. Vitale was wearing black work pants, and a black shirt, and a lightweight black jacket.

"If it isn't Slappy," Vitale said as he approached.

"I never laid a finger on you," Slater said. "You must have been talking to Bender."

"He said you slapped him around."

"That's a lie. I gave him a kovac. A simple double tap to focus his attention." Slater mimed the action, twisting his palm back and forth.

"I've heard that called the paintbrush."

"East of the Mississippi, maybe. In Cali it's definitely a kovac. Did Bender mention that he was asking for it?"

"Who's your girlfriend?" Vitale said.

"I'm not his girlfriend, you dope," Etta said, scowling at him. "I'm an operative."

"I'm not sure why the insurance company needs you two along. I think I've got this handled." He casually set his hands on his hips, revealing the butt of a handgun in a holster at his belt.

"And yet you actually haven't been able to handle it with the cargo vans," Slater said. "It's been one fuck-up after another. That's why we're all here."

His brow furrowed. "I'm going to check on the aircraft." Vitale walked under the tail and up the cargo ramp.

"Is he flying this crate?" Etta said.

"I'm sure he's never seen it before today. He thinks he's an Argonaut."

"On Monday you didn't even know who Castor and Pollux were. Now you're citing the myth."

Slater frowned. "I can read. I just mean that Vitale thinks he's in charge."

"I guess if you're the only one with a weapon, you are in charge," Etta said. "He wasn't shy about showing us he's armed."

"That's the equivalent of flashing his dick. And he's set up to cross-draw. That's reserved for people who are never going to win a gunfight."

A lanky dark-haired guy in a blue jumpsuit walked under the wing and introduced himself as Sánchez. "Russell is just finishing his walk-around."

"Who's Russell?" Slater said.

"The pilot. I'm in the right seat today."

"What kind of airplane is this?" Etta said.

"It's called a Sherpa. It's meant for cargo. Real smooth in the air. We're flying empty, so takeoff will be a little steeper than in a commercial aircraft."

"I'm not sure I like the sound of that," she said.

Sánchez chuckled. "Statistically it's safer than your car trip to get here. Why don't you get buckled in?"

He gestured to the interior, and they followed him up the ramp. The ceiling was just high enough that Slater didn't need to stoop.

"You can stow your gear in the mesh pockets," Sánchez said.

Attached between a couple of the curving metal ribs was a stretchy black webbing. Slater tucked the backpacks into it. It was actually a good design—they weren't going to shift around. Unpainted and with regular holes cut in them, the ribs made the cabin look industrial and unfinished, like wood framing before the drywall went up.

On the left side, just in front of the lone row of seats, was a passenger door, currently propped open, and in front of that was the cockpit bulkhead. Vitale was already in one of the seats, against the window on the far right. Etta dropped into the one next to the door, and Slater sat beside her.

"Is anyone else joining us?" Slater called to Vitale.

"This trip is just the pilots," he said, "and security, and you two boobs."

"Who's working security?" Slater said, and frowned. "I haven't seen anyone like that."

Vitale scowled and looked out the window. In front of Etta, a pasty blond in a blue flight suit stepped in the door.

"You must be Russell," she said.

"That's right." He grinned as he pulled the door closed and latched it. "Did anybody bring earplugs? It gets a little noisy. It helps to wear them."

"I never thought of that," Etta said.

As Russell got into his seat, Slater could just see his shoulder. Sánchez was in full view, and he turned around and met Slater's eye.

"Head's up," he said, and tossed three little packets.

Orange foam earplugs, Slater saw, and tossed a pair to Vitale. Etta pressed hers in, and soon the engines started, and revved up. A hydraulic whine came from behind them, and Slater looked back to see the cargo gate slowly rise into place, blotting out the daylight.

The engines got louder again, and Slater pressed in his earplugs. The pilots had left the cockpit door open, and as they started taxiing, he had a view of the airfield in front.

The aircraft was taxiing alarmingly fast, and made a couple of sharp turns. The engines roared louder, and the plane picked up speed until the ground pulled away. They were rising at a sharp angle, but it wasn't scary, although Etta was breathing hard and staring intently out the window. The golden light of dawn painted the mountains now, and the plane turned toward them, climbing higher.

It was too loud to talk, so Slater closed his eyes, lulled by the gentle vibration and the drone of the propellers. A while later the sound of the engines changed, and the nose started to drop. Out the window it was broad daylight now. They were over a mountainous desert landscape, but it looked different than the familiar Mojave. Darker, maybe.

As they descended, out the cockpit window he saw they were aiming for a playa, white with minerals. Dried-out ancient lakebeds, these were scattered all over the desert Southwest, and they were perfectly flat—an ideal place to land an airplane.

The white expanse slowly rose to meet them, and after the thud of the wheels connecting with the ground, the engine noise changed again, and the plane slowed. In the distance he could see a cluster of structures on the bajada, where it met the playa, and farther away a field of shiny black panels angled to the sky. That must be the cutting-edge thing Della talked about. From here it looked like a run-of-the-mill solar farm.

He lost sight of them when the plane turned toward the structures. Eventually the engines powered down, and Sánchez climbed out of his seat and stood in the cockpit doorway.

"It gets windy here," he said, "so we're not going to lower the cargo door until we're ready to load."

Slater got up, and pulled the backpacks out of the webbing, and handed Etta's to her.

"Your matching bags are adorable," Vitale said, on his feet now. "Did you get those at Girl Scouts?"

"I know several Girl Scouts who could kick your ass," Etta said.

"You shouldn't react to him," Slater said. "It's not his fault that he's got a microdick."

Sánchez stifled a laugh as he pulled open the door and folded down the little two-step ladder. Etta followed him out, and then Slater. He was struck by the cold air. Good thing he'd worn a jacket.

Even though the propellers weren't moving anymore, they looked dangerous, so he walked a few yards away from the plane. Once he'd stretched, and did a neck roll, he looked around. The buildings were actually a collection of trailers, the kind you'd see at a construction site. They were set up to be here for a while, with support jacks at each corner, the tires wrapped in white plastic.

Farther away, still on the edge of the playa, toward the solar farm and separated from the trailer camp by a few hundred yards, was a jumble of shipping containers in an array of colors. That had to be where the mining was happening. Next to them was a trio of vertical tanks on the ground and a row of smaller ones mounted horizontally on wooden platforms. Parked at the edge of the playa were some heavy vehicles—a bulldozer, and a loader, and a dump truck.

In front of the camp the playa stretched a long way across to the next mountain range, and parallel to this edge of the playa, the flat expanse met the misty horizon, miles away. Slater stooped briefly to pick up a pinch of the crunchy white dust. It wasn't very deep, with brown clay just below. Studying it in his palm, he touched the white minerals to his tongue.

"Why are you eating it?" Etta demanded.

"It's bitter, not salty. That means this is an alkali playa. In some places they're salt playas."

Slapping the dust off his hands, he looked out across the expanse. There were dark splotches on the alkali, he saw, not far past the solar farm, where the surface layer had been disturbed. But it hadn't been excavated, not to any depth.

"It doesn't look like a mine," Etta said. "I expected a hole in the ground."

"Apparently they're using some new technology."

Glancing back at the aircraft, he saw that Vitale was standing with the pilots, the three of them in serious conversation.

Nothing grew on the playa, but there was vegetation dotting the bajada around the camp. Most of it was one shrub, a kind of amaranth that he'd heard called shadscale. The few creosote bushes he could see had very dark leaves—that meant they hadn't seen moisture for a long time.

From the direction of the trailer camp a woman strode toward them, dressed for the desert, in jeans and a heavy plaid jacket. Her graying hair was in a utilitarian cut, and there was a smattering of freckles across her face.

"I'm Mo," she said, and smiled. "You must be from Cudahy Mutual."

They told her their names, but Mo's attention shifted to Vitale, who walked past, ignoring them, toward the camp. Her face clouded at the sight of him.

"Not a friend of yours?" Slater said.

Mo folded her arms. "Since you're here to do an investigation, I suppose I can be candid."

Slater gestured impatiently.

"He's a damn fool," she said, lowering her voice, even though Vitale was well out of earshot now. "All the shipping delays are because of him."

"How do you figure that?" Slater said.

"We can get into it later. Let me show you around." She turned and walked toward the trailers. "This is where we eat and sleep. The work gets done over there."

Mo headed toward the shipping containers, and they kept pace with her, walking abreast.

"I can't believe I've got cell service here," Etta said, looking at her phone.

"It only covers the camp. Technically it was easier for us to set it up that way than to put everybody on Wi-Fi. When you get half a mile from the mine, it fades out."

"It simplifies things for us too," Etta said.

"Those are such interesting backpacks. They look like solar cells."

"To charge our electronics," Etta said. "It looks like we don't really need them out here." She gestured to the rows of shiny black panels in the distance. "You have enough of your own. Those are the size of a football field."

"The array is actually much bigger than that," Mo said. "Direct current is key to our process. We pump groundwater from under this basin and mix it with the minerals on the salt pan. Our patented electrical technique extracts the palladium from among the many minerals and metals. The entire process is powered by renewable energy from the sun."

"What do you do with the wastewater?" Slater said. "You can't put it back in the ground. You'd pollute the aquifer."

Etta pointed into the distance. "It looks like they're just dumping it on the playa."

"The water evaporates," Mo said, "and the minerals go right back onto the salt pan where they came from."

"But you're depleting the aquifer."

"Nature put it there. Nature will recharge it."

"And the feds signed off on this?" Slater said. "I assume this is BLM land."

Mo looked at Etta and furrowed her brow. "Why do you call it a playa? It's a salt pan. Doesn't *playa* mean 'beach'?"

"Enforcing English vocabulary in this part of the world feels kind of colonial," she said. "But I don't actually speak Spanish. Slater, why do we call it a playa?"

"I only speak taco-cart Spanish, but in the Southwest, in English, this"—he waved his arm at it—"is called a playa."

"I grew up in Marin County," Mo said, "and I've never heard that word."

"Marin County isn't really the Southwest, though, is it," Slater said. "It's more like a gated little garden for rich folks. Play ranches for Wall Street types."

"And horse manure," Etta said. "I remember it was everywhere up there. On all the lawns. Beverly Hills is like that too. What is it with rich folks and horse manure?"

Mo huffed but held her tongue. Her job today was PR, Slater knew. She wasn't going to snap back at them.

"Why would you call it a salt pan?" Slater said. "It's alkali."

"Technically alkali compounds are salts," Mo said,

shooting him a thin smile. "Although I'm no scientist."

As they walked past the big tanks set up near the shipping containers, he saw there was no berm around them, and no hazard warning signs. That meant they were for water, not chemicals or fuel.

"Where's the well and the pump?" he said.

"In one of these units. We're using renewable energy and recycled shipping containers."

She gestured to the containers, arrayed in tight configurations spaced a few yards apart. Some of them had been cut open and connected, Slater saw, as they were stacked tight together.

Mo stopped and held up her hand like a crossing guard. As they watched, a loader rolled by, its bucket full of brown and white earth, presumably scraped from the surface of the playa. The driver, wearing a hard hat and sunglasses, waved to them as he passed. The vehicle disappeared among the containers.

It was hard to see from here, but there were definitely broad sections of the playa where the alkali had been scraped away. Farther away a thick pipe ran out across the surface, and beyond it were more discolored patches. That's where the wastewater went.

"Where do you do the magical electrical extraction process?" he said.

"That's right here too. I can't show you because it's proprietary technology."

"I bet it's in the sea can with all the cables running into it. That looks like a lot of juice."

"We have over a megawatt of energy coming in from the solar panels," Mo said. "They cover about five acres. The process uses no solvents, no drying pools, and it works fast, so it's economically viable."

"Until the aquifer runs dry," Etta said.

"The solar panels are completely portable." Mo held

her gaze. "When this resource has been exploited, we can move it all to another site with similar conditions."

"And deplete another aquifer," Etta said. "You have to love capitalism."

SIXTEEN

"WHY ARE YOU DOING it here?" Slater said. "Why not closer to civilization? These alkali playas are all over the desert."

"Not every salt pan has palladium," Mo said. "It's valuable enough to be economically viable here, but the other minerals aren't worth the effort of extraction. It's actually quite unusual to find palladium in this concentration. We think it leached out of nearby deposits in these mountains."

She turned back toward the trailers, walking along the edge of the playa, and stopped at a red shipping container that sat on its own, not far from where the airplane was parked. It had big double doors in the middle, and a mini loader with a forklift attachment parked at one end.

Digging out a key ring, Mo opened the padlock on the doors, then pulled one open a little, and took a moment to snap the padlock closed on the hasp. She'd been trained in security, Slater realized. You never left a padlock hanging unlocked. Someone could replace it with their own, and you'd put it on, unaware. The crook could come back and rob the place at their leisure.

Pulling the door wide and then stepping inside, Mo flipped on the light. "This is the finished product. Ingots of pure palladium."

In the middle of the space sat a wooden pallet stacked with gleaming bars. They had the shape of construction bricks, flat and oblong, but they were smaller. Stacked in three layers, they didn't fill the pallet, and there were fewer of them in the top layer.

Stepping closer, Slater picked one up. It was much heavier than he'd expected, and he had to use two hands. The surface was smooth and even.

"I bet this weighs exactly twelve kilograms," he said.

Mo nodded. "That's right—twenty-six point four pounds."

"Check this out," he said, and handed the ingot to Etta.

"Whoa," she said, taking hold of it.

Absently watching her, Slater thought about the numbers. Twelve kilograms explained a lot—the weight discrepancy in the shipments was exactly two or three of these ingots each time.

"It's insane how heavy this is," Etta said. "It's like a hunk of cast iron."

"Palladium is actually fifty percent heavier than iron for the same volume," Mo said.

Etta met her gaze. "Do you give these out as free samples?"

"Funny," she said, her expression deadpan. "You're holding seventy thousand dollars' worth of product in your hands."

"So they're heavy," Slater said, "but how hard can it be to put these in a van and drive them to LA? What's with all the delays?"

Her expression clouded. "Ask your friends at Seligman. No matter what we tell them, it gets garbled. They don't show up when we ask them to, and when they do show up, we're not expecting them."

Etta set the ingot with the others. "I'll catch up later," she said, and stepped to the door.

"You should probably stay with me," Mo said.

"I'm just going to look around." She held up her

hands and flipped them around to show they were empty. "I promise I won't steal anything."

Mo groaned and watched her leave, then followed Slater out, and relocked the doors with the padlock. The sun was higher in the sky, and it was getting warmer, but it still felt like winter.

"When are we going to load this stuff on the plane?" Slater said.

"That's up to the pilots. They'll let us know."

"So what exactly is your position here?"

"The way Mott does things is a little different," Mo said. "We don't really have job titles. We find them limiting."

Slater put his hands on his hips. "You really have bought in to the Silicon Valley mythology." He waved an arm. "Is any of this real, or is it some kind of aspirational scam?"

"What are you talking about?" She frowned. "Of course it's real. We ship the product regularly."

"Not regularly enough. Otherwise I wouldn't be here."

"That doesn't mean it's a scam. I just showed you three thousand pounds of 'real.'" She waggled her fingers to put air quotes around the word.

That was true, he had to admit. There were over a hundred ingots on that pallet. That meant Mott wasn't lying about their rate of production.

"If you don't have a title," Slater said, "what exactly do you do?"

"I'm office staff. Mostly payroll and accounting."

"And PR tours."

"That doesn't come up very often," she said, "but sure."

"You prepare the bill of lading for the shipments?"

"Usually Hilda does that. But I sign them. It's pretty basic."

"Is Hilda around?"

"I assume she's in the office."

"Does she have a bill of lading made up for this shipment?"

Mo sighed impatiently. "I'm sure that's in the office too."

"Do you weigh the ingots yourself, or does Hilda?"

"Whoever signs the bill of lading counts them. We don't need to weigh them because they're always the same weight. That's part of the extraction process. It's automated to make them uniform."

"Why does Hilda prepare the bill of lading in kilograms? Just now you were talking about pounds."

"Metric is the industry standard," Mo said, and waved a hand. "Even the military uses it now. There's no mistaking the meaning of a liter or a kilogram. Not so with other ways of measuring things. British ounces and gallons are different from the American versions, for example. Why would we borrow that kind of trouble?"

"The people who buy the stuff keep track of it in pounds, and so does the transport company."

"You're not a scientist, are you, Mr. Ibáñez."

"I'm also not a grifter shilling some secretive magical world-changing technology."

Mo scoffed. "Magic is the opposite of science."

"Why do you let Vitale wander around like he owns the place?" he demanded.

"I can't really lock him up. He's been here before. The only real risk to us is industrial espionage concerning the extraction process."

"In those sea cans."

"We call them shipping containers. Vitale won't get anywhere near them."

He watched her for a moment. "I need to talk to some of your people."

"Most of the staff are at work in the processing area.

They won't be available until dusk."

"I guess I'll catch up with them then."

Mo frowned. "You'll be long gone by then."

"So I've been told. How many people work here?"

"About thirty staff are on site at any given time. Every week we rotate some out, and they take a week off."

"Your people work every day?"

"While they're here it's dawn to dusk. They get all their days off when they leave."

"Where do they go?"

She waved a hand. "Wherever they want. Most people bring their own vehicles. We recruit in Twin Falls and Salt Lake. Both are about four and a half hours' drive. Most of our workers are from those cities."

"That explains why everybody's white."

Mo frowned. "That's not true. Hilda's from India."

Slater walked away, across the open space toward the trailers. It struck him that there were no vehicles around except for the heavy equipment. If the employees drove, their wheels must be parked elsewhere.

Nobody was around as he walked among the trailers, but farther up the row he saw Etta stepping out of one, closing the door behind her. She walked over to join him.

"You were right," she said quietly, her eyes bright. "We're not leaving here today."

"Who says?"

"Russell. The pilot. He's pissed. Apparently there's no fuel."

"I knew it would be something," Slater said. "Where did you see him?"

"He's in the canteen trailer. I think he's stress eating."

"Where's that at?"

"It's the one I just came out of. The only one with a double door. Most of them have four single doors." She gestured to the nearest trailer. "Four separate sleeping spaces."

"I'll go talk to him. Mo said everybody's working until dusk."

"I'm going to poke around anyway. I had to turn on my satellite modem too. The data speed on the network here was too pokey."

"How is it working?"

"So far it's great. As long as I'm outside."

Slater walked over to the canteen trailer and stepped in. Most of the space was filled with worn white plastic tables and chairs. A counter at one end made it look like a roadhouse diner. It smelled like cooking, and a glass-fronted cooler with sandwiches and muffins and fruit sat near the door, next to a soda machine.

Russell was sitting at one of the round tables, wearing a dark jacket over his flight suit. Gazing at the screen of the laptop open in front of him, he looked flushed, and he had a cell phone jammed to his ear with one shoulder. He didn't look up when Slater stepped inside.

Surveying the food case, nothing looked especially appetizing, but Slater grabbed an apple and bit into it.

"I don't care whose fault it is," Russell said. "You're going to pay me golden time ... That's what I'm saying ... All right. Just keep me in the loop." He set the phone on the table and took a deep breath.

"I can't believe they have to pay for soda," Slater said, and waved to the machine.

Russell looked up at him, as if just noticing he was there. "Just press the button. You don't have to put money in it."

"What's up with the return flight?"

"There's no freaking jet fuel here," he said intently. "It was supposed to be waiting for us. My company's sending a fuel truck right now. It won't get here before sundown. We can't fly in the dark, so we're tits-up until morning."

Slater bit into his apple, and spoke with his mouth half full. "Why isn't it here already?"

"Somebody at Mott Minerals thought we could fuel up an aircraft with diesel or automotive gasoline. Even though they were told we needed Jet 1A."

"Somebody who?"

"I don't know. My company told these clowns what we needed, and they messed it up."

"Did you deal with anyone here?"

Russell frowned. "What's it to you?"

"It might inform my research." He gestured with the apple. "If we're stuck here overnight, we'll have to come up with something to do. You seem stressed. I might be able to help with that. You know—work out some tension."

His eyes narrowed. "Are you hitting on me?"

"That depends," Slater said. "It gets cold in the desert. It seems kind of sad to sleep alone."

"That's never going to happen, cowboy."

Slater tossed his apple core into the trash bin. "Your loss."

Stepping out, he walked down the row of trailers. Like Etta said, most of them had four doors, and each was numbered. One of them had to be the office.

He found it at the end of the encampment, in the last unit before the open space that fronted the production area. A sign mounted next to the door declared MOTT MINERALS, along with the corporate logo.

A loud hum came from the shipping containers. He hadn't heard that when they'd walked over there with Mo. A pump, maybe? Looking out at the playa, he couldn't see any water discharge. But it was too far away to see much of anything.

Pulling open the door, he stepped into the trailer. Only one of the desks was occupied, by a woman, younger than Mo, with her wiry black hair styled out to the side. He couldn't tell if the look was intentional or just what the desert did to your do when you'd been out here for a while.

Her brow furrowed as she looked up at him. "Can I help you?"

"I'm with the insurance carrier."

"I've already been interviewed by the other one."

"Etta?" Slater said.

"I don't recall her name. She's Latina and pushy."

"She's actually Samoan, if we're playing guess my ethnicity. Someone told me you were from India. You sound like you're from here."

"My grandparents were from India," she said. "I've never even been there. Who told you that?"

"Etta is actually one of our top operatives. Highly skilled at conducting interviews and uncovering the truth. Did you tell her the truth, Hilda?"

"You make it sound like I wouldn't tell the truth."

"We all know somebody's messing around," Slater said. "They sent me here to figure it out. Did you handle the aviation company's request for jet fuel?"

"That's nothing to do with me. It went through head office."

"In Denver."

"Close," Hilda said. "Colorado Springs."

He spread his palms. "So of course nothing is your fault."

"Have you ever worked for a corporation?" she said, and sat back.

"Not full-time."

"I've worked for plenty. Small companies and publicly traded entities. Let me tell you—the larger the organization, the more irrational it is. Maybe it's because there are fewer interconnections. The people over here don't know what the ones over there are doing. And once a company starts trading itself on the stock market, that's it—everything stops making sense."

It had the ring of truth, Slater decided, watching her talk.

"Have you prepared the bill of lading for this shipment?" he said.

"It's ready to go. If the shipping company can ever get their act together."

"Do you double-check the bill of lading when the truck gets loaded?"

"I hand over the bill when they close the doors on the truck," Hilda said. "Our rule is that two Mott employees witness the transfer. That's usually Mo and me. Then we hand over the paperwork."

"You do a final count of the ingots?"

"I make sure they're all there, and we tie it down with a tarpaulin, and load it on the truck."

"Why do you prepare the document in kilograms?"

She waved a hand. "Our machines operate in grams and kilograms. It's an unambiguous international standard. Why wouldn't we use kilograms?"

"What about the hairy apelike creature?"

Her expression shifted, concern in her eyes. "What about it? Some of the workers have seen what they describe as bigfoot. It was in the production area. Around the equipment. One night they found the discharge pipe had been damaged."

"Damaged how?"

"Dented and disconnected," Hilda said. "Like it had been kicked or punched. It wasn't serious enough that it needed to be replaced."

"You've never seen the creature yourself?"

"No," she said flatly, and frowned.

He walked out, closing the door behind him. Interesting that Hilda claimed she hadn't seen the creature, when Hernán said she had. But then Hernán wasn't the most reliable witness.

Slater headed into the open space, toward the production area, and glanced over his shoulder. There was no one around to stop him. Hilda wouldn't be able to see him from this angle unless she got up and looked out the window.

Ahead he saw the loader roll out of the production area, piloted by the same driver, making tracks toward the playa. As he approached the lane between containers where it had appeared, he saw the worn tracks of innumerable loader trips on the ground, running out onto the playa. Turning the corner around the end of a container, he found a guy squatting with his back to the metal box, a cloud of vapor above his head.

When Slater stepped into view, he palmed his vape pen and stood up. A big guy, he had a rugby build, with red hair and ruddy cheeks, either from the cold or from embarrassment. He wore a quilted plaid jacket, and jeans, and yellow work boots. Totally fuckable, he decided.

"How you doing, Hoss?" Slater said.

He frowned. "Who told you that was my name?"

"It's not?"

"I'm Zed."

"Is that short for something?"

"It's a nickname," he said, raising his eyebrows. "I'm from England, and I'm often told I say things wrong, like 'lorry' instead of 'semitruck,' and 'alu*mini*um' instead of 'alu*minum,' and 'zed' instead of 'zee.'"

"That explains it," Slater said. "I was trying to place your accent. I guess you can't really help it—it's not your language."

"Oh! Such slander." He cracked a wry grin. "I know you're joking. You and I share the language of Shakespeare and Maya Angelou."

"If you sounded like Shakespeare, I'd have no idea what the hell you were talking about, and if I sounded like Maya Angelou, I'd have a much better job."

He laughed. "Can I ask your name?"

"Slater. I'm here on an investigation." He pointed to Zed's hand. "I'm not here to bust you for vaping."

Zed showed the pen, and twiddled it between his fingers, then tucked it into his breast pocket. "We're not supposed to. What are you investigating?"

"Several things. Do you have any connection to shipping the product?"

"That's not my area," he said. "I'm an engineer. I keep my head down and work on my small part of it."

"What would that be?"

"I'm sure you've been told that we can't talk about it."

"Of course. Cutting-edge intellectual property."

Zed gestured to his backpack. "I see you're solar powered."

"You can laugh, but my phone never goes dead."

"I'm not laughing. I think it's kind of ingenious. I want one."

"It's custom," Slater said. "So what do you know about the creature that comes around at night?"

"I haven't seen the beast, but I've heard several reliable people speak of it."

"Where do they see it?"

"Around the equipment at night," Zed said, "and on the salt pan."

"In case you want to improve your English," Slater said, and gestured widely, "that there is actually called a playa. Why would you call it a salt anything? It's alkali. I tasted it."

"Most of the staff are from Utah. Perhaps they're accustomed to saltier features. Like the Great Salt Lake. Whatever the reason, my employers call this a salt pan."

"Your employers are ill-informed dipshits."

"You're kind of rude. Did anyone ever tell you that?"

Slater could see that he wasn't really offended. That gleam in his eye, and the hint of a smirk—there was more going on.

"Almost continuously, Zed." Slater pointed a finger at him. "I'll see you later."

SEVENTEEN

WALKING BACK THE WAY he'd come, Slater crossed the open space to the trailer camp. Over on the playa, the passenger door of the airplane was hanging open. A figure in black climbed inside and pulled it closed. It was too far away to see his face, but Vitale was the only one around dressed like that. What the hell was he up to?

As he walked past the office, Mo appeared from between the trailers farther up, walking toward him. She tried to mask it, but when she spotted him, her expression shifted to a scowl.

"Hold up," Slater said. "What do you know about the jet fuel thing?"

"Just that nobody's willing to take responsibility," she said. "What a screw-up."

"So who's to blame?"

"Head office, or the aviation company. I never heard anything about a fuel truck. Now I have to find lodging for you and your friend, and the pilots, and the gunman."

"I might have a place sorted out already," Slater said, "but Etta will need a bed."

Her eyes narrowed. "What, you're going to sleep in the plane? You'll freeze. When the sun's gone it gets really cold, really fast."

"Later, Mo," he said, and stepped away. He walked to the canteen trailer and stepped inside.

Russell was gone, but there was another guy here

now, with a military-short haircut neatly pomaded into place, eating a bowl of something with broccoli and rice. Slater grabbed a muffin from the food case and sat across from him.

"How's the chow?"

He gestured with his fork. "Same as always. You must be one of the insurance people."

"Are you involved at all in shipping the product?"

He raised his eyebrows. "I do maintenance, and drive the forklift, so yeah, I load the pallet onto the truck. But the delays are happening way above my pay grade."

"What about shrinkage? Do you know anything about that?"

"You think someone's stealing? If they are, I never heard about it." He leaned toward him. "I'm never left alone with the product, if that's what you're asking. Mo is the only one who can open the vault."

"You mean the red shipping container with the padlock on it."

He waved his fork. "We call it the vault."

"So what's the problem with the transport company?" Slater said. "The late deliveries?"

"How should I know?" he demanded. "I fix the plumbing. I don't know who arranges the shipments. It's nothing to do with me."

"Do you drive the loaders and the diggers for the mine?"

"That takes a different qualification. I went to forklift school, but I can't operate the heavy equipment."

"Have you seen the creature that comes around?"

He sat back. "Actually, I have. I don't think he's got anything to do with the shipping delays either."

"Where did you see it?"

"Out on the salt pan. In the dark. It was late—after midnight. This dark shape was loping, not quite running, right where the discharge pipe is. I couldn't believe it."

"How tall was it?" Slater said.

"No idea. He was far away. I couldn't even be sure it wasn't a person, except that it was so dark. All the same dark, like fur, not like clothes. I got a pretty good look because the moon was out. Bright and high in the sky. It's like a spotlight out here around full moon."

"You said it was loping?"

"Hustling. In a hurry. And he walked funny—you know how people look when they're using snowshoes?"

"Was that the night the pipe got vandalized?" Slater said.

He shook his head. "Someone else saw him that time."

"Why do you say 'him'?"

"I guess there's no evidence that it's a him or a her. But if he's out there sabotaging equipment with brute force, that sounds more like a guy thing."

"Why do you think he would sabotage this place?" Slater said.

He leaned forward and lowered his voice. "We're disturbing the land. Pumping out the water and letting it dry up in the sun. If this was your place, you'd be pissed too. I don't know who the local Native Americans are, but if you talked to them, I bet they'd know exactly what's going on."

"How do you suppose something that big could survive out here? There's not a lot to eat."

"Some people think it's paranormal. Like it can phase in and out of our plane."

"I've heard that before too." Slater rose and took a bite of his muffin.

Outside, he walked behind the office trailer, toward the production area. If Zed had gone back inside, maybe he could look around uninterrupted this time.

As he was crossing the open ground beyond the

trailers, a golf cart appeared from over by the big tanks, moving fast and headed right for him. The driver was wearing a navy-blue jacket and a ball cap, and as he got closer, Slater saw the sidearm strapped to his belt.

He half expected the guy to stop right in front of him, blocking his path like an officious bully, but instead he pulled up beside him. Slater stopped walking to look the guy over. His graying hair was visible under his hat, and it wasn't very long, but it looked unctuous. His brow was fixed in a permanent squint. He smiled as he stepped off the cart.

"You must be one of the insurance people."

"And you're camp security," Slater said.

"The name is Cutter. Where are you headed?"

"I wanted to have a look at the production area."

"Unfortunately the company doesn't want you to do that."

Slater gestured helplessly. "I guess that's fair."

"How is your investigation going?"

"About that—you must know how this place operates. What's the reason for the shipping delays?"

"No idea," Cutter said. "I just keep an eye on things."

"So where are all the cars?"

"Half a mile that way." He waved toward the solar farm. "Only production vehicles are allowed on the site."

"I would think your workers would rather drive right up to their sleeping quarters."

"I know they would," Cutter said. "But that's the rule. My thinking is maybe management doesn't want it to be too easy to steal from the mine. Those ingots weigh damn near thirty pounds each. You couldn't walk away with one in your shorts, but it would be easy to throw one in the back of your car."

Slater nodded. "That sounds like a reasonable assumption."

"Can I give you a ride back to the residential area?"

"Do I have a choice?"

Cutter chuckled. "You know the drill."

He sat behind the wheel of the golf cart, and Slater climbed on the other side, and they drove the few hundred yards along the edge of the playa. In the distance, gleaming in the sun, the airplane's passenger door was open again. It looked like someone was sitting in the cockpit.

Slater climbed off the golf cart when Cutter stopped.

"Mo will set up a room for you," he said cheerfully, and drove away.

Pulling out his phone, he texted Etta:

Where you at?

A moment later her reply came:

Canteen.

When he walked into the food trailer, there were four people sitting at different tables, including Etta, eating a bowl of soup.

"How did you get fed?" Slater said, sitting in the adjacent chair.

She pointed toward the counter with her spoon. "You just have to ask Cookie. He's back there somewhere."

"So what have we learned?"

Etta lowered her voice. "Well, three people tried to buy my groovy backpack."

"Not useful."

"Even though we're here to interrogate them," she said, "they seem so nice. It's actually a little weird."

"It's the small-town effect," Slater said. "You have to be nice in a small community because everyone knows everything you do."

"It's like that in Samoa." She set her spoon down. "I

think the one named Hilda is kind of suspicious. She works in the office. Sweet and flirty on the surface, but watch out for the poison under the gravy."

"I actually met her. She didn't strike me as especially sweet or dangerous."

"Two different employees told me off the record that she's the type who'd easily screw up the scheduling if she had a hand in it."

"I wonder about the weight discrepancy. Mo claims she and Hilda both count the ingots before they hand over the bill of lading."

"There's another office staffer. Karen. Hilda said she does the paperwork sometimes."

"I haven't heard that name before."

"She's not back here until tomorrow afternoon," Etta said. "I wish I could interview her."

"I don't think you'll get the chance. Our ride will likely leave at first light."

Etta folded her arms. "Mo says we can each have our own room. I looked into one. They're not very big but they're clean, and they're heated."

They both glanced up as a couple of guys walked in, dressed for manual labor, and stepped over to the counter.

"Someone told me there's a midday shift change," Etta said, "except they don't call it a shift for some reason. That's why these people are here. But once it gets dark there's no work to do, so everybody will be here."

"That's hours from now." Slater sat back. "Does this place feel kind of claustrophobic?"

"It's the opposite of that. Did you not notice the massive playa? It couldn't physically be any less closed in."

"I think I'm going to walk up that ridge," Slater said. Etta frowned. "Why?"

"To get out of this place. Maybe clear my head."

"Do you know how to do that?"

"Walk? Yes, I have some experience."

"I mean hike in the wilderness," Etta said. "You're kind of urban."

"I'm just going to climb up part of the way. I won't even lose sight of the playa."

"All right. I guess I'll keep grilling these knuckle-heads."

Slater chuckled. "You're starting to sound like Max."

Near the counter he found a spigot, and zipped open the top of his backpack, and filled the water bladder. Pulling it on again, he adjusted the shoulder straps to balance the added weight, and snapped the connectors of the chest strap together. Outside, he walked toward the base of the mountain ridge, half a mile away at the end of the gently rising bajada. He hadn't made it far outside the trailer camp when Cutter rolled up in his golf cart.

"Where are you headed?"

"Up the ridge," Slater said. "You can't accuse me of trespassing on it. I know it's BLM land." He didn't actually know that, but it was a reasonable guess.

"There aren't any trails or anything. Just rocks."

Slater flashed his palms. "I won't need a trail."

Setting off again, he tried out the mouthpiece on his backpack. It took a minute to figure out how to get the water, as he had to bite down to make it flow, and the water tasted a little plasticky, but it worked well enough.

The rocky hillside was slippery with scree in the steep places, and he gradually made his way higher, stopping occasionally to take in the view. Breathing hard from the climb, Slater sucked at his water, and sat on a rock to look out over the landscape. The playa really was huge, and the disturbed part where they were harvesting the alkali was bigger than it looked from the bajada. Acres and acres of the surface had been scraped away, leaving the brown earth below, stretching halfway to the next mountain range.

There were two loaders at work, he saw, one out on the playa now and one headed back to the production area. Farther away a broad wet spot fanned out in a semicircle from the end of the discharge pipe, from here just visible as a thin hairline across the white surface.

Nobody had any answers about the shipping problems. The blame was always elsewhere. The weight discrepancy felt like it wasn't about the mine, but farther down the line, either with Seligman or Hernán or the buyers. Somebody was stiffing Mott, and it seemed like Mott hadn't even noticed. Why was he even worried about that when Della didn't care? It was Mott's problem. But maybe it was somehow intertwined.

It was quiet up here, and not actually cold in the sunlight. He pulled open his jacket, and closed his eyes, and turned his face to the warm sun. This felt good—nature knew how to organize things, how to create calm. Not like the mess they were making down below.

The shadow of the mountain range was gradually approaching the black field of solar panels, he saw. Once they were in shadow the work would stop. It wouldn't be that long. Rising, Slater sipped at his water and hiked down the slope.

Dusk was just setting in when he got back to the camp. Stepping inside the office trailer, he found only Mo, sitting at one of the desks.

"I suppose you want to know about your accommodations," she said. "You and Etta are in units 14 and 15. I left them open. You won't need a key."

"You never clarified why Vitale is responsible for the shipping delays," he said, and sat across the desk from her.

She leaned back. "I've given him direct instructions and he pays no attention. Vitale acts like he's in charge, but he's not very good at it."

Slater nodded. "He's definitely that guy."

"Vitale told me to call him when we needed to set up a shipment date. So I spoke to him about it, but he missed it by a week."

"You contacted him instead of the Seligman office?"

"Both. I emailed Rita at Seligman and I called Vitale. They still screwed it up."

"What do you know about Rita?" Slater said.

"Nothing. She's my contact at Seligman. My sense is that she's more competent than Vitale, but then I've never met her."

"Tell me about Karen."

"What about her?"

"Is she sloppy with the paperwork? The type who'd leave an ingot or two off the bill of lading?"

Mo frowned. "I know she's never done that. We check each other's work. If you think she's trying to steal the palladium, there's no way she could pull it off."

"Unless you're working together."

She closed her eyes for a moment, and pressed her palms flat on the desk. "I know this is your job, and I know the delays have caused issues for your client. But it's not because of anyone here."

"And yet nobody seems to be able to explain it. Seligman blames you, and you blame Seligman, or maybe it's Vitale. Does anyone cross-reference the bill of lading with the bill of sale?"

"I assume someone at head office would do that. The sales part of it doesn't affect us."

"Not your problem," Slater said. "Not your fault."

"You do understand. Finally." She shot him a thin smile. "You might be smarter than you look."

"How late is that canteen open?"

"Until everyone's done with it," Mo said, waving a hand. "Usually around nine o'clock."

EIGHTEEN

USK HAD FADED TO twilight, in that crisp intense way that things happened in the desert. There were downlights at the corner of each trailer that had switched on. When Slater walked into the canteen, lots of people crowded the tables, still dressed for work, in denim and overalls and thick jackets. Most of them were men. Vitale was sitting with the pilots at a table in the corner, and he recognized the maintenance guy, and Hilda, sitting with a couple of other women. There was no sign of Etta or hot Zed. Several pairs of eyes checked him out as he stepped inside, but mostly they ignored him and continued their conversations.

Behind the counter was a guy with a little blond mustache, wearing a hairnet and a food-stained white apron. Etta had called him Cookie. This place was so not like the city—even the food-service people were white and Anglo.

"What's for dinner?" Slater said.

His accent was a lot like Svetlana's. "A sausage on a roll with grilled onions and peppers."

"Hold the sausage."

"Do you want some broccoli on the side?"

"Hit me."

"Does that mean yes?"

Slater nodded. "It does."

Once he had his plate, he grabbed an apple from the case and set it on his tray. There were several fuckable guys, he saw, scanning the room, and walked over to an open seat where there were two of them, next to the table where the pilots and Vitale were eating. Slater took a chair with his back to the pilots and a view of the door.

He hung his jacket on the back of the chair and tucked his pack under the table, then greeted the two guys. At close range they weren't quite as interesting. One of them looked sunbaked, and tired, and had watery pale-blue eyes. The other was still in his twenties, his long hair tucked behind his ears.

The food was actually not that bad, he found, starting into it, considering it had been prepared for thirty people.

"So what do you guys do here?" Slater said.

Blue Eyes met his gaze. "We can't talk about it."

"Even your job description?"

"We're basically engineers."

Slater glanced up as the door swung open, and Etta walked in. She nodded to him and stepped over to the counter.

"That's your partner," Blue Eyes said. "I heard tell that you and her were private investigators. Is someone stealing product?"

"You tell me," Slater said. "Are they?"

"I've never heard that," the one with long hair said. "I can't see how you'd do it."

"So if it's not theft," Blue Eyes said, "why are you here?"

"It's about the shipping. Endless problems getting the product out of here."

"Have you figured it out?"

"Nobody here seems to know anything about it," Slater said. "But if your corporate masters are to be believed, the transport company is trash."

Behind him he heard a chair scrape on the floor, and

Vitale stepped around in front of him, his face contorted with anger.

"It's you," he growled, and poked Slater in the chest. "You're the trash. You."

"Touch me again," Slater said evenly, "and I'll dislocate your shoulder."

Vitale lifted the tail of his jacket to reveal his sidearm. "You try it, and I'll blow your head off."

"With that little pop gun? I was wondering where that came from. Did you get it as the prize in a box of breakfast cereal?"

Vitale lunged at him, hands grasping at his throat, but Slater was ready. Grabbing him under his arms, he heaved upward, leveraging his whole body, and flipped Vitale over his head. As a wrestling move he would have been able to balance the momentum of the throw with his legs, but sitting down, that was impossible. His chair toppled backward and Slater crashed to the floor. Flat out on his back, Vitale's feet had landed on an empty chair, and he looked a little dazed. Twisting around, Slater quickly got up, and straddled his pelvis, and punched him in the jaw.

"Why do you make me do this to you?" Slater shouted, and struck him again with a left.

His eyes glassy, Vitale wasn't even trying to fend him off. Slater forced himself to stop. At least he was still conscious. Slater yanked his firearm out of its holster.

"Whoa," someone shouted. "Slow down." Another voice called, "Don't shoot him."

Looking around, half the crowd were on their feet. Etta was standing close by. He handed her the weapon.

"Get it out of here," he hissed.

Etta grabbed it by the grip and shoved it in the back of her belt as she turned and headed for the door. Slater rose, and stepped back, and took a breath. No one was talking—every eye was on him and Vitale. The door swung open, and Cutter stepped in, and looked them over, but he didn't say anything either.

"The one in black started it," Blue Eyes called to him. "I saw it happen."

Vitale sat up and rubbed his jaw, recovering his senses. When his gaze fell on Slater, he glared at him and said, "Asshole."

Slater jutted his chin. "Settle down."

"Give me back my piece."

"Why would I do that? You just threatened to blow my head off."

Cutter stepped between them. "See, this is why I don't like outsiders hanging around."

Slater picked up his chair and set it at the table, then scooped up his jacket and hung it on the back.

On his feet now, Vitale looked to Cutter and jabbed a finger at Slater. "This psycho is out of control."

"Shut the fuck up," Cutter snapped. "I'm in charge here. Elijah—what happened?"

"He flipped him right over his head."

Slater looked toward the speaker, one of the few women in the room.

"Everyone shut up," Cutter said, raising his voice. "Everyone except Elijah." He looked to the long-haired guy who'd been sitting at the table with Slater.

"Well, the bald one came over and picked a fight, and then the Mexican one finished it."

"Where's his weapon?" Cutter said.

"The Mexican woman took it and left," Elijah said.

"She removed the firearm to deescalate the situation," Slater said.

Vitale raised his voice. "Give me back my piece."

"If you started it," Cutter said, "you have no right to be upset. You'll get your weapon when I say you do.

Right now you can calm the fuck down."

Vitale scoffed and pushed his way through the crowd toward the door.

"What are you all standing around for?" Cutter demanded. "Your food is getting cold."

Slater took his seat again, with Elijah and Blue Eyes, and dug into the grilled peppers and onions. It actually was cold, but he shoveled it in anyway.

"I can see why he was upset," Elijah said. "You did call his company trash."

Slater met his gaze. "I can punch you out too if you'd like. Just keep talking."

Elijah looked down at his plate. "No thank you."

"I could show you some other stuff," Slater said. "Do you sleep alone here?"

He looked up. "What are you talking about?"

Blue Eyes chuckled. "He's flirting with you."

Elijah's eyes grew wide. "I'm married."

"To a woman?" Slater said. "She's not here, is she? How would she ever find out?"

"Cutter was right. You people are trouble."

"Us Mexicans?" Slater raised his eyebrows.

Ignoring that, Elijah rose and carried his tray toward the counter. Blue Eyes was grinning like an idiot.

"What?" Slater demanded.

"The culture clash. It's entertaining. We don't get much of that out here."

"I'm not actually Mexican. I have as much right to be here as you or any of the other white folks."

"That's not what I'm talking about," Blue Eyes said. "It's the bedroom talk. That boy is from a little Mormon town in the countryside."

Slater set down his fork. "Well, at least he'll have a story to tell when he gets home."

Zed stepped up to the table, and set down his tray,

and pulled out a chair. Up close Slater could see that the stubble of his beard was the same electric orange as his hair.

"Howdy, Hoss," Slater said.

"Is it true?" Zed said, scooting his chair closer to the table. "You beat the shit out of that gunslinger?"

"As true as steel," Blue Eyes said. "I saw it with my own eyes."

Slater scoffed. "I hit him twice. Nothing's broken. If I'd wanted to beat the shit out of him, he'd be on life support right now. All I did was invite some peace into his life."

Blue Eyes laughed and got up, lifting his tray. "Remind me never to piss you off."

"Word travels fast," Slater said, eyeing Zed.

"Gossip is the only thing in the universe that exceeds light speed."

He lifted his dinner from his plate, the roll and the sausage and the grilled peppers and all, and bit into it like it was a taco. Slater watched him take a few bites, enjoying his gusto.

"You told me before that people here had seen the creature," Slater said.

"I don't think they're lying," Zed said, once he'd finished his mouthful. "Just mistaken."

"So it's the wind that caused the damage? Or some disgruntled employee?"

"I don't think so. We're pretty well paid. It has to be feral hogs. That's the real-world explanation that fits best."

"Fits what best?" he said. "The way people described it?"

"The damage. I saw some of it. There were broken pallets over where I work. It was quite eye-opening. Solid boards turned into toothpicks. A person couldn't have done that." Zed wiped his hands on a napkin and met his gaze. "Listen, Slater, everything about this place is as dull as ditch water—even the bigfoot stories. I'm here for weeks at a time and every day is exactly the same. You're from the outside world. Tell me about that solar backpack. You said it's not a consumer product."

"It's for the backcountry. A woman I know builds electronics. She attached the solar panels. There's a battery pack in it. The idea is to keep my phone charged."

"It's nice to have a full battery, but the limitation is that there are no mobile phone towers in the backcountry. You couldn't get online. I guess you could still use GPS and maps if you downloaded them ahead of time."

"You said this place was dull," Slater said. "Do you have your own room? I'm thinking we could do some stuff that's a little more interesting."

He sat up straighter. "Are you talking about a game of pinochle or blackjack or poker in which you relieve me of my cash?"

"I don't do that," Slater said. "I mean something more personal. As in, I could climb you like a tree. If you're up for that."

Zed cracked a smile. "I'm very much up for that." He glanced furtively at the people sitting at the next table and spoke quietly. "I need to shower first. Give me half an hour. I'm in unit 9."

Slater double-clicked his tongue, and stood up, and pulled on his jacket and his backpack.

Before he walked away, he met Zed's eye, and spoke intently. "I am going to wreck you."

Zed's eyebrows shot up, and he inhaled sharply.

Once he was outside, Slater paused at the corner of the trailer and pulled out his phone. He needed to talk to Etta. She'd already texted him:

You OK?

He thumb-typed a response:

Where you at?

A moment later, she replied:

Unit 14.

Slater walked into the next lane, eyeing the numbers beside the doors. There was enough illumination from the downlights to read them, and he soon found the one marked 14.

When he rapped on the door, Etta pulled it open and waved him in.

"It's warm in here," he said, looking around.

It was like a small hotel room, with a single bed, and a desk with a chair, and a closet rail with a wire storage rack underneath it. Etta sat on the side of the bed, and Slater turned the desk chair around to face her.

"What the hell happened?" she said.

"Vitale came at me." Slater explained the scuffle. "Where's the weapon?"

"Cutter dropped by a few minutes ago and took it. He was actually quite polite about it."

"I'm sure he was happy you'd removed it from the middle of a dustup. Nobody got shot on his watch."

"Apparently Vitale had the safety off."

Slater scoffed. "Idiot."

"Cutter said he was going to lock it up," Etta said. "I just hope he doesn't give it back to Vitale. That nut job will pop you."

"Vitale won't get it back tonight. Cutter's got security experience—he knows better. What else is going on?"

"I interviewed a couple of other people," she said, and they talked about what she'd learned.

"So there's no indication the shipping delays originate here," Slater said finally.

"Nobody knows anything about the weight discrepancy either. I guess it was a wasted trip."

"It's never a waste if you learn something." He threw up his hands. "We learned plenty."

"These people go to bed early because they start work at dawn," Etta said. "Are we going bigfoot spotting?"

"In a couple hours. I'll text you."

Etta frowned. "What are you doing for a couple hours, in the middle of the desert, in the dark?"

"Conducting an interview." Slater stood up and tucked the chair under the desk.

"You slut. Who is it?"

"Don't ask, don't tell, Etta," he said, and walked out.

NINETEEN

OST OF THE LITTLE residences had light in the windows, Slater saw, walking up the row of trailers. In the next row he found unit 9 and knocked on the door. It opened a crack, and then Zed pulled it all the way open, and Slater stepped in. Zed looked even taller in the small room. He was wearing only a pair of snug low-rise underpants, the blue fabric a stark contrast to his pasty redheaded skin. He was built solid, with a bit of flab on him, and from here, his junk looked impressive.

Slater pulled off his backpack. "You lost your pants."

Zed giggled like an eight-year-old. "I figured I was going to lose them anyway."

As he pulled off his jacket, Zed stepped close, and unbuttoned his shirt. Leaning in, he mouthed Slater's neck.

"You're warm," Zed said, and pulled back.

Slater ran a hand into his hair. "You're totally not afraid of me."

"Should I be?"

"There's no reason to be. I'm just not used to guileless people. It's actually kind of hot."

"I'm a big guy, so I'm not often physically intimidated. And I grew up in a place where people don't carry firearms."

Slater grabbed his biceps, and pulled him close, and leaned into his mouth. It was firm and warm and intense. Unbuckling his belt, he popped his fly, then sat on the bedside to pull off his boots, then his jeans.

Zed slid off his underpants, revealing his raging woody.

"Jesus," Slater said. "You're huge."

"You think?" he said, and pulled him onto the bed, and mouthed his ear and his jaw. Slater wrapped a hand around his cock and squeezed it, and Zed groaned, and folded his thick arm around his neck.

"What do you want to do?" Slater said.

"Well, since you ask, I like the feeling of being piled on. It's something about the weight on top of me. You said it in the canteen—you could climb me."

"Do you want me to fuck you? I have a condom." Slater reached for his bag and dug it out.

"Let me do it."

Slater leaned back, and watched as Zed stroked him until he was rock hard, and then rolled it on. Zed stretched out on the narrow bed and flipped onto his belly, and Slater climbed up to straddle him. Starting slowly, Slater worked his way into him, running his hands along his back as Zed moaned.

Once he was thrusting into him, Slater stretched out, lowering his weight onto his frame, increasing the tempo until he was pounding him. Slater reached under Zed's armpits, and pulled himself close, breathing in the scent of his damp hair, and came.

Once he'd rolled off, still panting, Zed turned to him, a silly grin on his face.

"Do you want to blow me?" he said, running a hand into Slater's hair.

"I don't know if that's physically possible."

"Guys always say that. It's not easy to be big sometimes."

"You poor thing," Slater said flatly, and shifted position,

and took him into his mouth.

"Can you face me? So I can watch. Unless that sounds controlling."

"It sounds like you know what you want."

Slater shifted again, positioning himself between his legs. Sitting up, Zed leaned back against the pillow and the headboard. Working him as best he could, and using his hands, Slater looked up to see that Zed was gazing at him, flushed and breathing hard. He held his eye, and that seemed to increase the intensity of it. A moment later, with a sharp yelp, Zed climaxed, his body spasming.

Slater shifted close to the wall and stretched out, folding his arm over his eyes, and caught his breath.

"That was so fucking hot," Zed said, moving close to him.

He slid an arm under Slater's neck, and with the other encircled his waist, pulling him onto his side. He notched his knees behind Slater's. It wasn't something that happened very often, getting manhandled like this, but he went with it, as the warmth felt good, and they lay that way for a while. Zed's breathing took on the regular rhythm of sleep, and before he drifted off himself, Slater sat up.

"Not a lot of room for two," Zed said.

"I need to go find the hairy biped."

He scoffed. "That's easy. Just look in the lost city of El Dorado, or hanging around the Fountain of Youth, or the sunken city of Atlantis."

"You sound like a skeptic," Slater said, pulling on his jeans.

"I'm a scientist. There's no scientific evidence that a nonhuman bipedal hominid exists in the Great Basin."

"I guess it'll be a quiet night for me, then."

Slater buttoned his shirt and gestured to a black-and-white photo that was taped to the wall above the desk.

It depicted Zed with his arms around a woman's neck, both of them smiling at the camera.

"Is that your wife?"

"That's my mother, you jerk. Why would I sleep with you if I was married to a woman?"

"I've heard of stranger things. Can I come back later?"

Zed beamed. "I'll leave the door unlocked."

"Like you said, though, there's not a lot of room. I won't mess up your sleep too much?"

"It's totally worth it."

Once he'd pulled on his jacket and his backpack, Slater leaned down to kiss him. "Bye, beautiful."

"If you step in bigfoot scat," Zed said, "leave your boots outside."

Most of the windows were dark now. Slater walked back to unit 14 and rapped gently on the door.

Etta pulled it open. "You're positively glowing."

"Let's roll," he said, and whirled his finger in the air.

She pulled on her jacket and her backpack, and positioned the night-vision goggles on her forehead. It wasn't a bad idea, he realized, and took his own pair out of his backpack, and pulled them on.

"So where are we going?" Etta said, under her breath, gently pulling the door closed.

"Where people said they saw it. Over by the production zone."

They walked onto the empty expanse beyond the trailers. The shipping containers weren't lit the way the trailers were, although the glow of a couple of lights somewhere among them outlined the nearest ones as sharp black rectangles. The crescent moon hung over one of the mountain ranges, and the dome of the sky was brilliant with stars.

"You don't see stars like that in the metropolis," Etta said.

As they walked he heard her sucking water from her backpack, and then the distinctive click of the mouthpiece reattaching to its magnetic clip. Before they were halfway across the open ground, Slater heard boots on the gravel behind them, approaching at a trot. There was enough moonlight to see that it was Cutter.

"Where are you two off to?" he said, his tone cheerful.

"I know you don't want us over there," Slater said. "We're not going to go inside. I need to see the hairy creature your people have been talking about."

"Are those night-vision goggles?" Cutter said.

"Busted," Etta said.

"I've never seen a pair so small. They must have cost a fortune."

"Check it out," Slater said, and pulled them off his head, and handed them over.

Once Cutter had positioned them and switched them on, he looked around.

"Damn—these are good."

They watched as he turned from the mountains to the playa.

"It's like broad daylight. The red won't mess up your existing night vision either. It's a great design." Cutter pulled them off and handed them back. "Here's the deal. The only way I'm going to let you walk around the production area is if I'm with you."

"Fine with me," Slater said, and they set off, walking abreast.

"So where have people actually seen the creature?" Etta said.

"It seems to hang around the discharge pipe," Cutter said. He pointed to the distance. "You can just make it out."

The containers at the edge of the playa appeared as black hulking masses. As they got closer, Slater saw the pipe snaking out across the bright alkali. At this end it hugged the ground, disappearing among the structures. Pulling on his night-vision goggles, he could see the darkened surface of the playa in the distance where the pipe ended.

"We might be here for a while," Slater said, pulling the goggles up onto his forehead. "Where can we sit with a view of the pipe?"

Cutter pointed to the container closest to the playa. "How about along that wall? It's in the shadow of the moonlight, so you'll have no glare."

They walked over and sat on the ground with their backs against the container. The earth was cold, and so was the steel against his back, even through his jacket.

"Should we watch in shifts?" Etta said. "That'll save battery life."

"I can see well enough without the goggles," Slater said. "If anything moves, we can pull them on to get a better look."

"Your eyes will get more used to the dark with time," Cutter said, "but you might need your goggles once the moon is gone. West is behind us, so it's on its way down."

"I'm thinking you have law-enforcement experience," Etta said.

Cutter chuckled. "You'd be correct."

"Isn't it a little slow out here? Apart from Vitale prancing around with his *pistola*. There can't be a lot of crime."

"This assignment is the definition of boring," Cutter said. "Every day feels the same as the last. I started making notes about the weather each evening, and then I stopped when I realized there basically isn't any weather. It's the desert."

"Why do you stay?"

"I'm getting too old to get shot at. That's what happens

on the police force. And I don't mind the people here. But it is hard to meet women."

"So you're not the guy Slater slept with," Etta said.

"Today?" Cutter said. "Really? One of the men? Who did you sleep with?"

"Don't ask me that," Slater snapped.

"I'm so curious now."

"Was it the forklift driver?" Etta said. "I could see him being your type."

"I don't have a type."

"I could make some educated guesses," Cutter said, "but it's probably easier to wait until breakfast. Somebody will know."

Slater huffed. "Stop talking about my sex life."

"You two certainly brought the excitement with you," Cutter said. "That dustup was the most action we've had in months. I didn't even get to see the best part."

"What did you do with Vitale's heater?" Etta said.

"It's in my gun safe. He'll get it back on his way out. By rights I should have taken it when you landed. I don't need an armed blockhead running around."

"It was a big old thing," Etta said. "I've spent time on the gun range, but I never saw anything quite like that."

"It looked like a Desert Eagle," Slater said. "It takes .50-caliber ammo. I wonder what he thinks he's going to be shooting at?"

"You know your weapons," Cutter said. "Were you in the military?"

"They don't recruit people like me," Slater said.

"Men's men? That's not true anymore."

"I mean crazy people."

"You don't seem crazy. A little high-strung, maybe. I'd say you've had manure on your boots."

Slater glanced at him sidelong. "What does that mean?"

Cutter chuckled. "I guess it's country talk. It means you know what real life is like. Physical labor."

"You don't need to explain it," Etta said. "He's literally had manure on his boots. I've seen it."

"That was fertilizer," Slater said. "I do some yard work."

Etta shifted position, pulling her knee and recrossing her ankles. "So do we trust Cutter enough to talk business in front of him?"

"What kind of business?"

"Well, I can get a ride to Salt Lake with one of the staff. She's leaving tomorrow night. I can fly home from there. That would give me a chance to interview the infamous Karen during the day."

"It must be a long drive," Slater said.

"Four and a half hours," Cutter said. "The first hour is on dirt roads."

"Hilda said four."

"Hilda drives like a hellhound."

"Is Hilda hot?" Slater said.

"You've met her."

"I mean hot to you."

"She's not uninteresting," Etta said.

"What do you say, Cutter?" Slater said. "Is Hilda hot?"

"At one time, maybe. I've been working with her for too long."

"It doesn't matter anyway," Etta said. "I'm exclusive with someone else."

"With a crazy person," Slater said.

"She's just emotional. I think I have to be more transparent with her. And I'm not sure we need to air my dirty laundry in front of Cutter."

"You're the one who wanted to talk business."

"So what should I do?" she said. "Wait to talk to Karen, or come back with you on the cargo plane?"

"Do you want to wait?"

"I don't mind. The drive and the commercial flight won't be that painful."

At this point Slater couldn't see the utility of interviewing any more of these knuckleheads, but it sounded like she wanted to stay.

"I guess you might learn something."

"Cutter, do you think Mo will freak out if I stay another day?"

"I doubt it," he said. "The crew were excited to be caught up in an insurance investigation. It's all they're talking about."

"That might be because I interviewed most of them," she said.

Cutter got up, grunting as he stood erect. "It's getting too cold for me. I'm going to turn in."

"You trust us not to break in and steal your trade secrets?" Slater said.

"The production units are alarmed, so I'll be alerted if you try."

"Good to know."

"So don't try," he said, and chuckled. As he walked away, he called, "Good night."

His shape was soon invisible in the gloom. It seemed darker now, and there were no shadows. Cutter was right—the moon had set. From his backpack he pulled out his flask, and twisted the cap open, and took a swig of beautiful sweet bourbon, then another. He offered it to Etta.

"Want a taste?"

"Is that the good stuff?" she said.

"It's just applejack."

Etta took a sip. "It tastes like bourbon, not apples."

"It's not really about apples. It just means cheap booze."

"I'd call that moonshine."

"That sounds Southern."

"I bet your ancestors weren't making booze out of apples either," she said.

"*Aguardiente,* maybe," Slater said. "In Central America."

"I've met Doris. Her people would have been making hooch or bathtub gin in their Lower East Side railroad apartments."

"I like that word," Slater said. "Hooch." He took another swig.

"Did you see that?" Etta leaned forward, her tone insistent.

"Where?" He tucked the flask away.

"Over by the loader. A shadow. It just … moved."

Slater stared intently at the vague outline of the machine, a hundred yards away, parked next to a water truck. Then he saw it too—an unmistakably humanoid form moved into view at the front of the loader. Etta inhaled sharply. Pulling on his night-vision goggles, he could see the machinery more clearly, but the creature was just a black shape, with a flicker of bright red as it moved—it's eyes.

It jumped onto the loader's scoop in one fluid movement. His heart started to pound. It was startling to watch mostly because the top of the scoop was at least three feet straight up, and the leap looked effortless. On all fours, the creature climbed up onto the engine cover, then banged its fists on the cab. The blows were audible, with the sound delayed slightly because of the distance.

Why couldn't these goggles resolve more than its outline? The creature looked like it was made of darkness. It was like watching a shadow, with nothing reflected, as if the ambient starlight just fell into it.

Slater got to his feet.

"What are you doing?" Etta hissed. She had her

goggles on too, and got up.

"I'm going after it."

Slater trotted toward the loader, keeping the creature in view. It paused its banging, and stood erect, the bright spots of its eyes looking right at him. Slater broke into a run.

The creature jumped down, landing light on its feet, and ran toward the closest shipping container, disappearing behind it. Just a few seconds later, Slater got there, and turned the corner. There was no sign of it. He ran to the end of the box, but saw only empty ground between it and the next one.

Rounding the end of the container, he looked both ways, then trotted to the next gap. When he passed the next box, Etta was there, and flinched at the sight of him.

"I thought you were bigfoot," she said.

"Did you see it run through here?"

"Not this way."

Slater went left, hustling past several more structures, some of the containers together in groupings of two or three, but there was no sign of it. When he turned the corner in front of the next structure, his vision went solid red. Breathing hard, he pulled off his goggles and winced in the bright light. A floodlight on this unit had switched on. He must have tripped a motion sensor.

Walking back toward the darkness at the edge of the playa, he found Etta.

"Where did it go?" she said.

"No idea."

"Was it even real?"

"I saw it too. You heard it beating on that loader, didn't you?"

"In the amplified light it still looked totally black," she said. "Could you make out any detail?"

"None," Slater said. "It was like looking into a void.

And it disappeared into thin air."

"It didn't look real. It didn't feel real. Would you call that paranormal?"

"You're not the first person who's picked up that vibe."

"What were you going to do when you caught up to it?" Etta said.

"I guess I hadn't thought that far ahead."

In the distance he heard the crunch of footsteps on gravel, and quickly pulled on his goggles to look. It was Cutter, walking over from the trailer camp, his eyes eerily glowing red.

"I thought we had a deal," he said as he approached.

"I didn't break into anything," Slater said. "I was following the creature."

His eyebrows shot up. "You saw it?"

"We both did," Etta said. "It ran between the containers and just disappeared."

"It didn't go inside anywhere," Cutter said. "I would have heard about it. All I got was the motion sensor."

"That was me."

"What the hell is that thing?" Etta demanded.

Cutter lowered his voice. "I think it's old."

"Like he gets Social Security and a discount on his pancakes?"

"More like it's an earth energy kind of thing. Like bigfoot has been here forever, in tune with this place, part of the land, and we show up and start trashing its habitat."

"I wouldn't have pegged you for a tree hugger," Slater said.

"I wish I'd seen it myself."

"It showed up not long after the moon set. Maybe you can wait for it tomorrow night."

Cutter heaved a sigh. "You two know reveille is half an hour before dawn, right?"

"It sounds like you want us out of the production area," Slater said.

"I'd say you're quite intuitive." He beckoned for them to follow. "Let's all get some sleep."

Walking back toward the trailers, Slater pulled off his goggles. "Has anyone said when the aircraft is leaving?"

"The last I heard was that the fuel truck driver wasn't willing to drive on dirt roads in the dark. He won't get here until well after dawn."

"I bet Russell had an aneurysm when he heard that," Etta said.

Cutter paused at the end of one of the trailers. "This is me. Can we agree on no more night prowling?"

"Rest assured," Etta said, "that we're both headed into the sweet embrace of Morpheus."

"I'll take that to mean no more night prowling."

Slater walked with Etta to unit 14, then went to Zed's door. He paused to take another long pull on his flask, then tucked it away and quietly let himself in. Zed's breathing didn't change as he got undressed and climbed onto the narrow bed with him. His skin was so warm. Slater pulled his arm around his chest, and Zed briefly stirred, and squeezed him, pulling him closer with his big meat hook.

Thinking about the dark figure, it was like it knew what Slater was going to do. It had reacted even before Slater had gone after it. He'd listened to that podcast *Sasquatch Search* for a long time, mostly at night, to take his mind out of the gritty metropolis, and zone out, and wind down before shut-eye. He never thought he'd actually see one.

TWENTY

A HARD MASS WAS PRESSING into Slater's thigh when he woke, and he felt hot breath on his neck.

"Can I fuck you?" Zed whispered.

"I'm not sure I can handle it. Do you have a permit for that thing?"

"It's not that big."

"Yeah, it is."

Zed mouthed his neck, and his ear, and caressed his chest with his big paw.

"Damn it," Slater muttered. "Why do you have to be so hot?"

"I've got lube."

"Are you wearing a condom, at least?" Slater said, and reached around to check. "Fine. Hit me hard."

Zed chuckled, and pressed into him, his arm tight around his chest. Wincing with the intensity of it, Slater tried to relax and get into it. To his credit the guy was being gentle, and it wasn't unbearable. Soon Zed was pounding him, and breathing hard in his ear, and yelped as he came.

Slater shifted to face him. Zed stroked his cock, massaging the back of Slater's neck with his other hand, and pressed their mouths together. Slater climaxed, and then pulled away, and flopped onto his back.

From under the bed Zed grabbed a towel, and gently wiped him off, and caressed his chest.

"Horse dick," Slater said softly, meeting his gaze.

Zed chuckled. "Is that why you called me Hoss?"

"No connection. I hadn't seen it yet."

Running a hand into Slater's hair, he leaned in and kissed him again, then pulled back and gazed at him. Slater knew that look, that irrational sticky infatuation. He snapped his fingers.

"Snap out of it. I'm not who you think I am."

Zed frowned. "What?"

"You're not seeing me. You're only seeing what's on the surface."

"I know you can defend yourself. That's not so terrible."

"It's more than that," Slater said. "I'm trouble."

"So you're a bad guy."

He held his gaze. "Real bad. I hurt people."

"We all do. It's part of the human experience. No love without pain."

"That's not what I'm talking about."

"It's worth it, don't you think? The good parts outweigh the heartache." Zed leaned in and nuzzled his neck. "I get to LA sometimes. Can I come and see you?"

"Sure." Slater squeezed his bicep. "What time is it, anyway? It's still dark out."

"Five thirty, maybe. I should get up."

"Is there food at this hour?"

"Of course. Most of us have to be at work when the sun hits the solar farm."

Once they were dressed, Slater walked to the canteen with Zed. Workers were streaming in and out, and just a couple of people were sitting at the tables. Brown paper bags were lined up along the counter, and Zed grabbed one, and walked out again.

Slater took a muffin and an apple, then paused at the spigot to refill the water bladder in his backpack, and sealed it again. He hadn't expected to be using it so much, but it really was convenient to have a water supply constantly on hand.

When he stepped outside, Zed was waiting.

"You never gave me your number."

Stater dug in his hip pocket for a business card and handed it over. Zed glanced at it, and tucked it away, then leaned in for a brief kiss.

"Good-bye, Slater," he said intently, and walked away.

The guy he'd sat with at dinner, Blue Eyes, walked past on his way from the canteen. He must have seen that exchange, because he had a silly grin on his face, and shot Slater a louche wink. Cutter was right—by sun-up everyone was going to know who he'd slept with.

Etta walked up and playfully punched him in the arm. "It was the redhead. I get it. That guy is totally stacked. Like, woof."

Running a hand through his hair, Slater huffed. "My mindfulness group leader would say 'you should go nourish yourself.' I took that as New Age code for 'piss off.'"

She laughed. "Let me get some grub."

As he walked toward the playa, twilight was brightening, and it was light enough now to see the workers trudging toward the production area, alone and in groups of two or three. Etta stepped up and stood beside him, a half-eaten muffin in hand, and gestured toward the plane.

"I wonder where the pilots are?" she said.

"If they're smart, they're still sleeping."

"I still can't quite believe we saw bigfoot last night. I've never really had a paranormal experience before."

"I've been thinking about that," Slater said. "Did it feel like a performance?"

"You think it knew we were there?"

"Exactly. Banging on the machinery was for our benefit."

Etta waved her muffin. "You'd have to be psychic to figure that out."

"Anyway, it's not for us."

"What does that mean?"

"It's not about our case. The shipping delays, the discrepancy in the documentation. The creature is something else. I'd like nothing more than to stay here and spend another night looking for it, but we can't get distracted by it."

"Fine by me," Etta said. "It kind of blew my mind."

"So you haven't interviewed anyone here that made you think they were involved in the delays, right?"

"Possibly through incompetence, but even then, there's really no solid evidence."

"That means it has to be somebody else."

"The transport company?"

"Rita and Vitale and Bender," Slater said. "I'm sure Seligman will be involved when the cargo lands at Van Nuys. I want to know where it goes from there."

"You're going to tail their van?"

"There's a better way. I'm going to plant a tracker on the shipment. We need to get access to that pallet before they load it."

They walked toward the red shipping container that the miners called the vault. The mini loader was parked here, but no one was around, and the padlock was on the door.

"If you had the right tools, you could get inside," Etta said.

"This guy drives the forklift." Slater nodded to the man walking toward them from the trailers.

Etta followed his gaze. "His name is Miguel," she said quietly.

"How do you remember that? You met so many people yesterday."

"I have to learn twice as many kids' names every term."

As he stepped up to them, Etta greeted him by name.

"We need to take a look at the shipment," Slater said. "Do you have the key to the vault?"

Miguel frowned. "Only Mo and Hilda can open it."

"That's not what I asked."

"I'm not supposed to."

"If anything goes missing, you can tell them it was the insurance company. You know damn well I can't stuff one of those ingots in my pants. They weigh thirty pounds."

"Actually twenty-six pounds, seven ounces," Miguel said. "I guess it's OK. I need to open the vault anyway. You know there's a camera in there, right?"

"Do Mo and Hilda keep track of that?"

"The feed goes to head office in Colorado Springs, I'm told."

Miguel dug out a jumble of keys, and twisted one in the padlock, and pulled it off. While he was folding the doors open, Slater slung off his backpack and dug out his vehicle tracker, and switched it on, then palmed it. It was meant for cars, so it had magnetic ribs to adhere to steel—but that wasn't going to work on the wooden pallet.

Once the doors were open, the three of them stood for a moment to take in the gleaming array of ingots. Miguel stood back and folded his arms, and Slater caught Etta's eye and subtly nodded to him. He could tell she understood what he meant—she raised her eyebrows and turned to Miguel.

Slater stepped in and squatted next to the pallet, not touching it yet, and listened to Etta engage him.

"So who covers it with the tarp?" Etta said.

"I'll do that," Miguel said, "but only after Mo or Hilda signs off on the paperwork."

While he waited, Slater counted the ingots. Two layers were the same size, and the top layer had half as many. Unless there was dead space somewhere in the middle, he came up with a count of a hundred and fourteen.

"What happens once it's wrapped up?" Etta said.

"I use the forklift to load it onto the truck. Today it's going on the airplane."

"I wouldn't call that a forklift," she said, and stepped toward it. "What is it really?"

As Miguel turned to explain it to her, Slater dropped to his knees and looked under the pallet's top deck, his head near the floor. There were a few inches of space between the two decks of the pallet, where the forks slid in to lift it, and as expected, there was no steel to attach the magnets to.

Reaching into the space with the tracker, he fumbled around with it. It was just a little wider than the gap between the boards. He tried to wedge it in sideways, but it was too big. Scooting closer to reach deeper, he set the device against the beam running along the center of the pallet and twisted it. There was just enough space to wedge it in, like kicking a chair under a doorknob. He pulled on it to make sure. It was seated pretty tightly.

Sitting up, Slater got to his feet and brushed the dust off his jeans. The only problem now was whether Miguel would dislodge it with the forklift. Hopefully he wasn't that sloppy. If he lifted the pallet from the middle of each gap, the forks wouldn't touch the tracker.

There was no point in opening Svetlana's software on his phone to see if the device was connected, he decided. It would have checked in via the cell network, but to determine its location, it had to be somewhere more crowded, where there were lots of Wi-Fi signals. The software calibrated its location based on public lists of the coordinates of Wi-Fi stations, not by overhead GPS satellites. The advantage was that the device didn't need a view of the sky, and the battery lasted a lot longer.

"Some people call it a skid," Miguel was saying. "At forklift school they called it a mini loader."

"I can't believe you had to go to school to learn to drive that thing," Etta said. "Can I try it out?"

She glanced at Slater as he stepped out of the container. He flashed her a thumbs-up.

"I might get in trouble," Miguel said. "You could damage something."

"It's a very cute machine. Maybe I'll have to sign up for forklift school."

Mo appeared at the end of the container, with a clipboard in hand, her jacket zipped to the top against the chill morning air. She frowned at the sight of them as she walked up.

"I see you got an early start."

"The investigators wanted to look at the shipment," Miguel said quickly.

"I needed to make an ingot count," Slater said. "Have you done that? How does it compare to the bill of lading?"

"I was just about to check."

Mo went inside the container and set the clipboard on the floor. Stepping onto the edge of the pallet, she squatted to lift some of the ingots from the center to look underneath. Finally she stood erect.

"A hundred and fourteen units, just like the paperwork says."

She picked up the clipboard again, and dug a pen out of her jacket pocket, and made a rapid scrawl at the bottom of the page.

Slater pulled out his phone and did the calculation.

If the ingots really were uniformly twelve kilograms, the total should be 1,368.

"Can I see the bill of lading?" he said.

Mo frowned but handed him the clipboard. "Usually Seligman's driver compares it to the ingot count. I guess today you're responsible for transport."

It was written up the same way as the ones he'd seen before, with Mo's signature, and the weight was listed as "1,368 kg."

He handed it back to her, and Miguel waved at the pallet.

"Should I wrap it up?"

"Let's wait for Hilda," Mo said.

"Because of the two sets of eyes rule?" Slater said.

Mo nodded, then looked past his shoulder and called out a greeting. Hilda was walking toward them, wearing a puffy orange winter jacket, her hair still an asymmetrical tangle.

"Are we ready to go?" Hilda said, and nodded to Etta, her gaze lingering on her for a moment after they exchanged a greeting.

"Do you want to do your count?" Mo said, and raised her eyebrows.

"Of course."

Hilda glanced at Slater and then stepped inside the vault. She made a perfunctory show of lifting up a couple of the ingots, then pointed at the array as she counted them under her breath. This was definitely for their benefit—it wouldn't be happening if he and Etta weren't standing here.

"I get one fourteen," Hilda said, and stepped out.

Mo looked to Miguel. "Let's wrap it up."

Miguel stepped inside the container and threw the tarp over the gleaming palladium. It was old-school, Slater saw, made of heavy canvas rather than plastic. He folded it double, and then double again.

"There's been another hiccup with the cargo plane," Hilda said.

Mo eyed her. "Like what?"

"One of the pilots can't get off the toilet. Daryl thinks it's food poisoning."

"Which pilot?" Slater demanded. "And who's Daryl?"

"The one named Russell. The other one, Sánchez, is fine."

"Daryl is a biologist on staff," Mo said. "He has his paramedic certification, so he's our unofficial medical practitioner."

"Did anyone else get food poisoning?" Slater said.

"Not that I've heard." Hilda waved a hand. "Apparently Russell brought some of his own food along. A day-old roast-beef sandwich."

"Another delay," Etta said. "It's the same as with the vans."

"They've actually come up with a workaround," Hilda said. "Sánchez can fly the plane, and Vitale can co-pilot for him."

"Vitale is licensed to do that?" Slater said.

"I guess so. The aviation company already signed off on it."

"They just want their plane back." Slater looked toward the playa where the aircraft was parked.

"What's the word on the fuel truck?" Etta said.

"I'm told it's thirty minutes out." Hilda raised her eyebrows. "So we can load the shipment now."

Miguel was tying ropes to bind the tarp to the pallet, looping it around the perimeter of the mass several times and heaving to tighten it. The rope looked old-school too, made of sisal or some other organic fiber. Since the ingots didn't extend to the edge of the pallet, there was a gap under the ropes on each side, but he'd lashed the tarp onto the mass of metal first. When he stepped back, it looked like a well wrapped and tightly bound package — you could flip it upside down and nothing would budge.

Mo whirled a finger in the air. "Let's move it."

Miguel walked over to the loader, and got it started, and drove it to the doors of the container. Watching him ease the forks into the pallet, it looked like he'd missed the tracker, and there was no telltale crunch of breaking plastic.

The four of them walked behind the little forklift as Miguel drove toward the playa, moving slowly on the rock-strewn ground. The cargo door under the plane's tail was down.

"You know that interviewing Karen probably doesn't matter, right?" Slater said to Etta. "You can fly back with me and the pallet if you want."

"I actually want to stay." She jutted her chin toward Mo and Hilda, walking in front of them. "Four hours in a car with that fox. Who knows what might happen?"

From inside the plane, Vitale walked down the cargo ramp. Slater could see from here that he had his weapon again. Standing with his hands on his hips, he watched the forklift approach. When they got closer, Vitale eyed Slater, and his lip curled in disgust. Slater wanted nothing more than to punch that look off his face, but if he did that, he'd wind up banished to that all-day road trip with Etta instead of flying back this morning.

Miguel maneuvered the forklift to the cargo ramp and stopped. When Sánchez appeared from inside, clad in his blue jumpsuit, he called out a series of precise directions to Miguel, guiding him up the ramp.

"Does it mean anything that Russell got sick and can't fly?" Etta said.

"It does seem awfully suspicious. But it hasn't changed anything. The shipment is still going to LA."

TWENTY-ONE

A SQUAT LITTLE TANK TRUCK rolled up from the direction of the production area, driving along the edge of the playa toward the plane. The livery on the side of the tank was for a fuel company in Elko, Nevada.

"Elko is nowhere near here," Etta said. "I was looking at the map when Hilda was explaining the drive."

"I bet Elko is the closest place they could get aviation fuel."

Mo stepped over to them, her clipboard in hand. "I'm told the bill of lading actually has to be given to the shipping company, not to you."

"Fine by me," Slater said. "I've already seen it."

Standing by the plane's passenger door, Vitale overheard them, and hustled over.

"I'll take that." He pulled the paperwork from the board and tucked it into his jacket. "You don't actually have to fly back with us, Ibáñez. You can wait with your girlfriend to meet Karen."

"That's not up to you," Slater said. "I'm going wherever the palladium goes."

"Your call." He shrugged, and walked over to the plane's passenger door, and stepped inside.

Once Miguel had set down the pallet, and had gingerly reversed down the ramp, Slater stepped over to look into the back of the plane. A pallet load of palladium didn't look like much in the big cargo space.

He stood with Etta to watch the fueling process, again with Sánchez keeping a close watch and giving instructions. Eventually the driver disconnected the hose and reeled it onto the truck.

Sánchez looked around, and caught Slater's eye. "All aboard."

"I'll see you back in civilization," Etta said, and clapped him on the shoulder.

Slater followed Sánchez up the steps and in the passenger door, and watched as he pulled it closed and secured it. Vitale was in the cockpit, in the right seat, with his headset on. Slater sat on the left where he could keep an eye on him. He'd forgotten to stow his pack in the webbing. But it would be fine here at his feet, he decided, and buckled his seatbelt.

The orange foam earplugs that he'd worn yesterday were still in his pocket, completely flattened, but he soon had them reshaped, and stuffed them in his ears.

Sánchez fired up the engines, and Slater heard a hydraulic whine from the back, and looked over his shoulder to watch the cargo ramp slowly rise into place. The pallet was right at the back, just inside the point on the floor where the ramp was hinged.

The engines revved, and the plane started rolling, then turned in the opposite direction. Slater peered out at the camp. No one was nearby now, and the fuel truck was gone. The propellers roared as their speed increased. Soon the rumbling of the wheels ceased as the nose pitched upward, and outside the windows the white expanse of the playa dropped away.

Slater settled into his seat once the plane started to level out. Vitale looked back at him for a moment, then reached around to pull the cockpit door closed. Why did they need privacy all of a sudden? Slater couldn't hear them anyway over the engine noise.

That look on Vitale's face. Slater thought about it. There was more to it than just his animosity. Something was up—he could feel it. His heart started to pound, and he popped open his seatbelt, and reached for his backpack, pulling it on and clicking the chest strap together. Absently sipping at his water, he glanced out the window. What the hell was going on?

He didn't have to wait long to find out. Vitale opened the cockpit door, and stepped out, and leveled that cartoonishly oversize handgun at him, an ugly grin on his face.

"Don't point your gun at me," Slater snapped.

"Hands," Vitale demanded.

He showed his palms. "What the fuck are you up to?"

"Get up, and walk to the back." Vitale waggled his weapon.

Slater rose, and moved slowly. If he was going to shoot him, he'd do it now, in the back. Instead Vitale spoke again.

"Stop there. On your knees, back to the wall."

Slater turned and looked him over. He was standing far enough away that he couldn't rush him—Vitale would plug him before he got there.

"What did I just say?" Vitale demanded.

He dropped to his knees, and sat back, next to one of the arcing ribs of the aircraft's frame, and glared at Vitale.

"Sánchez," Vitale shouted, and a moment later he stepped out of the cockpit. Vitale handed him the pistol. "If he goes for me, shoot him in the head."

Taking hold of the weapon, Sánchez pointed it at him.

"You're colluding with this creep?" Slater demanded. "What's the end game?"

Sánchez ignored him, and Vitale dug in his jacket

pocket and pulled out a set of white plastic loops—zip ties. So he wasn't going to get shot. At least not yet. Stepping next to Slater, he yanked his arm, and pushed his shoulder ahead. He felt the plastic tighten around one wrist, then the other.

As Vitale stepped back, Slater found that he couldn't reposition his hands—he'd looped the cuffs through one of the holes in the rib. Vitale took his rod back from Sánchez, and holstered it, and zipped up his jacket. Sánchez disappeared into the cockpit.

A few feet away, in the middle of the cabin, Vitale squatted and lifted a hatch in the floor, folding it open. He pulled out a heavy black canvas bag, almost as big as he was, and dragged it over to the pallet.

As he watched, Slater felt around with his fingers where the cuffs went through the hole in the rib. The metal wasn't sharp, but it wasn't polished smooth either. Pulling hard, he scraped the cuffs back and forth. He could only manage a small range of motion, but he could feel the resistance of the metal against the plastic.

Squatting at the pallet, Vitale used carabiners to attach the bulky bag to the ropes Miguel had tied around the shipment, first at one corner, then another. With a pocket knife he quickly cut the rope Miguel had used to lash the pallet to the tie-downs in the floor, first on one side, then on the other. He went back to mid-cabin and pulled an identical bag from another subfloor compartment, and dragged it over, and attached it to the ropes on the other two corners of the pallet.

"Three thousand pounds of palladium," Slater called to him. "You need more than one parachute."

Vitale met his gaze. "You're not as stupid as I thought you were."

"And I'm going down with the plane."

"It's not actually going down. It's going to run into

the High Sierra." He mimed flight with his hand. "Horizontally. With luck, no one will get to the wreck until spring. By then the condors and the coyotes will have picked your bones clean. Hopefully there'll be nothing left, and they'll assume all three of us were in the crash."

"That's why you didn't put a bullet in my brain," Slater said. "So it would look like an accident."

"This is a distinctive weapon." Vitale patted the big grip, visible at his waist. "It's my signature. But there's no need to draw attention to it."

"Don't you think somebody will notice that I was cuffed to the fuselage? Or that the palladium is missing?"

"It's not going to matter. I'll be on the beach in Brazil by then."

Stepping back to the hatches in the floor, Vitale pulled out two smaller bags. They had straps, and he quickly pulled one on, looping it around his shoulders and through his legs and pulling it tight. A parachute, Slater realized.

Vitale shouted to Sánchez, and he stepped out of the cockpit, and started to pull the other one on.

"Sánchez," Slater called to him. "You know this is murder."

Working with the straps for his chute, he scowled but didn't acknowledge him.

"Look at me," Slater shouted. Lurching forward, he used the momentum to amplify the bite of the metal on the cuffs. One of his hands was numb now, the circulation cut off by the tension.

Vitale chuckled and helped Sánchez with the parachute. Once he was strapped into it, he checked his watch.

"We're close. Get the door."

Sánchez went back to the cockpit, and a moment later there was a loud roar, and Slater's ears popped.

Leaning forward, he scraped the cuffs harder on the metal rib. Air rushed all around, whipping his hair, and a rectangle of brilliant daylight appeared around the top of the cargo door as it slowly started to open.

Vitale took hold of the overhead rail to keep his balance in the billowing air, and Sánchez followed him. They stood at either side of the pallet. When the ramp was level with the floor, it stopped its descent.

Slater felt the plastic snap. Finally his hands were free. Neither Vitale nor Sánchez noticed, as they were both focused on the pallet. Vitale was repositioning one of the big parachute bags.

Leaping to his feet, Slater rushed at them. Sánchez was on this side, and Slater struck him a body blow to his back. He yelped in surprise and pitched forward on the ramp, landing on his belly. Sánchez scrabbled with his hands, but he couldn't get hold of anything, and the momentum quickly took him out the yawning gate. With a scream cut off in the wind, he was gone.

The moment he struck Sánchez, Slater turned to Vitale, and stepped onto the pallet. Vitale was already reaching for his weapon. But his overconfidence was his downfall. It was stupid to use a cross-draw—it took too much time. Slater clobbered him with a hard left to the jaw, spinning his head. As he twisted away, Vitale drew the weapon, and Slater punched at it, hard enough that he dropped the gun. It clattered to the floor, and Slater hopped down to kick at it. It skittered out the open cargo door.

Watching it disappear, Vitale looked dazed. This moron had a glass jaw. Slater punched him hard in the gut, and he crumpled over, and stumbled back, toward the open door, his stupid hair whipping around his bald head.

Slater didn't actually want to throw the guy out—no way could he land this damn plane himself. Recovering his senses, Vitale straightened up, then reached for a handle on the wall, and pulled it horizontal. A grin spread on his face, and he stepped backward, and fell off the cargo ramp, and dropped out of sight.

"Fuck," Slater roared.

Something was happening now—it took a moment to figure it out, but the pallet was moving, sliding onto the ramp. That handle had activated a conveyor belt. The ramp was lowering itself too, its slope slowly dropping below floor level. He had to think quickly. There were two big freaking parachutes attached to this thing—it was his only chance.

Slater hopped onto the pallet and sprawled out, face down, feeling the layer of hard metal under the tarp. He slid his arms into the spaces under the ropes that bound the bundled ingots to the pallet, and spread his knees, and tried to dig his boots into the ropes at the other side.

Wincing in the rushing air, he felt the pallet tip forward as it slipped off the cargo door. The engine noise faded away. He was free-falling, and the rushing air made it hard to breathe.

The release mechanism for the parachutes, he realized. He had to find them. But Vitale hadn't planned to ride with this load. The chutes had to be automated. Before he could shift position to look at one of the bags, he heard a pop, quickly followed by another, and loud fluttering as the chutes deployed. He grabbed tighter to the ropes, and a huge g-force pressed him down, his body yanked left and then right.

The rocking back and forth soon stabilized, and he took a breath, and looked around. In the distance the horizon was level with the pallet. That had to be a good sign. Twisting his neck to look overhead, he could see thin lines running up to four big billowy parachutes, made of tan-colored fabric, filling the sky.

The ground was coming up fast, and the pallet was stable enough now. He pulled his arms out of the ropes and crouched on top of the tarp, grabbing one of the parachute cables to keep his balance. If he stayed flexible, he might just survive this.

As the ground rushed up, way too quickly, he readied himself in a crouch to jump off, tensing his legs, but the left side of the pallet hit the ground first, before he could leap, and catapulted him sideways. He landed in the sand, on his belly, unable to breathe.

The sudden silence and inertia were disorienting. He hated the feeling of having the wind knocked out of him. It was like being paralyzed. He lay there for a while, waiting for his breath to come back. It didn't feel like anything was broken. Bruised, maybe, his knees and his ribcage. Besides his aching empty lungs, the only real pain was at his wrists, where he'd cut into the skin scraping through the zip ties.

Eventually he was able to flop over, but his backpack prevented him from lying flat. It was still full of water. He had to chuckle. Thank you, Svetlana. And thanks to whatever instinct had told him to refill it this morning.

He got to his knees, then stood up, and slapped the dirt off his shirt and the sleeves of his jacket. Two little bright-orange cones sat on the ground. His earplugs. The impact had knocked them right out of his head. Grunting with the effort, he scooped them up, then looked around. There was just a slight breeze, and the parachutes were all lying flat, one draped inelegantly over a bush. This was a typical Great Basin plain, with a little more rainfall than at the Elmer Mine, as there was sagebrush dotting the landscape. Mountains were visible on three sides. That was also typical—Nevada was mostly that, mountains and more mountains, range after range.

Slater climbed on top of the pallet. It only gave him a

little more height, but now he could see another swatch of tan fabric lazily fluttering in the distance. It didn't quite match the color of the earth but it was close. Vitale wasn't armed anymore, and Sánchez had never flashed a piece. Slater would have seen it under that snug little flight suit. He hopped down and headed toward the distant chute, limping at first, and paused for a moment to stretch his thigh where the muscle was cramping.

At the end of the parachute lines he found Vitale, lying on his back, his head propped on the bag the chute had been in. His eyes were open but once again he seemed a little dazed. Looking him over as he approached, there was no blood, but one of his legs was at an odd angle.

"I'm injured," Vitale said. "You have to go for help."

Slater put his hands on his hips. "I'd say you busted your femur."

"It didn't break the skin. But I can't move."

"You're getting that broken-bone buzz," Slater said. "I can see it in your eyes. It must be something in the bone marrow, don't you think? I know that feeling. When it hits your bloodstream, there's not much pain relief, but it makes you dopey."

"This is all your fault. I was cramped up after you punched me. I lost my bag on the way down. There's a satellite phone in it. It has to be nearby. If you can find it, I can get us both out of here." He lifted a hand. "Start walking outward in a spiral. You'll find it."

"Was that your plan?" Slater said. "Call an accomplice with a truck to pick up you and Sánchez and the palladium?"

"We jumped too soon. It'll take him hours to get here. First I need to call and tell him where we are."

"Where do you suppose Sánchez got to?"

"He went out before I did," Vitale said, narrowing his

eyes, as if he were having trouble focusing them. "He's probably a mile or two that way. He wasn't unconscious, was he? If he was out, he wouldn't have deployed his chute."

Slater shrugged. "Either way."

"Ibáñez, listen—my bag. It's black. It's hard to miss."

"A minute ago you were going to kill me in a plane crash. I'm not feeling a lot of sympathy for your plight."

"Come on, man," he said, raising his voice. "You'll die if you try to walk out of here."

"If I let you call your truck driver, you'll just grease me anyway, as soon as he got here. I've got plenty of water. I'll take my chances."

"You can't leave me here."

"Actually, I can," Slater said, raising his eyebrows. "The thought of you baking in the sun warms my heart. Puts pep in my step. I actually wish it was a little hotter for you. The sun is nice and bright, though. You should pull in your parachute and use it for shade. You might live a little longer."

"Just listen to me," Vitale said. "The plane crash was Sánchez's idea. I tried to talk you out of coming with us, remember?"

"Blame the guy who's miles away, and potentially a red splat on the sand. That's pretty low. You know, I forgot one thing." Slater stepped closer, and straddled Vitale's waist, and leaned down. He wound up and punched him, a hard right to the jaw. "That's for pulling a gun on me." With a sharp left he snapped Vitale's head the opposite way. "That's for trying to kill me."

Vitale pounded at his shins. "Motherfucker."

"Why do you make me do this to you?" Slater shouted, and stepped back, and kicked the knee of his broken leg.

Howling in pain, Vitale arched his back and flapped his arm. Slater forced himself to stop, even though he wanted nothing more than to kick him again. Vitale's face was contorted, his eyes screwed shut.

"Idiot," Slater muttered, and turned away, and walked back toward the other parachutes.

"Ibáñez," Vitale shouted.

When he got to the pallet, Slater climbed on top of it. Shading his eyes with his palm, he scanned in a slow circle, looking for the other parachute, but there was no sign of it. He hopped down and pulled out his phone. It was working, he saw—it had survived that breathless belly flop into the dirt. That was a relief. Plan B to get out of here would have been to hunt for Vitale's satellite phone.

The map showed his location as a dot in the middle of a broad expanse of nothing. He copied the latitude and longitude into a note and tucked the phone away, then walked in the opposite direction from where Vitale had landed. Once he was far enough to be out of earshot, he stopped and slung off his backpack. This was the other moment of truth. Zipping open the top pocket, he powered on the satellite modem, then looked at his phone again.

The lone Wi-Fi point in range was labeled "спутник," and he tapped on it, and almost instantly saw that he was online.

"Yes," he hissed, and took a deep breath.

It seemed like weeks ago now, but just yesterday he'd taken a photo of the aircraft. He pulled it up and then dialed 911. It took a moment, but eventually a woman's voice answered: "Sheriff's office."

His phone must have shared his location data, he realized, and fleetingly wondered which sheriff this was, what county he was in.

"There's an airplane with no one on board, and it's going to crash," Slater said. "A propeller cargo plane. It's called a Sherpa." He read the tail number from the photo.

"How do you know that?" she said.

"I just jumped out of it. That's not the lead here. Some lowlifes set the autopilot to crash in the Sierra."

"What's your name?"

"That's not important right now. The flight plan was from a playa in rural Nevada to Van Nuys Airport in California."

"Sir, I need your name."

"Just look for the transponder for that tail number," Slater said. "Nobody's on board."

He ended the call and studied the map again. With a data connection the local topography quickly filled in, but it still showed no human-made features, only the empty desert. But as he zoomed out, a road appeared. It was on this side of the next mountain range, only about six miles away. When he switched to the satellite view, and zoomed closer, he could see the dashed yellow line in the center of the dark strip. A paved road. That meant regular traffic. He had to smile. This was very good news.

Scrolling around on the map, he saw there was a settlement on the highway, a little farther south—a cluster of buildings marked with a gas station logo. In the overhead image it looked like semitrucks were parked there. He spent a minute messing with the map, and eventually lined up the gas station with one of the mountain peaks on the horizon. If he walked cross-country rather than directly to the highway, it was just over eight miles, and the intervening terrain looked to be pretty flat—he wouldn't have to navigate over any mountains.

Piece of cake—he had plenty of water to walk that far. It wasn't even that long ago that he'd had breakfast.

TWENTY-TWO

WALKING IN THIS DESERT was easy. There wasn't a lot of vegetation, and most of what was growing was sagebrush. Slater caught a whiff of it once in a while.

He pulled out his phone and dialed Etta.

"You can't be in LA already," she said when she picked up.

"I'm in the middle of nowhere. Vitale pulled his damn six-gun on me." He explained what had happened.

"Bloody hell. I'm so glad I didn't get on that plane."

"Me too."

"So you're just wandering in the desert right now?"

"Not aimlessly," Slater said. "I'm close to a highway. Two hours' walk from a gas station, and I've got lots of water."

"Your backpack. I get it. I'll never question your faith in the Russian again."

"I wanted you to know where I was," Slater said. "Sooner than later you're going to hear about the airplane going down."

"I'm assuming I should keep this information to myself."

"That's always the best plan."

"Maybe I'll tell Max," she said, "in case he hears about it."

"Make sure you're somewhere that you won't be overheard."

Next he called Della, glad that she picked up.

"The aviation company told me you were delayed overnight," she said.

"It gets better. Seligman's armed guard tried to hijack the shipment and kill me in the process."

"Vitale?" she said, her voice rising.

"I'm not sure if he's working with someone else at Seligman or with his own crew." Slater explained the morning's events. "I'll text you the location where the pallet landed. Vitale had a truck waiting out here somewhere to scoop it up, but I don't think they'll be able to find it now. If you're on the hook for it, Cudahy Mutual needs to pick it up before they do. Or tell the mining company where it is. You can't trust Seligman anymore."

"I'll get someone on it," Della said. "Where's Vitale?"

"He's with the pallet. He has a broken femur. Whoever picks up the palladium will find him, or maybe his carcass."

"Did you call an ambulance?"

"I'm not going to do that. He tried to kill me. I guess you could call it in, if you want to prioritize assisting a lowlife, but he's been ripping off Mott, and ripping off your company. I suspect he orchestrated all the shipping delays to divert attention from his thievery."

"What are his prospects?"

"He doesn't have any water, but it's not that hot out here," Slater said. "He can probably survive overnight. The important thing is the cargo. It weighs three thousand pounds, and it's on a pallet. Unless you want to load it brick by brick, you'll need some way to lift it onto a truck. Like a winch and skids. The site is a few miles from a paved road, and it's open country—you should be able to get there with a four-wheel drive."

Once he'd ended the call, he texted her the latitude and longitude of where the pallet had landed, then took a minute to pull off his jacket and hang it over his backpack. He took a long pull on his water tube. Even with that hint of plastic, it was the best-tasting water ever.

He was sore from his crash landing, but he realized he felt good—euphoric, even—walking in the near silence of the wilderness, the bright sun overhead, the scent of sagebrush in the air. Maybe he was high from the adrenaline rush, buzzed from falling out of the sky.

Eventually he could see the gas station in the distance, and then the dark ribbon of highway shimmering in the heat, stretching off in both directions. A couple of semitrucks were parked nearby, and along the top of the building big red letters said FUEL and DINER.

Walking across the highway, devoid of traffic in both directions as far as the horizon, he couldn't wipe the smile off his face. He pulled open the door and stepped inside. Two men were sitting at a table with plates of greasy food, and a third was parked on a stool at the counter. Slater sat a few stools away and set his backpack at his feet.

The server came out of the back. Still in her fifties, maybe, she wore a mint-green uniform and a name tag that said HELEN.

"You look overheated, honey," she said, her brow furrowing. "Do you need some orange juice?"

"That sounds great. And some oatmeal. Hold the milk. And whatever fruit you have. And Helen—I'll need java."

She jotted it down on a little pad. "You got it."

Feeling the gaze of the guy sitting farther down the counter, Slater looked over. He had a bushy beard, and baggy jeans, and an embroidered oval patch on his jacket that said DEX.

It was more than curiosity in his eyes, Slater realized, and double-clicked his tongue. Dex quickly looked down at his plate.

When he finished his oatmeal, and the most delicious hunks of melon and pineapple he'd ever tasted, he dropped a sawbuck on the counter for Helen and walked to the register with his check. Dex was standing there with his own check, and subtly glanced at Slater's crotch as he walked over.

"You see something you like down there?" Slater said.

Dex coughed, covering his mouth with his fist.

"You don't have to be embarrassed."

"That's quite the backpack," he said.

"It's solar powered." Slater waved his arm. "I have to tell you, Dex, I'm having a really good day."

"Did you win the lottery or something?"

"It's just great to be alive, you know?"

Helen hustled over and rang up Dex, then took Slater's check as Dex stepped outside. Once he'd paid, he went out to find Dex standing nearby, hands shoved in his jacket pockets. He'd waited for him. That meant he was already halfway there.

"Tell me," Slater said. "Are you headed east or west?"

"South."

"Excellent. Can I get a ride? I can pay you for it."

Dex frowned. "How did you get here without wheels?"

"It's a long story. I can tell you all about it on the road."

He groaned. "I don't know. You're not high, are you?"

"Sober as a judge. Is that your rig?" Slater gestured to the nearest semitruck. "It looks like it has a sleeper in the back. Would you accept payment in kind? I could smoke you."

"Jesus," Dex said, his eyebrows shooting up. "Cash and sex. You really want to get out of here."

"It's more than that. You're a handsome fellow."

"Bullshit," he said flatly. "But what the hell. Come on."

Slater walked with him toward the cab of the semitruck. Painted on the door in black letters was DEXTER LOWE TRUCKING, along with a license number.

"Do you want to do some stuff before we roll?" Dex said. "It's private. Nobody can look in."

"If we do that now," Slater said, "how do I know you won't just throw me out? Leave me lying flat on the pavement in the middle of Nevada? I feel like I shouldn't pay you before you've held up your end."

"I'd give you a ride even without the sex. It gets tedious on the road with no one to talk to." He walked around the front of the vehicle. "Let me open the door."

Dex climbed in and pushed open the passenger door. As Slater stepped up, and set his backpack on the floor at his feet, Dex started the engine.

"You're not going to rob me, are you?" he said, eyeing Slater.

"I wouldn't get away with it. Helen has my face on her security cameras. But I can demolish you." He glanced into the sleeper compartment behind the seats. "Do I have to take my boots off first?"

"I thought you wanted a ride before we did that."

"Wouldn't we both be calmer if we went for it now?" Slater said. "The instructor in my mindfulness class said I should be inviting calm into my life."

His eyes narrowed. "You take a mindfulness class."

Slater waved dismissively. "Court ordered."

"Aren't you a barrel of monkeys." He reached down to untie his shoes. "Yes, boots off."

Slater climbed into the back, a dim windowless space with bedding and padded walls, and sat back on his elbows. Dex followed close behind him. There wasn't much room, but they both fit.

"It has to be something easy," Dex said, squatting on his haunches. "Like that blow job you mentioned."

Holding his gaze, he tentatively reached for Slater's crotch, and massaged his junk through his jeans.

"If you blow me too," Slater said.

Dex chuckled and shifted position, and Slater unbuckled his own belt, and popped his fly. He was half hard already, and Dex took him into his mouth. Gasping at the intensity of it, Slater shifted onto his side to unbuckle Dex's belt, and zipped open his jeans, and went down on him. Dex quickly got hard, and they worked each other in unison, the tension building as they both got closer. When Dex came, he strained into him.

Pulling back, Slater closed his eyes and let him work. He was good at this, intuitive and gentle. When Slater came, he yelped and reached for Dex's shoulder to get him to stop.

"That was amazing," Dex said, leaning back, red-faced and breathing hard.

Slater murmured assent as he folded his arm over his eyes.

"Now, get the hell out of my rig."

Slater lifted his arm to look at him.

Dex laughed. "The look on your face. I'm just messing with you."

"I guess I'm the one who started it."

"We should get on the road."

Dex climbed into the front, and Slater buckled his belt, then sat up and followed him out. By the time he had his boots on, Dex had pulled the rig onto the highway.

"So what are the next major towns we're driving through?" Slater said.

"There's Clinnel, and then Ardo, and eventually Ely. That's the end of the line."

"I've heard of Ely. Do you know if it has an airport?"

"Not one with commercial flights."

"How long till we get to Ely?" Slater said, and pulled out his phone.

"Two hours. But you won't get cell service out here."

"I don't need it."

He zipped open the top of his backpack and pulled out the modem, then set it on the dash, close to the windshield glass. That would give it a view of half the sky at least. It was enough—when he checked his phone, he was online.

A couple of aviation businesses were listed at the airport in Ely, and he dialed the number for the one that mentioned charter flights. A woman's voice answered.

"Can you fly me to Van Nuys Airport today?" Slater said.

"Where's Van Nuys Airport?"

"Los Angeles."

"Well, I don't love flying in that airspace. Southern California is awfully crowded."

"But you can do it."

"What time do you want to leave?"

"Two hours from now," Slater said. "What is it going to cost me?"

"Let me check the mileage."

Slater could hear her clacking at a keyboard.

"I'm going to have to say twenty-five hundred," she said. "I can't really do it for less. I'll have to turn around and come right back to make it before dark."

"Deal. I'll see you in a couple hours."

"You'll need to pay me up front. Do you have a credit card?"

"I've got cash. You'll get it when I get there. How will I find you?"

"It's not a big airport," she said. "Ask for Ruthie. What's your name?"

"Ibáñez," he said, and ended the call. He turned to

Dex. "Do you know Ely? Is the airport far from where you'll drop me?"

"I can take you there. It's not out of my way."

"Right on," he said, tucking his phone away. "Dex, you're a mensch."

"That's not a word I hear every day. Are you Jewish?"

"I don't hang around schul on Friday," Slater said, "but my mother is, so technically I am."

"Interesting. My father was. I mostly grew up around his people. One of my cousins said my primary role in the family was to shift the bell curve back to the left."

"What does that mean?"

"I'm not much of an achiever compared to my well-educated and well-paid relatives."

"It looks to me like you've achieved plenty," Slater said. "I saw your name painted on the side of the cab. That means you're working for yourself." He gestured to the windshield. "You've got the freedom of the open road. The whole world at your feet, while your nebbishy deskbound relations stare at screens all day under artificial light."

"I should get you to write that down. I'll send it to my cousins."

"So what's in the back of your truck?"

"I'm rolling empty," Dex said. "That's why we can make good time. I'm more interested in what you're doing alone in the middle of the desert."

"Well, Dex, I'm here, on the ground, and I'm loving the sunshine."

"I get it. It's good to be alive."

"I think I needed to be reminded of that. You have to get out of town once in a while, you know?"

"That's Los Angeles, you said on the phone," Dex said. "How did you wind up at the diner?"

"I started out the morning with some other people. It

didn't go so well. I think ditching them kind of put me in a good mood." Slater looked over at him. The best evidence of that, he realized, was that he didn't want to punch Dex in the face right now.

TWENTY-THREE

THEY CHATTED MOST OF the way to Ely, and eventually Dex rolled up to the driveway of the airfield. Slater could see a fire truck in the distance and a couple of hangars with light aircraft in front of them.

"I guess this is it," Slater said. "Thanks for the ride."

"Thanks for the diversion. That was nice."

Slater climbed out, and pulled on his backpack, and walked toward the hangars. The sign next to the door on one of them was for the business he'd called, so he headed toward that one. A dusty SUV was pulled up out front, and nearby was a single-prop airplane, painted white with a blue stripe down the side.

Before he reached the door, a woman stepped out, clad in jeans and a dark windbreaker. In her fifties, she had that sun-weathered look that lots of desert rats had.

"Ruthie," he said.

"Mr. Ibáñez. I wasn't sure you were for real."

"Call me Slater."

"I filed a flight plan. We need to get in the air. But first there's the matter of payment."

"Right." Slater slung off his backpack, and found his wad of cash, and counted out twenty-five C-notes.

Ruthie took the bundle, and riffled through it, then met his eye.

"That's a lot of scratch. You're not crazy, are you?"

"I can't answer that objectively. I've been straight with you, though—I just need to get to Los Angeles."

She eyed him a moment longer. "I have to lock this up. Give me a second."

Stepping back into her office, she was only gone a moment. When she came back, Ruthie locked the door behind her and waved him toward the little airplane.

Once she'd climbed in, Slater got in the opposite side, ducking under the wing. She pulled on a set of black can headphones with a little mike attached and motioned for him to put on the other pair. They covered his ears completely, and Ruthie reached over to position the mike at his lips. Even with the heavy cans, the engine was loud when she got it running.

"Buckle up," she said, her voice even and clear through the headphones.

By the time he got his backpack stowed at his feet, Ruthie was taxiing, the aircraft moving fast.

"What kind of plane is this?" he said.

"It's called a 172. Let me focus on getting us into the air. We can talk then."

The engine got louder, like an angry lawnmower, and the plane rolled faster, soon leaving the ground at a steep angle. Slater watched the dusty asphalt sink away. This was the second time today he'd been on a dinky aircraft. With luck this trip would have a better ending.

Once the plane had leveled out, Ruthie spoke. "What was your question?"

"How long to Van Nuys?" It was odd to hear his own voice in the headphones.

"About three hours. We have to go a little out of the way. The feds set up a temporary flight restriction around the Quinn Canyon Range."

"Why did they do that?" Slater said.

"An aircraft went down. I don't know the details. I guess they want the sky clear of traffic for the investigation. Not to worry—we'll fly around it."

"Where's Quinn Canyon?"

"About eighty miles from here. Southwest. On the way to Southern California."

It had to be the Sherpa, Slater knew. For some reason it hadn't made it to the Sierra. That sweet little plane had ended its days in a place like this—the Great Basin's endless mountain ranges. They were flying over a range now. The peaks looked small from here, so far below. It was pure luck that he hadn't had to hike over any of them to find that highway this morning.

Ruthie interrupted his thoughts. "Am I going to have any trouble with that cash?"

"It's real, if that's what you're asking."

"It looked brand-new."

"It's legit money," Slater said. "It's not missing from a bank or a payroll or an evidence locker. In my work I mostly get paid in cash."

"Fine with me. People who pay cash usually don't take kindly to lots of questions."

"You can put it in the bank. It won't cause you any problems."

"So why were you in the middle of the desert with no car and all that money?" Ruthie said.

"What happened to the thing about no questions?"

She laughed. "I guess my curiosity overcame that bit of wisdom."

"I got a ride this morning with a couple of guys," Slater said. "They turned out to be difficult people. So I left them behind."

"Fair enough."

After a while Ruthie started to talk on the radio, in clipped exchanges with air traffic control, interspersed with long periods of silence. She pointed out Death Valley, and then the snowcapped Sierra off in the distance. Once they were over the Mojave, Slater could feel her stress level rising as she made the terse radio exchanges a lot more frequently.

Eventually they were over the metropolis, the familiar local mountains, and then lined up with the runway, a void in the surrounding concrete sprawl of the Valley. Slater watched it get closer and rise toward them as Ruthie spent most of the time talking to the controllers.

When they touched down, even on the ground she was on the radio, and eventually she pulled to a stop in front of a squat building, and killed the engine, and took a deep breath.

Slater pulled off his headphones. "Do you need a coffee or something?"

"Thanks," she said. "I just need to refuel and get out of here. Cities stress me out."

Slater climbed out and walked toward the nearby hangar, then to the vehicle gate in the fence beside it. As he approached, the gate rolled open for him—either a sensor or someone at the switch who saw him coming.

Out on the street, he had to walk several blocks to find his car. It felt like a warehouse district, only denser, and with regular glimpses of the tall security fence that protected the airport. Finally he came to the Thunderbird, patiently waiting for him, sleek and black and cherry.

When he got behind the wheel, and twisted his key in the ignition, it felt quiet after all those hours sitting next to a lawnmower engine.

Looking at his phone, he opened Svetlana's app, and checked for the tracker he'd wedged into the pallet. There was no sign of it since they'd left the mining camp—the shipment was still in the wilderness with no access to the cell network. It was also possible that the hard landing had damaged the device, and it was never going to show up.

Or worse, someone had found the tracker. That would put the pallet out of his reach. He dialed Della's number.

"Where are you?" she said when she picked up.

"Van Nuys. Did you get the palladium?"

"It's not good news, Slater. There was no sign of the pallet or Vitale at the coordinates you sent."

"Damn it," he snapped. "I was so sure it would work. Maybe my phone was calibrated wrong, and I gave you the wrong location numbers."

"It was the right place. The parachutes were still there. I talked to the head of the recovery team. He said they were the same color as the ground."

"Those are the ones. But the pallet was gone."

"There were tire tracks," Della said. "Someone drove in to pick up the pallet and Vitale."

"It has to be Vitale's cohorts. They were able to carry out their original plan. He must have found a way to contact them."

"Or Sánchez did. Either way, the palladium is a loss, and those two are in the wind."

"Don't write it off just yet," Slater said. "I might have a way to track down the shipment."

"How?"

"Don't ask me that. Just give me a day or two before you make any decisions."

Slater ended the call, but before he could shift the car into gear, his phone rang, with the most annoying ringtone of all: "*No wire hangers! I buy you beautiful dresses, and you treat them like they were some dishrag …*"

"Damn it," he muttered, and picked up. "What do you need, Doris?"

"Where are you?"

"In the Valley, if it matters. Van Nuys."

"Did you jump out of an airplane today?" she demanded.

Slater groaned. "In a way. I kind of fell out. How did you know that?"

"Conrad told me. Are you OK?"

"Of course I'm OK. How did Conrad know?"

"Why don't you join us and ask him yourself? He's on his way over. We're planning to sit out and use the fire pit. The sun will be gone soon."

"You're meeting him because of me?"

"It's not a meeting, and not everything is about you. Come over and have some lemonade. I just squeezed a bunch of lemons from that tree."

Slater ended the call and backed into the street. His plan had been to go to his pad and just sleep while he waited for the tracker to come online. But those were awfully good lemons.

Accelerating onto the freeway, he headed east, and onto the streets of hilly Mount Washington, and pulled into Doris's driveway. Her Buick was here but there was no sign of the stupid midlife-crisis Boxster that her stupid boyfriend Albert drove.

As he walked up to the front door, Doris met him, and pushed open the screen, her brow furrowed. Slater leaned in to kiss her.

Once she'd embraced him, Doris grasped his hands and studied his face. "What have you been up to?"

"Let's wait for that deadbeat cop. That way I only get interrogated once." Slater followed her into the kitchen.

"Why would you call him a deadbeat?" she said. "Does he owe you money? Conrad's not crooked. Unless you know something I don't."

"I suppose I'm exaggerating. There's a long list of terrible truths about that man—a file cabinet's worth—but 'crooked' isn't one of them."

"Let's sit out back," Doris said, and handed him a stack of big glasses, then lifted the pitcher off the counter.

Slater held the back door open for her, and they went outside, and sat at the cast-iron patio table.

"The yard looks great," she said.

"I put down some mulch last week, and I fertilized the lemon tree."

The latch on the side gate rattled, and Conrad strode in, clad in chinos and a long-sleeved shirt.

"There's the detective," Doris said, and Conrad greeted her, and leaned down to kiss her cheek.

"Don't be slobbering on her," Slater said.

Doris shot him a look. "Don't give him grief about who he can kiss."

"You have to admit it's a little creepy."

Ignoring that, Doris eyed Conrad. "You're still wearing your badge."

"I came from work," he said, and took the chair next to her. "I didn't want to leave it in the car."

"What's with the hair?" Slater said.

Conrad ran a hand through it. "You like it? I'm leaving it a little longer. With the new job I need to look more white-collar."

"You also need to spend more than eight bucks on a haircut."

"It looks great," Doris said. "The cut is very professional." She sat up and twisted the handle of the pitcher toward him. "Can you pour the lemonade?" Eyeing Slater, she added, "Why don't you set up the fire?"

Slater huffed and got up. "Once a teacher, always a teacher."

"It's called delegating," she said. "Why would I do the heavy lifting when I've got you two stalwarts?"

From the pile behind the shed, Slater picked out some of the smaller logs, and tucked them under his arm, and then grabbed a handful of kindling from the bag. Arranging them in the fire pit, he crouched beside it, and lit the kindling with the stick lighter.

"Where's that old gonif who's been hanging around here?" Slater said.

"Albert is my age. He's out of town visiting his kids."

"I knew it," Slater said. "He has a secret family somewhere." He blew on the kindling, but it was plenty dry, the flames already licking at the bigger pieces, so he went back to his chair.

"He's a widower," Doris said. "I knew about his kids from the start. There's nothing secret about it."

"Do you know how his wife died?"

"I think it was cancer."

He eyed Conrad. "Can you order up an exhumation? In case it was something else. Run some basic tests. Just to be sure."

Conrad scoffed. "I'd need a damn good reason to do something like that. And a judge to sign off on it."

"Albert isn't a murderer," Doris said flatly.

"Has he asked to be added to any of your bank accounts, or the deed to your house?" Slater said. "Have you noticed any of your stuff going missing? I mean, does he steal?"

"Stop trash-talking Albert," she said, raising her voice. "What happened to you today?"

Slater picked up his glass of lemonade. "I'm on a case." He outlined the events of the day, in broad strokes, glossing over some of the details, like punching Vitale and hooking up with Dex.

"They wanted you dead," Conrad said finally. "You're lucky you got out of that plane."

"It wasn't personal. I just got in the way. It was actually my own mistake—it was stupid of me not to connect the dots and figure out that Vitale was the one behind the shipping problems and the cargo discrepancy. He was orchestrating the delays to divert attention from him pilfering the shipments."

"It's not your fault that somebody tried to kill you," Doris said.

"I'm just glad I was able to hold on to that pallet. More significantly," Slater said, and jabbed a finger at Conrad, "how did you hear about it?"

"A sheriff's deputy in Elko County, Nevada, called to find out what we knew about you."

"You have a flag on my file."

"I can't really confirm or deny that," he said. "It falls under ongoing police business."

"That makes me sound like a lowlife."

Conrad raised his eyebrows and shrugged, then averted his gaze, and reached for his glass of lemonade.

"How did the sheriff know who you were?" Doris said.

"I called in to report the unpiloted aircraft," Slater said. "Somebody needed to know about it. I used my own phone, so I'm sure they just looked me up that way."

"You were smart to jump out," Conrad said. "They shot it out of the sky. It was a whole thing. I'm sure it'll be in the news."

"I wondered about that. Whether they'd just let it crash or not."

"They scrambled fighter jets. The pilots saw the cargo door hanging open, and they used heat-sensing tech to see that there was no one on board. No one alive, at least."

"It's amazing that that's possible," Doris said, and set her glass on the table.

Conrad frowned. "You know, that part might actually be confidential. Maybe don't go talking about it. Or at least don't say you heard it from me." He eyed Slater. "You're going to have to talk to the feds. Interviews and statements and depositions."

"I figured. But I'm not going to do their job for them. They can come and find me." He waved a hand. "Why did they bother shooting it down? It would have crashed in the Sierra wilderness anyway."

"It actually takes pretty high-up clearance to fire on a civilian aircraft," Conrad said. "The story is that they were afraid it was going to hit the major metropolis of Beatty, Nevada."

"That's not a big community," Doris said. "And how could they tell it was going to come down there? It seems unlikely it would crash in that specific town."

"Beatty is the official reason," Conrad said. "I also heard it was going to fly right over Area 51. That place is a hard no-go."

Doris nodded. "That sounds more like it. Bring it down in a controlled way before it got close to anything sensitive."

"It's actually kind of sad," Slater said. "It was a sweet little airplane."

They talked some more, and Doris brought out a fruit salad and some crackers for them to snack on, and they watched the little fire flicker as the daylight faded. When it was reduced to glowing red embers, Conrad rose to leave, and leaned in to kiss Doris.

"Love you," he said.

"Whoa." Slater sat up. "Slow down, Seabiscuit. You don't get to say that."

Conrad frowned. "You don't get to tell me what I can say."

"Settle down," Doris said, eyeing Slater. "He's my friend."

"He's my ex. It's sleazy that he's creeping around here, cozying up to you." He scowled at Conrad. "What are you trying to pull?"

"I don't creep around."

"Whatever you're upset about," Doris said, "you need to smash it. There's no ulterior motive."

Slater pointedly looked him up and down. "I'm not so sure."

Conrad threw up his hands, then walked toward the gate to the driveway. "Good night, all," he called back to them. "Both the crazy and the sane."

Slater put the cover on the fire pit, then helped Doris carry the glasses inside.

"I should go too." He leaned in to kiss her.

Doris had tears in her eyes, and pulled him into a hug. "My beautiful son."

"What's with the waterworks?" Slater demanded, studying her face.

She squeezed his arms. "Just—be careful."

———·———

WHEN SLATER CLIMBED INTO his car, he checked his phone again for the tracker on the pallet, but there was still no signal. If it came within range of cell service, even without Wi-Fi signals to triangulate its location, it would still report in that it was alive. Maybe whoever had recovered it really had found the tracker.

Once he was up in his apartment, Slater dropped the solar panel–studded backpack on the floor. It felt heavy— it still had water in it. That bag had saved him today.

He pulled off his boots, and grabbed the bourbon bottle from the kitchen cupboard, too tired to bother with a glass. Once he was stretched out on the sofa, he took a long pull, then set the bottle on the carpet.

The hookup app, he thought fleetingly. It was that time of day. But then he'd hooked up with Dex earlier, and Zed first thing this morning. But it had been dark out, so it really didn't even count as today. He was too exhausted for that, he decided. The warm glow from the amber elixir was already suffusing outward from his belly.

Lying there, zoning out, he remembered something

Zed had said. Love without pain. Digging out his phone, he scrolled through his contacts and dialed.

"Hey, buddy," Pike said when he picked up. "I'm surprised to hear from you. It's late."

"Did I wake you?"

"I wasn't asleep. What's going on?"

"Have you heard the idea that love stories end badly?" Slater said. "It's a saying. 'Love stories usually end badly.'"

"What are you talking about?"

"There are no happy endings. You either break up and hate each other, or you die. People die. It's a thing."

"If that's the yardstick you're using," Pike said, "life doesn't have a happy ending either. For anybody."

"I'm a mess, Pike. I'm a drunk, and I'm angry, and I'm selfish."

"You don't sound drunk right now. But I guess I saw some of that."

"And yet there's a statue of Pollux sitting on my desk. It's like you didn't see it correctly."

"I've got Castor on my desk," Pike said. "I've been thinking about you a lot."

"Somebody tried to grease me today."

"Damn it." He sighed. "That sucks. It's a rough business we're in."

"It kind of made me appreciate not being dead," Slater said. "Afterward I was walking around in the sunshine, and I was thinking, you know, sunshine is kind of great. Is that messed up?"

"In no way is that messed up."

"Castor and Pollux faced death every day. All the Argonauts did. It was their whole orientation."

"Things didn't end well for them either," Pike said.

"I think we should do something. Try something. Otherwise we won't know what we missed."

"I'm down for that. Unequivocally, Slater. What do you want to try?"

"I don't know. We'll figure it out. I've got some money I need to do something with."

"Maybe we'll aim for something less brutal than the Argonauts," Pike said.

"Going in," Slater said, "you need to accept that I'm fucking crazy, and I cannot be fixed. If the willpower of the entire LA public school system couldn't fix me, you won't be able to either."

Pike laughed. "Like you said—we'll figure it out."

TWENTY-FOUR

I N THE MORNING SLATER woke to daylight streaming in the window. Somehow he was in his own bed. His head felt clear. He must have crashed before he drank too much.

His muscles were stiff when he sat up, but that wasn't the effects of bourbon, it was about jumping out of the sky and trekking across the desert yesterday. He did a neck roll. A flood of memory struck him then—he'd talked to Pike. Had that been a mistake? He ran through the conversation in his mind. A little sticky, maybe, but no, not a mistake.

A notification sound from his phone, he remembered. That's what had just woken him. Slater grabbed the device and saw that the alert had been from Svetlana's app. Finally—a signal from the tracker. Zooming in on the map, it was in town, and nearby. He'd half expected it to turn up at Seligman's truck yard, but it wasn't there. The marker was in a warehouse district, near the 10, just south of downtown.

The accuracy wasn't precise with this tech, and when he zoomed in on the street, the map showed a green circle that covered two adjacent buildings. He quickly found the street numbers for both and sent a text to Della:

The pallet showed up. It's at one of these addresses.

Next he texted Conrad:

Seven million bucks of palladium stolen from that aircraft is at one of these buildings. You should pick it up. I anticipate Vitale's coconspirators will be well armed, because he was. I'm headed over there. Tell your people not to shoot the hot guy in the black shirt.

Slater was hurriedly pulling on his jeans when Conrad's reply came:

Don't go in there. Wait for law enforcement.

He sent a quick response:

Your people will take their sweet time, and you know it. The palladium might be gone by then.

Stepping over to his closet, he found a black shirt to wear, just in case, then hustled down to his garage and headed to the warehouse district, driving hard.

As he pulled up on the location, he glanced at his phone. The tracker was still here. Before he climbed out he looked around the street. A van with a Colorado tag was parked in front of one of the buildings. It was unmarked, but he knew that vehicle. It was one of Seligman's down-low vans, with the armor on the inside, and the fake tinted window. Seligman didn't have bases outside town, so the out-of-state plate had to be an attempt at obfuscation. That's why the tracker had been offline—it had been inside the signal-blocking steel cage in the back of that vehicle all the way from Nevada. They must have just unloaded it.

The building had an oversize garage bay, and the shutter was rolled down, but the pedestrian door beside it was propped open with a cinder block. Slater took a moment to start the audio recorder on his phone, then dropped it into his shirt pocket. If he did wind up getting shot, at least there'd be some evidence of how it had gone down.

He climbed out of the Thunderbird and walked to the doorway. It was darker inside, but he could see it was a cavernous warehouse space with a high ceiling. In the middle of the floor sat the pallet, its load unwrapped now, the array of ingots gleaming white in the fluorescent light. Somehow it looked weightier now than it had at the mine, more significant, taking up more room.

Instantly there were handguns pointed at him—one by a short man he'd never seen before, standing next to Rita from Seligman, her hair bound tightly back, wearing a gray jacket. Sitting in a wheelchair, with dark bruises under his eyes and his leg in heavy white plaster, Vitale pulled the other. Even in his battered condition he was wearing his holster.

"Grab a little air, Ibáñez."

Slater flashed his palms at his sides. "You're looking well, Vitale. I guess stupidity can't keep a murderous thug down for long."

Rita was scowling at him. "Such a nosy little fuck. You just won't let it go. How did you find us?"

"You're sloppy, Rita," Slater said. "It's your downfall."

She scoffed. "We tried to croak you in that airplane, but here you are, back for more, the very next day. Don't count on your luck running so well the second time around. Speaking of stupid, showing up here alone definitely falls into that category."

"So it was your idea to have me go down in the crash."

"The plan to transport the cargo by air was really fortuitous. It made it much easier for us to acquire the whole shipment. In the vans we could only risk smurfing two or three bricks at a time."

"You're extremely lucky nobody noticed the missing ingots," Slater said.

"I almost can't believe that myself." Rita waved a hand. "But that's the thing about paying people minimum wage. It makes it a lot less likely they'll give a shit about your precious property."

"You knew I'd be on that plane. You planned to kill me from the start."

"Vitale came up with that idea. It was risky, and it took some work, but it meant we could get all this at once."

"You're ambitious, I'll give you that," Slater said. "That's definitely the American disease. But I can't believe this goon came up with that plan. You're obviously the brains, Rita. He was strapped into a parachute and he still broke his leg."

"Fuck you," Vitale snapped. "This is a collaborative effort."

"You found another heater, I see," Slater said. "It makes me think you're trying to compensate for something."

"I should ventilate you right now."

"Not here," Rita said.

"So who picked you up in the desert?" Slater gestured to the guy with the handgun. "This bozo? How did he find you?"

The guy scowled at him but didn't speak, the aim of his weapon unwavering.

"Sánchez had his satellite phone," Vitale said. "It turned out he wasn't that far away. He spotted the parachutes."

"I assume he's still ambulatory," Slater said. "He didn't strike me as the kind of idiot who'd break his leg on a routine jump."

"Keep pushing, Ibáñez," Vitale said through his teeth. "I've got a lead slug with your name on it."

Slater frowned. "That's so bad for the environment. You really should switch to steel ammo." He eyed Rita.

"It's a shame Sánchez couldn't join us today. Where's he at?"

She scoffed. "Why would that matter to you? You're not going to see another sunset."

"What about Bender? Is he working with you?"

"That guy is a straight arrow," she said. "Square and black like a little chocolate wafer. I don't think he could stomach this kind of work. Not having him on this run made things a lot easier."

"So what's your plan for the palladium?"

"We'll melt it down, like we've been doing," Rita said, and grinned. That expression didn't suit her face, and it came off as eerie. "Sell it to scrap dealers bit by bit. I'm not greedy—we won't have to tax those shipments anymore. I've earned enough with this lot to pay off my ranch in Arizona."

"Interesting that you and Wheels here are both stealing to buy real estate." He jutted his chin at Vitale. "I saw your house in the hills. It's pretty bougie."

"How did you know about that?" Vitale demanded.

"Why would you plant a *benjamina* out front? It's almost like you want trouble."

He frowned. "What?"

"Arizona," Slater said, eyeing Rita. "Personally I wouldn't be able to leave Cali, but hey, smoke 'em if you've got 'em."

Rita looked toward the door to the street, and her eyebrows shot up. Turning his head, Slater saw a stream of black-uniformed cops rush in, one after another. They were wearing helmets and aiming rifles. One of them shouted, "Hands, hands," and then, "Drop your weapon."

Slater didn't budge, and extended his palms at his sides. The guy with Rita quickly ditched his handgun, and it clattered on the concrete floor, but then he turned and bolted farther into the warehouse. One of the cops ran after him, moving a lot faster, followed by another, and a moment later they tackled him.

"Drop your weapon," one of the cops shouted.

Vitale leaned forward and tossed his handgun, then held up his hands. His face was contorted with anger.

The same moment that a cop went for Rita, and pulled her arms back, one of them grabbed Slater's wrists. There was no point in resisting or protesting, he knew, and heard the distinctive ratchet click of the cuffs going on.

When the gunman was frog-marched back over, his hands cuffed behind his back, his jacket was askew and his jeans were covered with dust.

Someone shouted "Clear," and Conrad stepped in from outside, along with a woman dressed the same way, in bland office civvies, with their badges and sidearms at their hips. Presumably she was another detective. Slater took a deep breath to dispel the adrenaline. He could feel the electricity in the air already starting to ebb.

"Are you in charge?" Rita called to Conrad and the other detective. "You're making a mistake. I work for Seligman Trucking. We transport this material for the mining company. It went missing, but I was able to recover it today. I was just about to call you people."

"It won't work, toots," Slater said. "I recorded our conversation." He wanted to pull out his phone and wave it at her, but with the cuffs on, and the cop behind him with a firm grasp on his bicep, he couldn't.

Conrad gestured to Slater. "Unhook him. He's not part of this."

As the cop started to unlock the cuffs, Slater frowned at Conrad. "It took you long enough."

Once his hands were free, Slater stepped over to Vitale. A helmeted cop was squatting behind his wheelchair, and had Vitale's arms pulled back. Maybe he was having trouble cuffing him in that position. Slater punched Vitale hard, snapping his head.

"That's for pointing a gun at me again," Slater shouted. Leaning in, he punched him in the crotch. "That's for trying to grease me again."

Vitale howled and pulled his knee up, folding it over the one in the cast, and arched his back. One of the cops grabbed Slater from behind and hauled him back.

"Knock it off," Conrad said sharply. "Do you want to wind up with charges too?"

Letting himself be pulled off, Slater took a few steps backward, but the cop didn't let go.

"It's OK," Conrad said. "He'll behave."

Slater looked to the cop squatting behind Vitale's wheelchair. "It's just a broken femur. He doesn't really need that chair. You should make him walk."

"Let's get them out of here," the other detective said, gesturing to Rita and the thug, and the uniforms hustled them toward the door. She followed them out, and Conrad stepped toward Slater.

"I told you to wait," he said quietly.

Slater waved at the gleaming mass on the pallet. "I thought they might unwrap the cargo and split up the palladium. It looks like they were about to, but it's all here. Good thing Rita was so proud of stealing it. She took the time to explain it to me."

"Seven million clams doesn't actually take up a lot of space," Conrad said, looking it over. "How did you find these numbskulls?"

"Work. It's what I do."

The cop behind Vitale's chair finally stood up, and they both watched as he was wheeled out. Vitale yelped as the wheelchair bumped against the door frame.

"I can't believe you dick-punched him in front of a

bunch of cops," Conrad said, and chuckled.

"He deserves worse."

"You can take solace in the knowledge that he's going to be eating baloney sandwiches in jail for a while. We'll get the pilot too."

"You'd damn well better."

"It's what we do." Conrad looked at him. "You know, you're pretty good at this. The work."

"I'm not sure if that's true. I spent the last week spinning my wheels when the perps were right in my face the whole time. But I do think it's good for me. It makes me feel alive."

"Still."

Conrad held his eye for a moment. It took Slater a second to parse his expression. Not desire; something else. Respect, maybe. He'd never seen that from Conrad before.

Standing taller, Slater jutted his chin. "Yeah, well, wipe the drool off your chin, bub. You might learn something."

The moment evaporated, and Conrad clapped a hand on his shoulder. "You're a lot of man, Slater."

———·———